DYING TO BAKE

A RIGHT ROYAL COZY INVESTIGATION
MYSTERY

HELEN GOLDEN

DREW BRADLEY PRESS

ALSO BY HELEN GOLDEN

ISBN (P) 978-1-915747-21-1

Edited by Marina Grout at Writing Evolution

Published by Drew Bradley Press

Cover design by Helen Drew-Bradley

First edition March 2024

To Emily B-S,
My friend. My sing-along-in-the-car partner. My Harrods
sale buddy. My support team. My greatest cheerleader. I love
your big hair and your big heart.
Thank you for being my ELLP.

NOTE FROM THE AUTHOR

I am a British author and this book has been written using British English. So if you are from somewhere other than the UK, you may find some words spelt differently to how you would spell them, for example Scottish whisky is spelt without an e. In most cases this is British English, not a spelling mistake. We also have different punctuation rules in the UK.

However if you find any other errors, I would be grateful if you would please contact me helen@helengoldenauthor. co.uk and let me know so I can correct them. Thank you.

For your reference I have included a list of characters in the order they appear, and you can find this at the back of the book.

1

JUST AFTER 11 AM, MONDAY 19 APRIL

"So I'm thinking green would work well in the dining room," Lady Beatrice, the Countess of Rossex, said to Perry Juke as they descended the stone steps leading away from the Breakfast Room at Francis Court with Daisy, her small West Highland terrier, trotting between them. "What do you think?"

"Bottle, sage, or grass?" her best friend asked as they turned right, skirting along the high stone wall at the back of the Old Stable Block.

"More of a highland green."

Perry pulled a face. "What's highland green when it's at home?"

"It's more tree green than grass green. Like this…" They stopped, and Bea showed him a photo on her mobile phone.

"Ah," he said, nodding. "Yes. That will work well. It says stately but not boring."

"Indeed," Bea replied, pocketing her phone and calling Daisy, who had her face stuffed in one of the squat rhododendron bushes that lined the stone wall. The large white flowers shook as Daisy extracted herself and joined them. They began walking again.

The morning sun cast a warm glow on the path ahead as they turned away from the Old Stable Block. Walking around a 'Closed' sign, they skirted the carefully manicured grounds beyond it. In the distance, on the left, the newly restored Old Barn came into view as they rounded the corner. Currently being used to host the popular television show *Bake Off Wars*, the building was surrounded by outside broadcast vehicles and temporary cabins. Bea sighed. Two weeks into filming and everyone on the estate seemed to be obsessed with the show. And no one more so than Perry.

She glanced at her business partner walking beside her. His eyes had turned dreamily towards the area of the Old Barn. She knew he'd been there most of the weekend with his husband, Simon Lattimore, winner of *Celebrity EliteChef* and good friend of Ryan Hawley, the new judge on *Bake Off Wars*. Bea had first met Ryan last summer at the local Food and Wine Festival and had instantly liked the young, ambitious chef. Later, when he'd taken her fourteen-year-old son, Sam, under his wing, she'd liked him more, admiring his passion for good food and the way he encouraged her son to embrace his love of cooking. Poor Sam had been gutted when he'd had to go back to boarding school last week, meaning he'd missed Ryan's *Bake Off Wars* debut.

Perry tore his eyes away from the building and looked at her, his body fairly shaking with excitement. Unlike Perry, who loved reality television, since they'd unintentionally become involved in several murder investigations over the last twelve months, Bea didn't need any more drama in her life. But… *Alright, Perry, I'll ask…* "So how did filming go over the weekend?"

"Well," Perry replied, his eyes bright. "Ryan was quite nervous, but he kept it together really well. It was the first weekend of filming with the contestants, so all twelve teams were there. Everyone seemed a bit on edge initially, but once they got into the swing of things, it was smooth sailing. Or baking, rather." He grinned.

Bea rolled her eyes before furrowing her brow. *What about the other judge?* Vera Bolt, the sixty-six-year-old pastry chef known as the Queen of Bakes, was a national treasure, but it was well known that during the two weeks of rehearsals and pre-filming, the formidable judge had ruffled a few feathers on set. "And what about Vera Bolt?" Bea asked.

Perry raised an eyebrow. "Well, she's definitely straight-forward and to the point." He paused for a moment, his lips curling into a knowing grin. "But there's no denying her expertise with cakes, according to Simon."

They carried on past the Old Barn and made their way towards The Dower House. Bea's stomach fluttered when she spied the black metal back gate that led into the garden of the three-storey Georgian house in the distance. Daisy ran ahead, stopping occasionally to sniff the ground. *I bet she can smell the deer.* The estate had a mixed herd of deer that roamed freely, delighting the public who visited the gardens during opening hours.

The top of the seven-bedroom mansion, formerly the home that Bea had shared with her husband until his tragic death fifteen years ago, was just visible above the stone wall. *I can't wait to move back in.* After James' death, heartbroken and pregnant, she'd moved into the main Francis Court manor house at her mother's insistence and had ended up staying there to raise Sam. But now, with her son outgrowing their apartment there and with her newly found independence, she was keen to establish a home for the two of them and Daisy at The Dower House. If everything went according to plan, the kitchen would be up and running by the end of the week, and she could move in at the weekend.

"Fred was hanging around the show all day Saturday," Perry said, dragging her attention back to *Bake Off Wars*. "He really is rather taken with Summer York, isn't he?"

Bea smiled. Her elder brother, Lord Frederick Astley, had been smitten with the bubbly presenter of *Bake Off Wars* ever since they'd first met a month ago when she'd been on-site attending the initial set-up meeting.

"Is it serious?"

Bea gave him a knowing smile. "Well, he invited her to dinner with Ma, Pa, and Grandmama on Saturday night."

"Ooh…meet the parents and the former queen," Perry said, wiggling his eyebrows. "That's a big step."

Bea ducked her chin, recalling how nervous her normally calm and collected brother had been when he'd begged her and their sister, Lady Sarah, to be there for moral support. She smiled. "Summer charmed Pa easily, and even Ma appeared to warm to her." Perry raised an eyebrow. Her Royal Highness Princess Helen wasn't easy to impress. "Grandmama, however, kept inquiring about her parents." Perry nodded. Queen Mary the Queen Mother was a formidable woman who had very strong opinions on the type of background her grandchildren's friends should have.

"And did she pass the suitability test?" Perry asked, his eyes twinkling.

"Well, Summer's father is a surgeon, and her mother's the head teacher at a private all-girls school. It's hard to know if that's good enough for Grandmama, but it could definitely be worse." Bea's thoughts turned to Detective Chief Inspector Richard Fitzwilliam from Protection and Investigation (Royal) Services (PaIRS for short), who was currently recuperating in one of their estate cottages after having been shot during a murder investigation at Gollingham Palace ten weeks ago. Fitzwilliam's mother lived in a flat in Leeds, and his father had disappeared when he'd been young. What on earth would her grandmother make of that? She frowned. *What difference does it make what Grandmama thinks?* Admittedly, she and Rich had been spending a fair amount of time together since he'd been released from hospital eight weeks ago and had taken her up on her offer to recover in the tranquillity of the Francis Court estate. And, yes, during their gentle walks around the grounds, they'd got to know each other better. Maybe even a friendship was blossoming. But nothing for her grandmother to worry about. *It's not like we're dating or anything.* She stifled a huff. *That would be ridiculous.*

"It sounds like they make a lovely couple, but only time will tell if Summer can handle all the attention that comes with being involved with Fred," Perry pointed out as they approached the large wrought-iron gate that led to the back entrance to the grounds of The Dower House.

"Yes, that's going to be the true test," Bea agreed. She hoped for Fred's and Summer's sakes that they could keep their relationship from the press for a little longer and enjoy getting to know each other in private. Once it became public, it wouldn't only be her grandmother who would express her feelings about the king's nephew dating a TV presenter.

Woof! Daisy spun around and barked again.

Was that a scream? A shiver ran down Bea's spine as she turned.

Ana Halsall, the young runner for *Bake Off Wars*, emerged from the Old Barn, her eyes wide and frantic, searching. She saw Bea and Perry and shouted, "Help!" as she sprinted towards them.

"What on earth?" Bea murmured, exchanging a worried glance with Perry.

The distressed young woman struggled to catch her

breath, her feathered black hair dishevelled as she slowed down in front of them. "I… I don't know what to do," she stammered, tears glistening in her eyes.

Bea's heart jumped. "Take a deep breath and tell us what's wrong," she urged gently.

Ana looked rapidly from Bea to Perry, then choked out, "Oh, Perry. There's…there's a body."

Bea's heart rate increased. *No! Not again. Not another death at Francis Court…*

"I found her… There's blood everywhere," Ana stammered, tears now streaming down her cheeks.

"Oh my giddy aunt!" Perry gasped, his eyes wide as they locked with Bea's. Without hesitation, they both sprinted towards the Old Barn, Ana and Daisy following close behind them.

Police! "Ana, have you called the police?" Bea shouted over her shoulder.

"No! I didn't know what to do… I panicked!" Ana cried, her voice shaking.

"Alright, I'll let them know now," Bea reassured her, her voice wavering only slightly. Her hand delved into the pocket of her puffa jacket. She fumbled for her two-way radio, her hands trembling as she pulled it out and pressed the call button to contact Francis Court's head of security. "Adrian? This is Lady Rossex. Over."

There was a faint click, then a man's voice crackled back through the static. "My lady, this is Adrian Breen. Is everything okay? Over."

"We need you at the Old Barn immediately. There's been an incident. Over."

"Roger that, my lady. I'm on my way. Over."

"And Adrian?"

"Yes, my lady?"

"You'd best call an ambulance and the police. Over."

"Roger that. Out."

Bea caught up with Perry and Daisy just outside the building. Perry, panting and out of breath, was leaning against the wall. Bea stopped and inhaled deeply to regain control over her pounding heart. *Who?* She suddenly realised Ana hadn't actually told them who she'd found. She turned to Ana, who was breathing hard and furtively glancing towards the entrance of the Old Barn. "Who is it you've found, Ana?" Bea asked, keeping her voice steady for the young girl's sake.

"Vera Bolt…" Ana sobbed, her words barely audible. "And…and she's dead!"

TWO WEEKS EARLIER, MONDAY 5 APRIL

The Society Page online article:

Rehearsals Start at Francis Court for TV Show Bake Off Wars

Francis Court estate, the home of Her Royal Highness Princess Helen and her husband, Charles Astley, the Duke of Arnwall, is hosting the next series of Bake Off Wars. *The competition, which sees twelve bakery teams compete over ten weeks to win the coveted title of* Bake Off Warriors *and a twenty-five-thousand-pound reward, starts filming in two weeks. In the meantime, rehearsals and pre-production filming begins today with renowned pâtissière Vera Bolt (66) and her fellow judge TV chef Ryan Hawley (31), along with new presenters Hamilton Moore (41) and Summer York (35).*

Ryan Hawley, co-presenter of Two Chefs in a Camper, *and a regular host of BBC's* Sunday Roast, *replaces well-*

known chef Mark Jacobs (49), who was controversially let go at the end of the last series. Although no details of why Mr Jacobs was asked to leave have been made public, show insiders say that his departure was an enormous shock to many of the crew, amongst whom he was very popular. Jacobs has not made a statement about his departure, but rumours persist that he and Vera Bolt had a fractious relationship for the past two series. A source close to the show's production reports that the chef was making noises about the show needing a new format to 'shake it up a bit', while Vera insisted that the current format was what made the show so popular, regularly attracting audiences of ten million or more. Friends of Chef Mark report that an updated format proposal by him to the show's producers was rejected at the end of the last series after Vera stepped in and threatened to leave if any changes were made.

Hot on the heels of the announcement that Jacobs was leaving, comedy duo Claudia Sharp and Kit North chose not to renew their contracts with the show. Although at the time they said their decision to leave was to allow them more time to concentrate on a new television show they were writing, it later emerged that they supported Jacob's view that a change in format was what the show needed. When the proposal was dismissed and he was let go, they refused to stay in a show of solidarity with the chef. They have been replaced by Hamilton Moore, a well-known foodie and host of award-winning podcast Moore Food Please!, *and Summer York, comedian and presenter of future technology show* What's The Buzz?.

While the public are patiently waiting for Bake Off Wars *to be aired later in the summer, the critics are poised to record their verdict on the new judge and presenters, something the show's producers must be very conscious of.*

Meanwhile, Lady Beatrice, the Countess of Rossex, and

her business partner, Perry Juke, have almost completed the refurbishment of The Dower House in the grounds of the Francis Court estate where the King's niece lived with her husband, James Wiltshire, the Earl of Rossex, before his untimely death fifteen years ago. Lady Beatrice is moving back into the seven-bedroom mansion with her son, Samuel (14). Perry Juke (34) recently married Simon Lattimore (40), the crime writer and celebrity chef, in a lavish ceremony at Francis Court two weeks ago, and the couple were due home from their honeymoon yesterday.

3

BREAKFAST, MONDAY 5 APRIL

Bea sat at a table in the far corner by the window in the Breakfast Room in Francis Court, her green eyes regularly flicking towards the entrance. Daisy, her little white terrier, lay by her feet, occasionally snoring. The pungent aroma of freshly brewed coffee filled the air, mingling with the smell of newly baked bread and sizzling bacon. She took a sip of coffee, the warm liquid slipping down her throat. She let out a contented sigh, savouring the moment as she waited for Perry to arrive fresh from his honeymoon in Italy.

She scanned the restaurant. It was still early, and only a handful of tables were occupied. The Francis Court estate didn't open to the public until ten, so it was currently only staff tucking into their breakfast before they began their day. Free meals and drinks in either the restaurant or the Old Stable Block Cafe was one bonus of working at Francis Court.

The low sun was beaming through the large windows that spanned the two sides of the Breakfast Room, flooding the entire space with natural light. Bea peered out of the window next to her, searching the path leading along the front of the restaurant for the tall slim figure of her best friend. *Where is he?* She absentmindedly straightened the small vase of fresh flowers, hand-picked from the kitchen garden, that was in the middle of the table.

Taking another sip of coffee, she started when Daisy yipped excitedly and charged off towards the internal door that led into The Painted Hall, her tail wagging furiously. Perry strode into the room, his short spiky strawberry-blond hair perfectly styled, his blue eyes sparkling with happiness. A huge smile split Bea's face. He'd been gone for what had felt like forever. *I've missed him so much!*

"How's my favourite girl?" Perry said, bending down and picking up Daisy, who squirmed in his arms excitedly. "I've missed you too!" he told her, turning his face away from the barrage of affectionate licks. With a quick kiss on the top of her head, he gently placed Daisy on the floor and walked towards Bea, grinning.

She stood and leaned into his warm hug, inhaling the familiar spicy smell of his aftershave. "It's so good to see you," she said, squeezing him tight.

"I've missed you almost as much as I've missed Daisy," he mumbled into her mane of red hair.

She stepped back and tilted her head to one side. "That much?"

He grinned.

She grinned back. "You look amazing!" His slightly olive skin was still flushed from the Italian sun. "How was your trip?"

"Incredible!" Perry pulled out the seat across from her, and they both sat down. With a sigh, Daisy plonked herself by Perry's feet and closed her eyes.

Bea quickly looked around the room. Catching the eye of Nicky, their usual server, she nodded her head. "Tell me everything. As I haven't been to Italy for over fifteen years, I want to live vicariously through you!"

"Well." Perry took a deep breath. "Italy was absolutely stunning, and Simon's family was so welcoming."

Bea knew Perry had been nervous about meeting his new husband's Italian relatives for the first time. Simon's mother, Bella, had left Italy in her early twenties to work in a famous restaurant in London. It was there she'd met Simon's father, Ray. Much to her families' consternation, Bella had stayed in the UK, settling in Fenshire, where she and Ray had set up first a bakery and then a small pizzeria. Along with Simon's older brother, they now owned and managed three trattorias in Fenshire. However, every year, Bella and Ray, and their sons when they'd been younger, had spent their summer holidays with Bella's mother and aunt in southern Italy. Simon had said it was where he'd learned to cook.

Nicky approached the table with a cheery smile. "Perry, good to see you back. What can I get you?"

"Thanks, Nicky. Just coffee for now, please," Perry replied.

Bea frowned. It wasn't like Perry to pass on breakfast.

"Coming right up," Nicky said, then headed back to the counter by the kitchen access door.

Before Bea had time to ask Perry why he was skipping his favourite bacon rolls, he began to tell her of his time away. Bea listened intently, her imagination painting vivid pictures of the quaint small town in the Abruzzo region where Simon's family lived. She could almost taste the rich red wines of the area and feel the sun on her skin.

"And you wouldn't believe the food we had there, Bea. I swear I must have gained at least half a stone." He patted his stomach.

"Rubbish," Bea scoffed, her gaze appraising him from

head to toe. "You're as slim as ever." It was a bone of contention for her and Simon that Perry could eat what he liked and still have a super model's body. *And* he had a passionate dislike of exercise, so he maintained his enviable physique without it. Whereas Bea ran almost every day, and Simon reluctantly dragged himself to the gym four times a week.

A mischievous grin spread across Perry's face. "Well, in that case," he said, waving to Nicky, who was passing. "I'll have two bacon rolls, please, Nicky."

As they continued to talk about his trip, the restlessness that had settled on Bea during his absence lifted. Looking down at Daisy curled up at his feet, blissfully content in the presence of her two favourite people, Bea knew that life had returned to its proper balance once more.

Nicky returned with Perry's bacon rolls, the mouth-watering smell wafting through the air. Bea rarely ate breakfast. The thought of food this early in the morning made her feel quite nauseous, but she enjoyed the whiff of bacon and freshly baked rolls coming from Perry's plate. Daisy jumped up, her little nose twitching. With an indulgent sigh, Perry tore off a small piece of crispy bacon and held it out under the table to the little dog, who eagerly gobbled it up.

About to open her mouth to scold him for feeding Daisy titbits from the table (Bea was supposed to be watching Daisy's food intake since the vet had described the little terrier as 'chunky' at their last visit), she stopped herself. It was Perry's first day back, and Daisy hadn't had bacon since he'd gone away. She let it go.

"So how's things at The Dower House?" Perry mumbled with his mouth full of bacon roll.

"The work's coming along nicely," she said, excitement bubbling inside her. "Hopefully just a few more weeks, and

I'll be moving in. The kitchen's the biggest issue; it's been delayed a week already. I just hope they'll be able to make the new date they've given me. Sam's already picked the rooms he wants for his bedroom, sitting room, and games room. They're all on the top floor in the east wing. He's very excited and has some ideas about what he wants to do in terms of colour and furniture." She smiled and raised an eyebrow. "I've told him he'll have to run it by you first."

"That will be fun!" Perry exclaimed, clapping his hands together. "How's he doing?"

"He's still on Easter break, so you'll see him later," Bea replied, smiling fondly at the thought of her son still fast asleep upstairs in her apartment. "He's having a lie-in today. His best friend, Archie, is arriving later. They're both thrilled about *Bake Off Wars* being filmed here. They can't wait to see Ryan when he arrives." Ryan Hawley, the TV chef and new judge on *Bake Off Wars,* was a hero of Sam's and Archie's, having visited their school last year to give their cooking club a masterclass.

"Speaking of which," Perry said, wiping his mouth with a napkin and pushing his empty plate to one side. "Simon plans on swinging by later to catch up with Ryan as well. I'm sure he'll take the boys with him if you ask him."

"Perfect." Bea bobbed her head, pleased that everything seemed to be falling into place.

Perry picked up his coffee cup, his eyes twinkling as he leaned in. "So have I missed any juicy gossip while I've been away?"

Bea shrugged, grinning. "I'm hardly the right person to ask, am I? No one tells me anything. Claire's the best one to bring you up to date." Claire Beck, Francis Court's human resource manager, rivalled Perry in her appetite for celebrity gossip. "She and Ellie have been hanging around the *Bake Off*

Wars production set, trying to catch some behind-the-scenes titbits." Ellie Gunn, Francis Court's catering manager, at least had a legitimate reason to be there. She was helping the production crew source their ingredients from the estate and local producers.

"Ah, Claire always has her ear to the ground." Perry smiled like a proud father. Bea agreed. Claire's and Ellie's skills at finding things out had come in very handy last month when they'd been away for Perry's bachelor weekend and had become embroiled in a murder investigation. "What about Fred? Does he still have a crush on Summer York?"

Bea smirked. Her oh-so-cool elder brother was following around the new presenter of *Bake Off Wars* like a puppy dog. "Summer is staying in a rented house in the village over-looking the beach, just opposite Tappin's Teas," she told him. "Apparently, she's working on a TV show pilot when she's not on set. Anyway, Fred has commandeered the bedroom next to his apartment here and has turned it into a study. Suddenly, he's working from home most of the time." She gave Perry a knowing look. "He also seems to need a lot of fresh air these days, as he's been taking long walks on the beach."

Perry gave a wide grin.

"Talking of walking and fresh air. How's Fitzwilliam doing? Is he overdoing things?"

"How did you guess?" Bea gave a deep sigh, her brow furrowing. "I'm worried he's pushing himself too hard too soon." Although it had been eight weeks since Rich had been shot while confronting a killer at Gollingham Palace, the king's official residence, the doctors had told him that the damage caused by the bullet ripping through his torso would take at least twelve weeks to heal, longer if he didn't give himself time to rest and recover. "He's already itching to get back to work, but his boss has told him they won't even consider him returning until the full twelve weeks is up. He has to do two four-day courses of intensive physio and *then* he has to pass a fitness assessment to be allowed back on active duty. He's not happy."

She recalled their walk yesterday just before he'd left for his first stint of physio. He been unable to hide his frustration at what he'd called "being left on the side lines to fester". She'd tried to reassure him it was just PaIRS' back-to-work process, and he would need to be patient, but he'd huffed at her. He'd been quiet for the rest of their walk. She'd not badgered him. He needed time to come to terms with his disappointment.

"I can imagine," Perry said, nodding.

"Oh, and of course Em and Izzy were here for a few days." Rich had been happy when the detective chief inspector from PaIRS and her wife had stayed on in Francis-next-the-Sea for a bit after Perry and Simon's wedding. Although it had prompted Rich to tell Bea off when Em had given him all the details of Perry's bachelor weekend one night over dinner at Hope Cottage. There she revealed that Bea had gone chasing after a potential murderer on her own, something Bea deliberately hadn't told him when she'd given him her version of the events that had taken place at Chasingham Hotel and Spa. Bea had been pleased to see how much Rich had cheered up with his friends around despite them constantly nagging him to slow down and rest more.

"It was funny to hear Em telling Rich that he should rest when he'd spent all that time when we were at Drew Castle earlier this year telling her exactly the same thing!" Em had broken her leg at the end of last year during a foiled attempt to kidnap Bea's uncle, the king's brother.

Perry snorted. "I bet he didn't like that!"

"Oh, and Elise came to stay again. This time she brought her husband, Rhys, with her." Rich's sister had been a regular visitor when he'd first arrived, worried that he wouldn't be able to look after himself properly. But once she'd seen that Bea, Perry, and Simon were checking in on her brother regularly, delivering food, and, as he became more mobile, inviting him out for short walks, she'd relaxed a bit, and her visits had reduced in frequency.

"Well, I hope you've been looking after him too in my and Simon's absence." He raised an eyebrow, causing Bea to blush slightly. She'd checked in with Rich every day while they'd been gone, either inviting him to meet for a coffee or to take a walk in the garden with her and Daisy if the weather was dry.

"I've just… I've just been making sure he's alright," she mumbled, avoiding Perry's gaze as she focused on her coffee cup in front of her. It was funny how quickly she'd got used to seeing Rich every day. She'd even started looking forward to it…

Perry reached across the table, giving her hand a reassuring squeeze. "And I'm sure he appreciates it more than you know." *Does he?* He'd often seemed subdued on their walks, and it was hard for her to tell if he enjoyed her company or would rather be alone. "Oh, I have something else to tell you. It's a bit of a mystery, really."

Bea looked up and met Perry's shining eyes. *A mystery? That's intriguing…* "Do tell."

"Well, Dylan Milton, you know, the landlord of The Ship and Seal in the village, dropped a note through our door while we were away. Apparently, there was a girl, maybe in her late teens, asking after Simon at the pub. Dylan didn't give her any details, of course; he just told her Simon was currently away."

"Really?" Bea's curiosity was piqued as she leaned in closer to hear what Perry had to say. "Did she say what she wanted to see Simon about?"

Perry shook his head. "Dylan thought she might be a fan of Simon's books. Anyway, he wanted to let us know just in case she turned up at the house."

"What, like a stalker?"

"I don't think so." Perry frowned. "Although it never occurred to me she could be a stalker."

Oh no! I shouldn't have said that… "Well, I'm sure it's nothing to worry about." She smiled at him in what she hoped was a reassuring way.

"Um…anyway, Simon's planning to pop in and talk to Dylan about it later just to get a better idea of what she said."

"Good idea." Bea dipped her head, relieved that Simon had things well in hand. "As you say, it's probably just a harmless crime fan."

"Exactly," Perry said, finishing his coffee.

Bea let out a sigh of relief. He sounded less worried now. *Me and my big mouth!*

Perry glanced at his watch and rose. "Shall we head over to The Dower House now? I can't wait to see all the progress you've made."

"Indeed," Bea replied, downing the last of her own drink. As she rose from her chair, Daisy jumped up, her tail wagging frantically.

As they made their way out of the Breakfast Room, Bea's mind was still preoccupied with the mysterious girl who'd been asking after Simon. She shook her head, chasing the thoughts away for now. There would be time to discuss it later, after Simon spoke to Dylan.

4

7 PM, MONDAY 5 APRIL

Bea leaned against the marble island and gazed around the warm and inviting open-plan kitchen and dining area of Simon and Perry's home, Rose Cottage. Her son, Sam, and his best friend, Archie, were busy helping Simon prepare dinner. Both boys were lanky and tall for their age, with youthful faces alight with enthusiasm and pride in their culinary expertise. Bea smiled at their keenness as they moved with an easy camaraderie, laughing and joking as they cooked under Simon's watchful eye.

Perry stood by the wine rack, selecting a bottle to accompany the meal, while the new *Bake Off Wars* judge, Ryan, leaned against the kitchen counter, chatting amiably with Simon. *No wonder he's a television heartthrob*, Bea thought as she studied the charismatic chef. His dark skin was the perfect setting for his wide mouth and white smile, showcasing perfect teeth, and his shaved head made his brown eyes seem even more expressive.

"Food's almost ready," Sam called out.

"It smells amazing, darling," Bea said to him, watching

her son expertly dip his spoon in and taste a creamy-looking sauce. He nodded, then carried on stirring.

Perry grabbed two bottles of red wine and said, "Shall we move to the table?"

Heading over to the massive wooden table surrounded by eight sturdy chairs that dominated the dining space, she passed Daisy, her little white terrier, who had claimed her favourite spot in an armchair by the patio doors leading to the garden. Her compact form was almost lost in the plush cushions as she rested her head on the arm of the chair, watching the bustling scene before her.

"Sit wherever you like," Perry told Ryan, uncorking the wine bottle with a *pop*. Ryan took a chair on the other side of the table. Bea sat next to him. She had a good view of the kitchen, and she smiled as Sam and Archie followed Simon's guidance in plating up the starter. *They're like a well-oiled machine.*

Perry leaned over and filled Bea's wineglass. A soft glimmer emanated from the vintage chandelier above the table, casting a cosy light on the red liquid as it swirled around the wineglass.

The starters were delivered by Sam and Archie, who placed plates in front of them.

"So I've made a chicken poached in butter terrine, drizzled with a tangy lemon sauce, and accompanied by asparagus spears," Sam announced proudly. Archie cleared his throat. "Oh, and Archie helped."

Bea's mouth watered as she took in the aroma wafting from the dish before her.

"Wow, this looks amazing," Perry said, eagerly reaching for his fork.

"That's down to the boys here," Simon replied, gesturing

to Sam and Archie. With huge grins on their faces, the boys came and sat next to Bea and Ryan.

"It looks delicious, darling," Bea said, bumping Sam's arm with hers. He turned and smiled at her. *When did my boy grow up and become so accomplished?* Bea dug into the food, marvelling at her son's cooking skills as she savoured the delicate flavours.

"Ummm, that was an accomplished piece of cooking," Ryan said, after demolishing his plate of food with a speed that rivalled Perry's. Next to Bea, Sam broke into a huge grin, lapping up the renowned chef's praise.

When they'd all finished, Simon rose, and with Sam's and Archie's help, they cleared the table of the empty plates. "The main course will be a few minutes, so help yourselves to more wine," Simon said as he and the boys headed into the kitchen.

"So how was your first day of filming, Ryan?" Perry asked as he topped up the chef's wineglass.

"You wouldn't believe how much standing around and waiting there is," Ryan said, shaking his head in disbelief.

"Ah, the not-so-glamorous side of television," Bea said, her green eyes sparkling with amusement.

"Exactly!" Ryan laughed. "When I've been involved in filming for TV before, I've always been the one cooking, so there was plenty to get on with while they did set-ups and test shots, but here, I'm not doing anything but judging the finished product. It's very different. It's all about making sure it will work when we film." He leaned back in his chair. "Today, for instance, they did a test run of one of the skills challenges. Leah and Shelly, two of the team, had to bake and decorate a birthday cake from one of Vera's recipes within the same time limit we'll give the contestants."

"And did they manage it?" Perry asked.

Skills challenge? Bea leaned in, not completely sure what they were talking about but genuinely curious.

"Unfortunately not." Ryan sighed. "And Vera was livid. She tried to blame Leah and Shelly, saying they hadn't worked fast enough, but the producer disagreed and told her she would have to come up with an alternative recipe that *could* be achieved within the time. Tensions were high, to say the least."

"And I bet that didn't make Vera very popular," Perry added. Ryan raised an eyebrow and nodded.

———

After they'd eaten their main course of pan-seared sea bass with a walnut pesto and roasted vine tomatoes, Sam and Archie bustled about in the kitchen, preparing dessert.

Bea glanced over at Simon on the other side of the table. "So did you speak to Dylan about that young woman who was asking after you?"

"Yes. He said she's nineteen years old."

Bea raised an eyebrow. *How did Dylan—*

"He checked her ID when she asked for a drink."

Of course!

"Her first name is Isla, and she has a faint Scottish accent, apparently. Dylan said she seemed disappointed when he told her I was away."

Ryan frowned. "Any idea who she might be?"

Simon replied with a shrug. "I assume it's a fan or maybe a student looking for an interview. I've come across that before."

Bea tipped her head. That would make sense. Simon was after all a bestselling crime writer. Maybe there was no mystery about the girl after all.

Just then, Sam and Archie emerged from the kitchen, bearing bowls filled with shards of stiff white meringue topped with thick whipped cream and fruit.

"Here we have Eton mess with strawberries and blueberries freshly picked from the Francis Court greenhouse by me and my assistant," Archie told them cheerfully, setting the bowls in front of each person, then grinning cheekily at Sam.

"It looks yummy," Perry said, digging into his dessert with delight.

As they ate, Sam and Archie chatted with Simon and Ryan about food while Bea discussed with Perry an idea she'd had about the cloakroom downstairs at The Dower House. Eventually, Ryan glanced at his watch and pushed back his chair. "I should head back to Fawstead," he said, collecting his jacket from the back of his seat. "Thank you for a wonderful meal, Sam and Archie." He gave a small bow to the boys. They grinned back. "I'll see you at some stage tomorrow, no doubt." They nodded.

Simon showed Ryan out while Perry and Bea cleared the dishes away.

"Can Archie and I watch TV, mum?" Sam asked as she returned to the table.

Bea tipped her head with a smile, and they jumped up eagerly. Sam called Daisy to follow them into the sitting room next door, and the little dog eagerly trotted after the boys.

Perry returned to the table, a large pot of coffee in one hand and three mugs hanging off the fingers of his other. He placed the pot on the table and poured the steaming black liquid into the mugs. He handed one to Bea while Simon sat down and grabbed another.

"So from what Ryan said, day one of filming wasn't very smooth. How do *you* think it went today?" Bea asked Simon.

Simon sighed, running a hand through his short light-brown hair. "Everyone seemed tetchy, if I'm honest. Vera was particularly picky with Summer and Hamilton."

"It was their first day as presenters. You'd think she would've cut them a little slack," Perry said, raising his coffee mug to his lips.

"Indeed," Bea added. She took a sip of her hot drink. It seemed as if all was not well on set. "Do you think it's just first day nerves, and things will improve as the week goes on?"

"Well, Ana, one of the runners, mentioned to me there's a lot of bad feeling since Mark Jacobs left," Perry said, placing his drink down on the table. "Apparently, they blame Vera since she gave an ultimatum to the show's producers at the end of the last series. Her or Mark. Many of the crew think they should've let her go and kept him instead."

"There appears to be a bit of an atmosphere on set," Simon agreed. "But I'm sure it will all calm down once everyone settles in. We'll see how the rest of the week goes."

5

LUNCHTIME, TUESDAY 13 APRIL

Bea gazed out the large bay window as sunlight streamed into the Breakfast Room at Francis Court. The rays of sun cast a golden flare on the soft yellow walls adorned with elegant framed paintings. Outside, the blossoming trees swayed gently in the spring breeze, their petals dancing through the air. She loved this time of year, when everything outside seemed to wake up.

As she sipped her coffee, she looked around the table at her lunch companions. Claire, Francis Court's human resources manager, was wiping her mouth with a napkin as she pushed her empty plate to one side. The red glasses perched on her nose accentuated her full lips, which were coated in a vibrant red lipstick. Next to her, Ellie, the catering manager, was sipping her tea, her sparkling blue eyes framed by her heavily made-up lids. Perry, dressed in a smart blue suit jacket and designer jeans, was leaning under the table, feeding Daisy the remains of his sandwich.

Does he think I can't see him?

He glanced up and, seeing the look on Bea's face, gave her an apologetic smile and mumbled, "It was only a little piece." She raised an eyebrow. No wonder Daisy was getting chunkier since Perry had got back from his honeymoon!

"So did you go on set at *Bake Off Wars* this morning, El?" Perry asked, sheepishly looking away from Bea's disapproving glare and towards Ellie.

"Yes. I've got a list of ingredients they need for the rest of the week now. I think I can get them all locally."

"You wouldn't believe the tension on the set!" Claire exclaimed, her brown eyes widening behind her glasses.

Perry frowned. "What were you doing there?"

"Er, helping Ellie," Claire replied, blushing.

"Um..." Perry grumbled.

Bea suppressed a grin. She knew Claire was almost as massive a fan of the show as Perry was. They seemed to be having a little competition over who knew the most gossip about the production. She didn't want to encourage Claire, but she was curious. "Is there any reason for the tense atmosphere?"

"It's hard to say for sure," Claire replied thoughtfully, twirling a tight brown curl around her finger. "But it seems like some people aren't getting along too well behind the scenes."

"Ah, the ever-present drama of reality television," Perry remarked, nodding sagely.

"So nothing specific then?" Bea asked.

"Well," Perry said, leaning in. "I heard from Ana, one of the show's runners, that everyone thinks it's not as much fun since Mark left. He was very well liked by the crew. Vera's apparently become quite snappy, and poor Austin Matthews, the director, spends most of his time trying to placate her." Perry looked pointedly at Claire.

Bea tilted her head to one side. "Don't they like Ryan?"

She couldn't imagine anyone not liking the charming and good-looking chef.

"Oh, yes," Perry replied quickly. "It's not Ryan. I think it's Vera."

"Ryan is absolutely swoonworthy," Ellie chimed in, her generous lips curving into a broad grin.

"Definitely." Claire nodded, taking another sip of her drink. "You can practically feel the electricity in the air whenever he walks on set. I mean, you can see everyone's a bit on edge, but he just keeps on smiling and making jokes. He's lovely."

"Exactly," Ellie agreed, a dreamy look in her eyes. "His upbeat personality seems to be keeping everyone going."

"So is that what the two of you did all morning — follow Ryan around like love-sick puppies?" Perry asked slightly petulantly.

Claire laughed, sticking her tongue out at him. "He's just jealous, El," she said to her friend sitting next to her.

Perry huffed.

"We got to see one of the skills challenges they do for the show." Ellie shifted in her seat as she leaned forward.

"Oh?" Bea didn't really know much about how the show worked. Much to Perry's disgust, she'd never watched it, but she remembered a skills challenge being mentioned last week at dinner. "How does that work then?"

"Right, well." Claire pushed up her glasses perched on her nose. "So Vera or Ryan chooses a recipe, and with the help of Harvey—"

"That's Harvey Jury, the food producer," Ellie added.

"—they whittle down the cooking instructions to the absolute minimum." Claire bobbed her head.

"Then Leah Goldrich, the lead home economist, and Shelly Black, the food researcher, have to make the dish following those bare-bones instructions," Ellie continued, her eyes glimmering with enthusiasm. "They're given the same time as the contestants will have during the actual competition, and they do it in The Tent. It's like a trial run to ensure it's actually doable."

The tent? Bea frowned. There was no tent as far as she was aware. "What tent?"

"Oh!" Perry chimed in. "It's not an *actual* tent. It's how they refer to the main room inside the Old Barn where they film the show. In previous seasons, they filmed in a marquee in the grounds of a country house in Suffolk, which they called 'the tent', and it appears the name has stuck."

"I see," Bea said. "So did they do it within the time?"

"Not the one we saw," Claire said, leaning in conspiratorially. "Apparently, it often takes multiple attempts to get the right balance between the brevity of the instructions and a sufficient amount of time for them to complete the bake."

"The crew eats a lot of cake!" Ellie added, grinning. After a moment her blue eyes darkened with disapproval. "But Vera was downright scathing towards Leah and Shelly when they struggled to finish the dish on time and, according to her, didn't meet her exacting standards."

Ah! Now what Ryan had said at dinner after the first day of filming made more sense. "That seems rather harsh," Bea replied. "I thought from what you said that the whole point of them running through it was to see if it worked?"

"Exactly!" Claire cried, her brown eyes sparkling. "I'd hoped the firm but fair persona Vera presented on the show was just an act, but after watching her on set, I can't say I've warmed to her at all."

"Leah and Shelly seemed to take it all in their stride. I believe they've worked with Vera for years, so they must just be used to it," Ellie added, her lips tightening. "But if someone talked to me like that at work, I'd have a thing or two to say about it!"

"Maybe even take it to HR, eh?" Perry said with a grin, looking at Claire. Claire and Ellie laughed.

Bea felt a pang of sympathy for Leah and Shelly. *It must be hard to maintain one's dignity in the face of such criticism. Maybe you get used to it over the years?* Not that that was an excuse for Vera's behaviour.

Just then, Perry's gaze shifted to the entrance of the restaurant, where two people that Bea didn't know entered. With a grin, he called out, "Cleo! Ana! Over here!"

They turned and walked towards the table. The shorter of the two young women looked around, her red lips slightly parted. Her black glasses gave her an air of quiet intelligence, while her black T-shirt, with a fantasy image on the front, hinted at a geekier side. As she approached, Bea could sense her hesitation, and her pale cheeks coloured slightly as she stopped awkwardly before them. In contrast, her companion radiated warmth and openness. Her brown-skinned face lit up with a beautiful smile as she grinned at Perry, making Bea want to smile back. The woman cut an athletic figure, her short black hair framing her brown eyes perfectly. "Hey, Perry!" she greeted warmly, her voice brimming with enthusiasm. The younger woman offered a more subdued hello, her eyes flicking between Bea and the others.

Perry sprang up as Daisy unfurled herself from beneath the table. "Ana, Cleo, meet Lady Beatrice, the Countess of Rossex." Bea stood. "Lady Beatrice, this is Cleo Barrington and Ana Halsall. They're the runners on *Bake Off Wars*."

Bea smiled, holding out her hand. "Nice to meet you both."

The taller woman, now identified as Ana, grinned broadly

as she shook hands with Bea. "You too, my lady. We're so excited to be filming here. This place is just awesome."

Daisy, her black eyes shining with curiosity, was sniffing at the newcomers' shoes.

"I agree," Bea said, grinning back. "But then I *am* slightly biased."

Ana chuckled. Bea held her hand out to Cleo. She took it gingerly and mumbled, "Hello."

"And who's this?" Ana asked, crouching down level with Daisy, who was now sniffing Cleo's black jeans.

"This is Daisy," Perry said. "She lives here too."

"Aw, she's adorable," Ana cooed as she tickled Daisy under her chin.

"And this is Claire and Ellie, who you may have met already as they've been on set a few times," Perry added.

Cleo inclined her head while Ana straightened up. "Yes. I think I saw you both this morning."

"So what does a runner do?" Bea asked.

"Well, we sort of run around doing whatever needs doing. Like a personal assistant but to everyone," Ana replied.

"That sounds busy."

"It is, but we love it; don't we, Cleo?" Ana glanced at her young friend, who looked as if she wanted to disagree. Instead, she nodded. "This is my second series, and afterwards I'm hoping to become a production assistant."

Bea smiled. There was no doubt Ana enjoyed her job.

"What about you, Cleo? Is this your second series too?" Claire asked, sounding as if she was interviewing her for a position.

She shook her head. "No."

Claire waited. Cleo shuffled uncomfortably, then looked at the floor.

Well, she wouldn't get the job!

"It's her first." Ana broke the silence. "Anyway, we don't want to disturb you. It was nice to meet you all." She grabbed Cleo's arm and steered her away from them and towards a table in the corner.

Daisy sighed and curled up by Bea's feet.

"Ana's lovely," Perry said as he and Bea sat back down. "She's been really nice to me and Simon whenever we're on set."

"Cleo's a bit of a wet blanket though," Claire said, knocking back the rest of her tea.

"I think she's just shy," Perry said.

Claire checked her watch and gasped. "Goodness, look at the time! I'd better head back to work," she said, springing up from her chair.

Ellie rose too. "Yes, I'd better get this order in."

Claire bent down to ruffle Daisy's head. Then the two women said goodbye and slipped out of the Breakfast Room.

As they left, Bea glanced over at Cleo and Ana, who were engaged in a quiet discussion across the room. What must it be like working on such a high-profile television show, especially with the bad feeling that seemed to lurk beneath the surface?

"Right then," Perry said. "Shall we go to the office and look at those plans for the cabins at the Three Lakes rehabilitation centre?"

Bea nodded, her thoughts shifting from the mysterious world of *Bake Off Wars* to the more pressing matter at hand. Her older brother, Fred, an ex-Army officer, was the patron of the military charity Care for Heroes, which last year had launched the campaign Rehab for Heroes to fund the building and running of a purpose-built recovery complex for military personnel. The location in nearby Fawstead, aptly named Three Lakes because three lakes dominated the site, had already been donated by her family, and construction of the communal rehab centre and supporting ground structure had begun. She and Perry had volunteered their services to design the interior of the easy-access chalets being built on-site for those staying at the facility.

"Indeed."

"Did you have any particular ideas in mind for the cabins?" she asked Perry, her mind racing with possibilities. She envisioned cosy interiors filled with warm colours and soft textures, spaces that would provide comfort and solace to the residents.

Perry smiled, his blue eyes sparkling with excitement. "I've got a few thoughts," he admitted, his voice tinged with enthusiasm.

"Great, then let's get some of them together to present to the charity board next month, shall we?"

They rose as Daisy opened one eye, then slowly lifted herself onto her back legs and stretched.

As the three of them exited the Breakfast Room, Bea was invigorated by the prospect of contributing to the charity. The rehabilitation centre would provide essential support to many individuals in need, and she was eager for herself and Perry to play their part.

6

9:45 AM, FRIDAY 16 APRIL

Looking around at the tranquil beauty of Francis Court, Bea strolled alongside Richard Fitzwilliam. Daisy scampered ahead, weaving in and out of the trees and bushes, her nose glued to the ground. As they ambled in companionable silence, Bea was acutely aware of Rich's warm presence next to her as she caught a whiff of his musky aftershave. She glanced at him out of the corner of her eye. The sun played off his brown hair and highlighted the powerful lines of his face. *He looks quite handsome*, she thought as he walked beside her with his hands in the pockets of his wool overcoat.

She drifted closer to him without realising it until her arm brushed his. Startled, she sprang away, her cheeks glowing as the heat travelled across her face. *He must have noticed. How could he not?* It seemed to her like the entire world had stopped when they'd touched, yet he hadn't seemed to have reacted. She couldn't bring herself to look over at him and risk making eye contact, so she looked up as a flock of birds darted through the air in perfect synchrony above her.

Suddenly, a wasp buzzed past her face, and she jumped back with a start.

"Are you alright, Bea?" Rich asked, a frown across his forehead. "You seem antsy."

"Er, yes. It just took me by surprise." She gave a quick snort. *Oh my goodness!* She needed to pull herself together. *Change the subject...* "So how are you feeling after your first course of rehab?" Having not seen him for almost a week, the first thing she'd noticed had been the healthy bloom that had replaced his previously sallow complexion.

"Great. I'm feeling much stronger." He ran a hand through his short hair, peppered with grey at the temples. "In fact, I'm ready to go back to work."

Bea's heart sank. *Could he be leaving again so soon?* Surely he still had a few weeks before they would even consider assessing him to return to active duty? And anyway, didn't he still have one more session of intensive physio to do before that? She opened her mouth to remind him they wouldn't let him go back yet, then stopped. Wasn't he always pointing out to her she liked to tell him what to do? *You're not his mother, Bea!* She carried on walking and said nothing.

He sighed. "I can't bear sitting around, unable to do anything."

Is he bored with being here? She swallowed painfully. *Is he bored with me?*

Daisy suddenly darted off, her white fur a blur against the lush greenery. Her excited barks echoed through the air as she disappeared around a bend in the path.

"What's she up to?" Rich asked, an amused smile on his face.

"She's probably seen a squirrel or—"

Daisy reappeared, bounding towards them with two young boys in tow. Bea smiled. Her son, Sam, his reddish-brown hair tousled from exertion, and his best friend, Archie, a mop of curly brown hair topping his slender frame, were pushing their bikes towards them.

"Hello, you two," she greeted as they drew close. "I thought you were going into the village to check out the market?"

"Hi, Mum. We were, but Archie's got a flat," Sam said when he reached them. He turned to Rich. "Oh, sorry, Fitzwilliam. I don't think you've met my friend Archie yet. He's at my school. Arch, this is Detective Chief Inspector Fitzwilliam. He works for the Protection and Investigation (Royal) Services."

Archie's eyes widened as he stared up at Rich.

"Nice to meet you, Archie," Rich said, extending a hand to the boy.

Archie took his hand. "Do you have to stop Sam and his mum from being kidnapped?" he blurted out.

"That's part of my job, yes," Rich replied, attempting to suppress a grin.

"And he got shot a little while ago!" Sam told Archie, his eyes flashing with excitement. "Right in his middle! He's here getting better."

Archie's mouth opened to form an O shape. "Really? Did it hurt? Do you have a scar?"

Bea stifled a laugh. *Boys! They always get down to the heart of the matter quickly.*

"Er, yes. It hurt a bit, but I'm much better now. And yes, I have a scar." Rich shifted on his feet.

"Cool!" the boys chorused.

Bea put her hand up to her nose and mouth to cover a snort.

"So what seems to be the problem?" Rich asked, nodding at the bikes.

Archie gestured to his, where a deflated tire hung limply. "I popped my tyre, sir."

"We thought Mr Ward might help," Sam added.

Rich slowly crouched down, examining the damaged wheel with a critical eye. "I can show you how to fix this if you'd like. There should be some tools in the garage block we can use."

"Really?" Sam's brown eyes lit up with gratitude.

"That would be brilliant!" Archie cried.

"Okay. Then meet me there in fifteen minutes, and we'll get it sorted," Rich assured them.

With a nod and an exchange of excited whispers, the boys took off towards the garages, leaving Bea and Rich to resume their walk.

"Shall we?" He held out an arm and steered her towards the entrance of the formal gardens. Bea nodded as her thoughts drifted to the unexpected friendship that seemed to have developed between Rich and her son over the past eight weeks. Sam had briefly met Rich last October when they'd been involved in the messy business at Fenn House. Her son had been fascinated by Rich's job and slightly in awe of the senior police officer. But it had only been after Rich had come to recuperate at Francis Court that they had really got to know each other.

Bea smiled, recalling how Sam had pestered her to take him with her to visit Rich at Hope Cottage. She'd been reluctant at first, concerned that Rich would rather not have to entertain a curious fourteen-year-old boy. But he'd surprised her when he'd answered all of Sam's questions about his injury with patience and care, and in turn had asked her son about school and, in particular, the sports he loved. When it had turned out that Rich had played rugby for the Army, they'd chatted away,

Daisy happily sandwiched between them, about positions and game strategy. Since that first visit, Sam had regularly accompanied her or Simon to Hope Cottage or had joined her, Rich, and Daisy on a walk around the village or the estate.

It warmed her heart to see them so comfortable in each other's company. Another positive male role model in Sam's life was always welcome as far as she was concerned.

"Thank you for offering to help the boys," Bea said warmly as they strolled through the rose garden, the bushes just beginning to show their buds. "You really didn't have to."

"I don't mind," Rich replied with a smile. "My nephews are almost the same age as Sam, so I've done my fair share of bike repairs over the years."

Daisy suddenly barked and tore off towards a couple in the distance. Recognising the pair, Bea waved at her brother, Fred, walking next to Summer York.

"Is that the woman who's stolen Fred's heart?" Rich asked curiously, his brown eyes following Bea's gaze.

"Indeed," she confirmed, feeling a touch of surprise at her brother's openness with Rich. "Fred told you about her?"

"I bumped into him when I got back last night. He mentioned he'd met the woman of his dreams." Fred was another member of her family who seemed to have struck up a friendship with the chief inspector. The result of the arrest from the incident at Gollingham Palace, when Rich had been shot apprehending a killer, had led to multiple other arrests of organised crime suspects around the world. Fred, a special observer for MI6, the British intelligence service, had been working with her and Rich to expose them. Fred now seemed to consider Rich a buddy-in-arms.

How seamlessly Rich has integrated into our lives. Almost without me noticing.

As Fred and Summer approached, Daisy pranced around their feet, clearly delighted by the attention. Fred's face was alight with happiness. "Summer, this is Richard Fitzwilliam," Fred said, his voice full of pride. "Fitz, meet Summer York."

"Delighted to meet you, Summer," Rich said, his smile genuine.

He can be so charming sometimes.

"Thank you, Richard," Summer replied graciously, returning his smile. "Fred speaks highly of you."

"Does he now?" Rich raised an eyebrow. Fred shrugged. Bea suppressed a grin.

"Oh, by the way, Fitz, I've been meaning to invite you to come and look at Three Lakes, the rehab centre I was telling you about. You're ex-military, so I thought you might be interested. We're at the point where we can have visitors on-site now. Do you fancy it?" Fred asked.

Rich nodded. "Sounds good to me."

He turned and winked at Bea. "Maybe they can give me a few tips," he whispered, patting his midriff. Bea grinned.

"Excellent!" Fred clapped his hands together, not appearing to have heard Rich's aside. "How about we go in about an hour?"

"Great," Rich agreed. "I have a job to do over at the garages. Meet you there?"

Fred dipped his head, and he and Summer bid their farewells.

"They seem comfortable together," Rich said as Fred and Summer strolled around the corner and out of sight.

"I think they're very happy," Bea said. Then she frowned.

"But?" Rich prompted.

"I worry what will happen when the press gets wind of their relationship." She knew from last summer when she'd had a brief liaison with a famous chef just how brutal that scrutiny could be. "They can be ruthless, especially with someone as high-profile as Fred."

"Let's hope they can weather the storm," Rich said. "If they can get through that, then they'll get through anything."

"Um," Bea replied. "She hasn't met my grandmother yet!"

7

LUNCHTIME, FRIDAY 16 APRIL

In the Breakfast Room at Francis Court, Bea absentmindedly stroked the top of Daisy's head as the little dog sat quietly on her lap, her paws hanging over the side of her mistress' leg as she gazed out of the window that lined one wall. *On the lookout for squirrels, no doubt.* The bright and airy restaurant was filled with sunlight spilling in from the large windows, and a grand chandelier hung from the ceiling, casting a calming shine over those seated at the tables around the room. The clinking of cutlery against plates added a peaceful backdrop to the chatter that filled the restaurant.

Around their table, Perry perched on the edge of his chair in anticipation of his lunch being delivered while his husband, Simon, discussed this morning's filming with Ryan.

"We finally got it right on the seventh take," Ryan said, grinning. "I'm not sure why we have to do these little skits, you know. Hamilton and Summer are the funny ones. Vera just stares at the camera without smiling, which seems to be what they want, and I'm standing there like a wooden pole just manically smiling."

"I'm sure it wasn't that bad," Simon said.

Ryan raised an eyebrow.

"Well, not by the seventh take anyway," Perry chimed in. They all laughed.

Bea caught sight of two unfamiliar faces entering the restaurant. The men paused in the doorway, scanning the room for a table. Ryan noticed them too and waved them over.

"It's Harvey Jury and Austin Matthews from *Bake Off Wars*." Perry leaned over and whispered to Bea, "Harvey's the food producer, and Austin's the director."

Daisy wriggled in Bea's arms as they approached the group.

"Ryan, Simon," the younger of the two men greeted them. "Austin and I are just grabbing a quick lunch. The cafe is full, so we thought we'd try this place for a change."

"Yes, we're on a tight schedule today," Austin added, bustling with energy, his metal-framed glasses perched on his round face. "But we've still got to eat."

"Harvey, Austin, this is Lady Beatrice, the Countess of Rossex," Ryan said, gesturing towards Bea. "And this is Simon's husband, Perry Juke. You may have seen him on set."

"Nice to meet you," Bea said warmly, taking in their appearances with curiosity.

"Likewise," Harvey replied, offering her a small smile, then nodded at Perry.

"An absolute pleasure," Austin chimed in, his blue eyes glancing around the room as if he was already preparing to move onto his next task. "Well, we'd best find somewhere to sit."

"Enjoy your lunch," Ryan said as the duo left to claim a nearby table.

Bea watched them leave, noting the contrast between Harvey's stocky build and Austin's slight frame. As she turned back to her friends, she found Ryan and Simon exchanging meaningful glances.

"Is it just me, or does it seem odd that they're having lunch together?" Simon asked quietly, leaning in closer to the group. "I wouldn't have pegged them as friends."

"I don't think I've ever seen them speak to each other off set," Ryan added.

"Well, I've heard something that may shed some light on it," Perry said conspiratorially. "Apparently, Harvey and Austin were seen with Mark Jacobs in Windstanton a couple of evenings ago having a drink in a pub there."

How does Perry know these things? "Isn't he the judge you replaced, Ryan?" she asked.

Ryan nodded. "Why would they be meeting up?"

"And what's Mark even doing in the area?" Simon asked, his voice laced with suspicion.

"He and Austin were tight, according to Ana." Perry glanced over to the table where the two men sat. "Austin fought hard to keep him on."

Ah, so the young runner is Perry's source of gossip…

"I wonder what they're up to?" Ryan ran his hand across his chin.

The group fell quiet, a twinge of unease creeping into the cosy atmosphere, as if the two men at the restaurant hinted at something more significant than a simple lunch meeting.

Nicky arrived with their food, breaking the silence. Bea dropped Daisy gently to the floor as Nicky placed a tuna toastie on the table in front of her. "Thanks, Nicky," she said, opening her napkin and placing it on her knees.

Just then, a burst of deep laughter echoed through the restaurant. Bea's gaze followed the sound to the entrance, where two men stood. They looked very similar from a distance, both dark-skinned and sporting black beards. She instantly recognised the slightly taller of the two as Mark Jacobs, the well-known chef and ex-judge of the previous season's *Bake Off Wars*. The other man, dressed casually in joggers and a hoodie, looked familiar too, but she couldn't place him. Was he another crew member that she'd seen around the place?

"Talk of the devil," Ryan murmured under his breath, casting a sidelong glance at Simon.

"What's Mark doing with Hamilton Moore?" Perry asked, leaning forward to get a better look at the two men.

Who?

Perry saw the look on her face. "He's the other new presenter on the show."

"Ah." She smiled gratefully. Under the table, Daisy gave a low *woof*, and Bea leaned down to pat her on her head.

"No idea," Ryan replied to Simon, his brow furrowed in concentration as his eyes followed them across the room. The two men headed to a free table in the nearest corner. As they got closer, it was easier to make out the differences between them. Mark had a touch of grey at his temples. Hamilton was younger and athletic looking. Mark stopped as he spied Harvey and Austin. He tapped Hamilton on the shoulder and gestured towards the other two men, then he changed direction and, with Hamilton following, went over to join them. They greeted each other with enthusiastic handshakes and bright smiles.

"Something seems a bit off about this," Ryan said, a sandwich halfway up to his mouth.

"Could Mark be planning something?" Perry suggested, his voice barely above a whisper. "Like a coup."

"I hope not!" Ryan replied quickly, putting down his knife and fork. "Or else I'll be out of a job before the show even gets aired."

"I'm sure it's nothing to worry about," Simon reassured him as he cut his chicken salad baguette in two.

"Yes," Perry agreed. "They're probably just old friends catching up."

As Bea took a mouthful of food, she stole a look over at where all four men now sat. The light streamed through the windows, lighting up their table. Mark and Hamilton had both assumed a more serious demeanour, leaning in close as the men talked in hushed tones. Mark's eyes occasionally darted around the room, while Hamilton looked pensive, his hands clutching the armrests of his chair as though he were about to stand up any minute. Harvey and Austin seemed to be listening intently and nodded occasionally. *Whatever they're talking about, it seems serious. Certainly more than just a casual chat.*

Bea glanced around the rest of the room; no one else seemed to notice their presence at all. Everyone was too engrossed in their own conversations or too busy eating lunch to pay much attention to them. *Even so*, Bea thought, *if they were up to no good, surely they would've found somewhere less public to conduct their business?*

She returned her attention back to her table just in time to see Perry slip a piece of chicken underneath the table and into the open jaws of Daisy. He glanced up and caught her eye. She gave him a look. He blushed, and looking at his sandwich, he took a large bite.

Next to him, Simon was staring out of the window. *He looks worried.* Despite what he'd said to Ryan, did he think Mark was up to something? Bea stifled a sigh. After the craziness of the last year, she really just wanted a quiet life with no drama. Yet somehow she had a feeling that she wouldn't get what she wanted while *Bake Off Wars* was at Francis Court.

8

BACK TO 11:25 AM, MONDAY 19 APRIL

Vera Bolt? Bea stood dumbstruck, her green eyes wide as she stared at Ana Halsall. The words that had just escaped Ana's lips echoed in Bea's head, threatening to overwhelm her.

She looked over at Perry, who was leaning against the wall. His blue eyes were shining with excitement as he processed the news. "Who would have thought it?" he whispered, slowly shaking his head. "The nation's sweetheart. The Queen of Bakes. Dead!"

Ana bowed her head, wringing her hands anxiously. "I found her on the floor of The Tent. It's like something out of a nightmare."

Bea's mind raced, attempting to make sense of the situation. Was it an accident? Or could it be murder? Her heart pounded in her chest, refusing to calm down as dread seeped into every corner of her thoughts. *Not again!* Daisy gently nudged her in the leg, and she looked down into her large black eyes.

"There's blood everywhere," Ana continued, her voice cracking. She shook her head. "It's horrible." She moaned softly.

For a moment, no one spoke. Bea's head was thick with disbelief. *Get a grip, Bea! You need to check she really is dead. Now!*

"Right," Bea said, taking a deep breath to steady herself. "Ana, stay here with Daisy and keep watch. When you see either the police or estate security, direct them inside." She turned to her little dog. "Daisy, stay here with Ana," Bea instructed, her voice firm despite the turmoil inside her. "Good girl."

She turned to Perry. "We need to go in and see what's happened."

He nodded slowly, then grasped the door handle, pausing for a moment before pushing it open. They rushed into the building, their footsteps echoing loudly through the empty halls. "Where's The Tent?" Bea cried above the noise.

"End of the corridor, on the right," he replied, his face pale but focused.

She hurried on despite knowing each step was bringing her closer to the scene she dreaded. *Keep going, Bea.* As she entered the large barn hall, the room's grandeur struck her. High ceilings loomed overhead, making her feel insignificant in the face of tragedy. Windows lined both sides of the room, allowing the bright sun to cast an eerie light across the twelve cooking stations arranged neatly in two rows of six with a wide gap between them. There was a considerable amount of space left at the front and back of the room, presumably where the filming crew and presenters were based.

Bea stopped partway down the aisle, unable to tear her gaze away from the lifeless body lying between the cooking stations. She could feel the horror clawing its way up her throat, threatening to choke her with its intensity. A large deep-red patch of blood had spread across the floor, pooling on either side of the aisle in front of the kitchen units. *So much blood*... There was no question. Vera Bolt was dead.

"I'll check for a pulse, but…" Perry trailed off, placing a hand on her shoulder and giving it a squeeze as he walked past her. He knelt down beside the crumpled body sprawled on the floor and held his fingers to Vera's pale neck. After a few seconds, he turned to Bea and shook his head.

"Indeed," Bea whispered, then took a deep breath, forcing herself to ignore her churning stomach.

Perry stood and stepped away from Vera's colourless form. He hesitated for a moment before reaching into his pocket and pulling out his phone.

He's going to take photos of the crime scene, isn't he? Perry always did this when given a chance. He said Simon would find them useful for future books. It never failed to shock her at how quickly he became detached. She felt a sudden urge to laugh. *Simon must have a vast collection of real-life murder scenes to refer to now.*

She looked away and examined the room. "Look," she cried, pointing towards one of the work surfaces near Vera's body. A wooden knife block rested on the back edge of the bench, with two black handles sticking out. There was a gap where a third knife should be. She quickly scanned the other workstations. They all had knife blocks on them. None of them had a knife missing. "Was that the murder weapon, do you think?"

"Seems likely," Perry murmured, snapping a photo of the knife block. He paused, frowning. "The killer must have been very careful. There are no bloody footprints or handprints anywhere around here."

Bea dropped her eyes to the floor. Her mind raced with possible scenarios. "They must have gone out the way we came in."

"Or they could have gone around the workstations and out that way," he said, pointing to an exit on the other side of Vera's body.

The sharp sound of Daisy's bark outside made Bea start.

"Perry!" she hissed, her heart racing. "Someone's coming!"

Perry looked up from his phone, his eyes wide with understanding. He quickly slipped it back into his pocket, falling silent as they both turned towards the entrance behind them.

As Bea waited, the gravity of the situation hit her like a wave, filling her with dread. She needed to maintain her composure and cooperate with the authorities; now was not the time for amateur detective work. Anyway, she really didn't have the stomach for it. She thought back to Alex Sterling, who had died at Francis Court just a year ago. Another tragedy. Another senseless loss. The weight of it settled heavily on her chest, making it difficult to breathe. She didn't want to go through that again.

"Adrian." She stepped forward to greet the man in the black suit who had entered the room, followed by two uniformed men. Francis Court's head of security looked down at the floor, then back to Bea, his face etched with concern. "Are you alright, my lady?"

She gave him a sad smile. "Yes, thank you. Mr Juke checked for a pulse, but…"

Adrian Breen nodded, then running his hands through his short grey hair, he turned to the two men. "Secure the room. CID will be here soon." His eyes flicked between Bea and Perry as he gestured towards the door he had just come through. "I think it's best you both leave while we take care of things in here."

"Of course," Bea agreed, stepping back to give the offi-cers room to move past her. "Thanks, Adrian. We'll wait outside." She glanced at Perry, who returned a brief nod of reassurance, and they left the room.

9

JUST AFTER 11 AM, MONDAY 19 APRIL

Where are they? Bea stood outside the Old Barn, scanning the horizon for signs of the police arriving. She knew they would have to drive the back route to the staff cottages and then on past them to the Old Barn access road. Why couldn't she see them through the trees? She tapped her foot.

To her left, Perry fidgeted nervously with the cuffs of his light-weight coat, his blond hair catching the sunlight in a fiery halo. Daisy sat by his side, her ears pricked and alert.

Ana leaned against the wall, her face flushed as she clutched a crumpled tissue in her trembling hand. "Who could do such a thing?" she choked out between sniffles, her gaze drifting towards the barn door where a uniformed security man stood guard, his stern expression never wavering.

"Try not to worry too much, Ana," Perry said, moving over to her. He gave her a reassuring pat on the shoulder. "The police will get to the bottom of it. They should be here in a jiffy."

Questions swirled around in Bea's mind. *Who would want to hurt Vera Bolt? And why?* She shivered. This was different from the previous murders they'd encountered. This hadn't been made to look like an accident. It didn't appear the killer had tried to cover it up. Bea shivered. Facing someone, looking them in the eye and sticking a knife into them seemed so personal. *Was it a crime of passion?* Had Vera been able to incite that much hatred in someone that they could do that? *Or was it motivated by love?*

"Bea, do you hear that?" Perry whispered, dragging her away from her thoughts. Her eyes narrowed as she looked towards the cottages. The distant hum of an approaching engine was followed by the appearance of a black Volvo and a marked police car, gravel crunching beneath their tyres. Fenshire CID was here.

A few minutes later, Detective Inspector Mike Ainsley appeared around the corner of the Old Barn flanked by three police officers, two of them in uniform. Daisy jumped up and hurtled towards them. He stopped briefly and patted Daisy on the head.

Bea smiled as he walked towards them and held out her hand. "Mike, it's good to see you," she greeted warmly.

The man with the dark-grey hair and sharp features reached out and took her hand. "Lady Beatrice. It's always good to see you too," he replied, his deep voice resonating as he gave her a firm handshake. "Although I wish the circumstances were different." His eyes darted to the entrance of the Old Barn, then he turned to the shorter man next to him. "You know DS Hines, of course?" Bea nodded and smiled at the younger man.

His eyes crinkled in a genuine smile as he shook her hand. "Your ladyship."

The inspector turned to him. "Right, Hines, can you check in with Adrian Breen, please?" The sergeant gestured to one of the two officers in uniform to follow him, and they headed for the door.

Mike peered around Bea. "Ah, Mr Juke. How are you?" He held out his hand.

Perry scuttled forward. "Inspector. We must stop meeting like this," he said, returning the handshake with a wry smile.

Mike gave a dry laugh. "It's becoming a bit of a habit." His gaze flickered to Ana, who was now standing straight, her eyes wide as she stared at them.

"Oh, this is Ana Halsall, inspector. She found the body," Perry said, beckoning Ana over.

Mike greeted the young woman who stepped forward tentatively. "I'm sure this has all been a massive shock for you, but I'm afraid I will need to ask you a few questions." He gestured to the other police officer, and she joined them. "PC Fowler here will take you inside, where you can sit down and have a cup of tea. I'll be in to see you soon. Is that okay?"

Ana allowed herself to be steered towards the open door of the Old Barn by the officer.

The inspector turned back to Bea and Perry. "Of course, I've had to inform PaIRS of the incident." He smiled apologetically at her, knowing that the protocol of Protection and Investigation (Royal) Services taking the lead in any incident at Francis Court because of her families' position within the royal family had bothered her in the past. She nodded, having accepted a while ago that PaIRS had jurisdiction wherever there was or could be perceived to be a threat to royalty. After all, it was how she'd met Rich in the first place. *Will they assign him to the case even though he's still off work?* "They'll be sending someone over later."

"Do you know who?" Bea asked, glancing at Perry. "DCI Fitzwilliam is currently out of action." Mike raised an eyebrow, and Bea briefly told him about Rich's shooting.

"Oh," Perry cried, his eyes glinting. "Perhaps they'll send Em."

Detective Chief Inspector Emma McKeer-Adler was a colleague of Rich's, and they had worked with her on two investigations recently. *It would be great to have someone we know.*

"Whoever they send, I'm sure they'll be more than capable," Mike said reassuringly. "I'll let you know when they arrive. In the meantime, I need to take Miss Halsall's statement. I'll catch you both later."

They said goodbye, and the inspector disappeared into the Old Barn.

"So what do we do now?" Perry asked.

Bea hesitated. She really wanted a coffee, but part of her felt they should tell Rich first. Maybe he *was* well enough to lead the investigation. *Better the devil you know…*

She glanced at Perry. "Do you think we should tell Rich about this?" Perry tilted his head to one side, and she could see the uncertainty in his eyes mirroring her own.

"Well," he said. "I suppose we could. He's here, after all. And even if he's not well enough to take the case on, he might have some say over who they assign it to."

Good point. The last thing she wanted was a complete stranger at Francis Court asking questions and upsetting everyone. "Come on, Daisy. Let's go and see your favourite person."

"Hey! Don't you mean second favourite person?" Perry pouted, following them as they walked away from the Old Barn.

Bea smirked. "Yes, of course I do."

Perry huffed as he pulled his phone from his coat pocket. "I'd better let Simon know what's happening," he said, his fingers flying across the screen as he typed a text message.

"Ask him if he wants to meet up later. If he's not too busy writing, that is," Bea said as they crossed the Long Drive, the old carriageway that led to the front of Francis Court manor, and headed towards the cluster of stone cottages on the other side.

"He's just in the outlining stage of his new series at the moment, so he's fairly flexible." Perry hit send.

They walked to the end of the terrace of quaint white-washed cottages, and Perry opened the gate of the last one, Hope Cottage. Blooming flowers and lush greenery lined the path leading to the blue front door, but their beauty did little to ease the anxiety bubbling up inside Bea. Rich was supposed to be resting. *Should I be bothering him with this murder?*

As they neared the entrance, Daisy's tail wagged excitedly, and she let out a low *woof.* Perry rang the bell.

What if he's having a nap? Perhaps we shouldn't have come....

"Bea, Perry!" Rich greeted them warmly as he opened the door. "I wasn't expecting to see you today." Daisy nudged his legs, and his rugged features softened into a genuine smile as he leaned down and ruffled the fur on her head. He straightened and, pushing the door open, said, "Come on in."

Daisy darted ahead, and they followed her through the hallway and into the cosy living area. The interior was simple yet elegant, with a plush velvet sofa, warm-toned fabrics, and an inviting fireplace along the wall opposite the large bay window. Daisy, having finished her sniffing expedition of the room, jumped up onto an armchair by the large bay window and curled up with a sigh.

"Coffee. Tea?"

I'm desperate for a coffee. "That—"

"No thanks, Fitzwilliam. We're about to meet up with Simon," Perry jumped in.

But…

"We don't want to disturb you, but there's something we think you should know."

"Is everything alright?" Rich asked, a deep furrow creasing his brow as he looked from Perry to Bea.

"Er." She swallowed. "Rich, Vera Bolt has just been found dead at the Old Barn."

"Vera Bolt, as in the judge on the baking show they're filming here?" Like Bea, Rich hadn't really shown much interest in the TV show but had heard enough about it from Perry to recognise the name. His eyes widened. "How did it happen?"

"She was stabbed to death!" Perry told him triumphantly, then blushed and looked down at the floor.

"Murdered…" Rich muttered, sinking down to perch on the end of the armchair, his fingers absently stroking Daisy's head. For a moment, there was silence.

"Any idea who PaIRS will send to investigate?" Bea finally asked. "With you out of commission, I mean."

"Could it be Em?" Perry ventured, a hopeful tone in his voice.

Rich shook his head, his expression thoughtful. "No. She's currently with the king and queen on their tour of Wales." He paused, his gaze fixed on a small framed painting of a seaside village that adorned the wall above the fireplace. "Um, I wonder…" he muttered, rubbing his stubbly chin. He stood up. "I'll make a call."

Bea raised her hand to shield her eyes from the sunlight filtering through the delicate curtains behind him.

"I'll find out who they've assigned to the case," he said, moving towards a small table where a mobile phone rested on top. "Even better, I might convince them to let me take over the investigation, seeing as I'm already here." Determination was etched across his features.

Yes, but are you well enough? Torn between his wellbeing and her desire to have someone who they knew and trusted leading the investigation, she said, "You still have a couple of weeks before they said they would let you go back to work. Are you really well enough?"

Rich exhaled, running a hand through his hair. "Bea," he warned, his voice low. "I can make that decision for myself."

I know! I'm not your mother!

A glint of light flickered in his brown eyes as they met hers. She slowly nodded. He turned away and reached for his phone.

"We'll leave you to it then," she said with a breeziness she didn't feel. "Come on, Daisy."

Perry followed her out of the room. "See you later," he called over his shoulder.

As she gently closed the front door of Hope Cottage behind her, Bea let out a deep sigh.

"He'll be fine, Bea. He'll have help from Mike and his team, *and* they'll send him a DS to do all the donkey work," he whispered. "And it would be good if it was him. He already knows how to navigate an investigation at Francis Court."

It would be the ideal situation. *We won't even need to get involved*, she thought. *I can concentrate on moving into The Dower House and let Rich get on with it.*

10

A FEW MINUTES LATER, MONDAY 19 APRIL

Rich lowered himself into the armchair, his phone in one hand as he searched for a number from his contact list. He tapped on the name. Leaning back in the chair, he smiled when he felt the warm patch left from where Daisy had been curled up earlier. A pit opened up in his stomach as the phone rang at the other end. *Please pick up!*

"Richard," Superintendent Nigel Blake greeted him. The word reverberated in his boss' deep voice. "What can I do for you?" As usual, there was no small talk from the senior police officer from PaIRS.

"Er, sir. I understand there's been a suspicious death here at Francis Court," Rich said, rubbing his free hand along the top of the arm of his chair.

Blake said nothing.

"Er, so I thought that as I'm here already, I could—"

"No, Richard." Blake's response was clear and firm.

Rich stifled a sigh. *I haven't even finished.* "But, sir. I know the area. I know the site. I know the local police, the staff…" He trailed off.

An uneasy silence hung in the air. Then Blake spoke,

"No, Richard." His voice was low and calm. He sighed. "I'm sorry," he added.

What can I say to convince him?

"But, sir. The Astley family won't want someone they don't know—"

"Richard!" The superintendent raised his voice.

Rats!

"You are not available for active duty. For all sorts of health and safety reasons and insurance conditions, I cannot assign you to this job. Do you understand?"

"But if I had Spicer to do all the running around, and I just did the interviews…it would be light duties. I'm sure I can get the medical board to sign me back—"

"DCI Fitzwilliam!" Blake barked.

Rich's throat tightened. *Oh no, I'm in trouble now…*

A deep sigh came from the other end of the phone. "Look, Richard, I understand you want to get back to work. I know you must be frustrated. But there's a good reason they stipulate a period of time for rest and recovery. You were seriously injured during a traumatic event."

What's he saying? That I'm not up to coming back to work mentally? Rich swallowed. He hadn't told anyone about the occasional nightmares. *I'm dealing with it.* He'd be fine as soon as he had something to think about other than the moment he'd stared down the barrel of a gun, knowing he was going to die. His hands were clammy. He shifted the phone to his other ear and wiped his now free hand down the side of his jeans. *I just need to get back to normal…*

"How did your intensive physio go?" Blake asked.

Hasn't he seen the report? "It was fine. They said I'm doing well."

"Physically, Richard, yes. But you refused to see the trauma counsellor?"

So he has *seen the report.* "I don't need to, sir. I'm fine." He shifted in his seat.

"You know you need to be signed off by both the physio *and* the psychologist before you can return, don't you?"

Good grief! How hard can they make it to get back to work? "Yes, sir. And I'm ready."

"Not until they say so, Richard."

Doesn't Blake want me back? Do they think I'm not up to it anymore? He swallowed. "Yes, sir."

"And about this business up at Francis Court. I've already sent someone to head up the investigation."

"Can I ask who, sir?"

Blake told him, then with a sharp, "I'll see you in two weeks' time and not before," his boss cut the call.

Fitzwilliam stared at his phone screen. *Really?* He dropped the mobile on the table and wiggled his stiff fingers. *Of all the people!* His chest felt heavy. *Bea won't like this…*

11

2 PM, MONDAY 19 APRIL

Bea held the delicate china teacup in her slender fingers as she sipped her coffee, the rich aroma wafting up to mingle with the sweet scent of the dessert Perry was devouring next to her. The atmosphere around the table in the Breakfast Room at Francis Court was subdued, punctuated only by the sound of cutlery scraping on a plate as Perry scooped up another spoonful of Bakewell tart and ice cream and, sighing contentedly, popped it into his mouth.

Underneath the table, Daisy lay curled up between her and Perry. The little white terrier's soft snores punctuated the quiet conversations that filled the room from the few tables still occupied by staff members having a late lunch. As the afternoon sun streamed through the tall windows, casting a warm richness on the polished wooden floor, Bea glanced over at Simon and Ryan opposite her, who were both nursing cups of coffee and staring into space. *No doubt trying to come to terms with the reality of Vera Bolt's death.* It still seemed hard to believe that such a violent death had occurred only a few hours ago. What would happen to the TV show now? *Will they postpone filming? Cancel the show even?* She had no idea how these things worked. Poor Ryan, he'd only recorded one episode. "Ryan," she said gently, studying his face for any signs of distress. "I can't imagine how shocking this news must be for you."

Ryan's large hands trembled slightly as he clutched his coffee cup, his eyes wide. "It's…it's hard to believe. I was only with her this morning at the cast and crew debrief meeting, and now she's gone." He slowly shook his head. "When Perry texted Simon, and we read the message, I just didn't believe it at first. And the way she died…" His voice trailed off. He shook his head again.

So Vera had been at a meeting with everyone this morning. *Did anything happen there that led to her being killed?* "Was everything alright at the meeting this morning? Was Vera okay?"

Ryan sighed, putting down his cup and running a hand through his hair. "To be honest, it wasn't what I expected. It's a regular Monday morning thing apparently, where the production team and talent meet to review the first weekend and discuss any lessons learned before the judges and presenters leave. We're free then until we return on Thursday afternoon to film our segues and intros ready for the weekend. I thought it would be a casual roundup, but—" He stopped and looked down at the table.

"Go on," Bea urged gently. Her stomach fluttered. *Something must have happened…*

"Well, I don't like to talk ill of the dead, but Vera was brutal."

Really?

"She tore into Summer for her presenting style right in front of everyone. She said she was too chatty with the contestants, and she wasn't there to make friends with them," Ryan continued. "Poor Summer was really upset. Then Vera snapped at Cleo when she handed her a cup of coffee, telling her it had too much milk in and to remake it. Next she scolded Leah and Shelly in front of the entire group, saying that after she'd changed the timing because they'd moaned about not having enough time to complete the skills challenge, the contestants then had had too much time, and they'd all completed it well within the time frame. She told them it wasn't good television if they weren't rushing to beat the clock and making mistakes."

"Sounds like a rough morning," Perry murmured sympathetically.

"It was. But the strangest part was when Austin defended the decision, saying that it was his call what made good TV or not. Vera turned on him and said, 'And don't think I don't know what you two are up to,' and pointed at him and Harvey. It was all very awkward."

What does that mean? Bea recalled the conversation they'd had after seeing Harvey and Austin having lunch together on Friday. Hadn't Perry said that Harvey and Austin had been seen with Mark in Windstanton? *Is that what Vera was referring to?*

Perry, pausing mid-bite of his tart, said, "It seems like loads of people had a reason to want Vera dead, doesn't it?"

He was right. Ryan and Simon had reported that tensions had been running high over the weekend, and now it sounded like Vera had made no friends during the meeting this morning. A chill ran down her spine, making her shiver. Did someone at that meeting kill her? But then what had Vera still been doing on-site after the meeting had finished?

"So the judges and the presenters leave after the meetings and go back where?" she asked Ryan.

"Er, back to their lives, you know. Hamilton goes back to Bristol where he lives. Summer is staying on locally. I normally go back to London and do a few days of planning at Nonnina."

Bea had almost forgotten that Ryan was still the executive chef at the exclusive fine dining restaurant in Mayfair.

"And Vera goes back to her house in the Cotswolds," he finished.

Bea frowned. "But she didn't this time?"

Ryan shook his head. "She told me she was staying on to review the timings for this week's skills challenge before she left."

That would explain it. *Hold on…what about Ryan?* Her throat tightened. *Why is he still here?* "And you?" she asked tentatively. "Why didn't you leave after the meeting?"

Ryan exchanged a hesitant look with Simon. "I was in Windstanton with Simon."

Phew… Hold on. Bea raised an eyebrow. *Why?* She turned and looked questioningly at Perry.

He, in turn, looked at Simon. "You should tell her before she thinks you two are having an affair behind my back!"

"I never—" she cried, then noticed the grin on Perry's face.

Ryan, also grinning, nodded at Simon, saying, "Tell her."

Taking a deep breath, Simon said, "Alright, but it's top secret at the moment, Bea. You can't tell anyone. Okay?"

Her heart raced as she tipped her head. *What's going on?*

"We were looking at an empty restaurant for sale. Ryan and I are considering buying it as a joint venture."

Wow! Bea's face split into a huge smile, her earlier concerns momentarily forgotten. "How exciting. I'm thrilled for you. Did you like the place?"

"It has potential," Ryan said, smiling.

"It's right on the seafront, but it will need some work," Simon added, his eyes sparkling.

She could already picture Ryan and Simon bustling about in the new restaurant, their passion for food and hospitality radiating through in every detail. *And Sam will be beyond himself with excitement if it happens...*

"It's very early 'days," Simon added. "That's why we're not saying anything yet. Our next step is to take Charles with us to have a look."

Bea tipped her head. Charles was the building contractor who she'd previously employed to do local refurbishing work. He could tell them if what they wanted to do was workable.

"And I don't want to destabilise the investors at Nonni-na." Ryan pulled a face.

"Indeed," Bea said.

Perry pushed his plate to one side and picked up his coffee. "So getting back to Vera's murder—" Bea flinched. "—have they interviewed you yet, Ryan?" he asked, taking a sip.

Ryan shook his head. "No. I had a call from Austin to tell me Vera was dead, although of course I already knew from your text to Simon. He told me that the police wanted all of us to remain in the area, so he would arrange for my stay to be extended at the hotel in Fawstead, and he'd be in touch."

"They probably won't start interviewing properly until PaIRS arrives," Simon said.

"Rich was making a call when we left him to try to get assigned to the case," Bea told him.

Simon raised an eyebrow. "I thought he was still on sick leave?"

She shrugged. "He is, but he's here already, and he knows Francis Court and the people here. As long as they send someone to do all the legwork, then it would make sense, wouldn't it?"

He rubbed his chin. "I suppose so."

"Well, I, for one, hope Fitzwilliam takes it on. We can then get all the insider information and—"

"Whoa, slow down, Sherlock Holmes!" Simon interrupted Perry. "You're surely not contemplating getting involved in this investigation, are you?"

Perry opened his mouth and turned to Bea.

Sorry, Perry. Not this time. She shook her head slowly. "I'm afraid I agree with Simon, Perry." He closed his mouth, his wide eyes staring at her in disbelief. "Seeing Rich lying on the floor in a pool of blood at Gollingham Palace just a few months ago made me realise just how dangerous catching a killer can be. And anyway, I've had enough with the drama. I just want to finish The Dower House and get settled in there." She gave him a tentative smile. "And we've got the rehab centre at Three Lakes to get started on."

"But aren't you curious about what happened, Bea? Don't you want to find out who did it?" he pouted.

"Of course, but I'm sure Rich will work that out without our help. We'll find out in due course."

Perry sighed deeply and drained his coffee cup. "Okay," he said, tilting his head to one side. "If you really think you can keep your nose out, then…" He raised his beautifully sculpted eyebrow and pulled a face.

Of course, she could 'keep her nose out' as Perry had so kindly put it. She'd had enough of investigating murders to last her a lifetime. She was happy to leave it to PaIRS this time.

The phone in front of her buzzed, and giving Perry a wry smile that she hoped conveyed her determination to not get involved in this case, she picked it up.

. . .

Mike Ainsley, Fenshire CID: *PaIRS are here and the DCI would like to meet you. Are you free to come to the Old Stable Block, where we have been allocated the same office we've used previously?*

She smiled. This must be Rich's idea of a joke. Well, she would be happy to go and 'meet' him. She rose. "PaIRS are here and want to see me. I won't be long. Come on, Daisy." Her little dog stood up slowly and stretched. Bea grabbed her jacket and put it on, then with Daisy trotting behind her, she headed for the door. As she got outside and headed towards the Old Stable Block, a small seed of curiosity sprouted in the back of her mind, but she pushed it away. It was time to focus on new beginnings and let the professionals handle the mystery that had been forced upon them.

12

2:45 PM, MONDAY 19 APRIL

"Okay," Lady Beatrice murmured to herself as she hesitated outside the police's temporary office in the Old Stable Block. Her muscles tensed. She took a deep breath. Just in front of her, Daisy sniffed the worn wooden door. A soft breeze rustled Bea's long red hair as she ran her hand through it. Why did Rich want this formal meeting? Did he perhaps want to maintain a professional front before Mike and his colleagues so their friendship wouldn't be questioned or cause any awkwardness? *Yes. That makes sense.* She raised her hand and knocked on the door. She would play along, but she would also make it clear to him she had no intention of getting involved in the case this time.

"Come in," called a familiar voice from inside.

As she entered the room, her gaze swept around the office. Boxes cluttered the tables, and a whiteboard leaned haphazardly against the far wall. A woman was engrossed in something on a screen in the corner. Bea smiled. She recognised the long blonde hair cut into a bob. Detective Sergeant Tina Spicer. *This is great. She and Rich work really well together as a team. He'll be so pleased to have her on this case with him.*

Daisy, ever the social butterfly, ran up to Mike for a fuss, her tail wagging enthusiastically. "Ah, Lady Beatrice. Thank you for joining us," the detective inspector said smiling, although his blue eyes held a note of wariness. He bent down and scratched Daisy behind the ears.

What's wrong? Her eyes scanned the room once more, searching for Rich. *Where is he?* Then she saw it — a shadow moving in the kitchen at the back of the room. *That must be him.*

Daisy trotted over to the woman in the corner. Spicer turned, a bright smile spreading across her oval-shaped face when she saw Daisy. She reached down and patted the small dog's head, then she looked up and spotted Bea. She stood and smoothed down her baby-blue T-shirt, then she did up the buttons on the jacket of her slim-fitting black suit before walking over, grinning. "Lady Beatrice. How lovely to see you again." She held out her hand.

"Indeed," Bea replied warmly, taking it in hers. There was something familiar and comforting about having Spicer here. Some of the tension in her neck eased. "How are you? I hear you're waiting for the results of your inspector's exams?" Rich had told Bea weeks ago that Spicer was hoping to get a promotion soon, having recently sat for the exams. As he'd talked, it had been clear to Bea that he would miss his DS, but he'd also sounded proud that she'd done so well. *At least they'll have this last case together.*

Spicer pulled a face as she ran her hand through her blonde hair. "I should hear in the next few days."

"You'll be fine, I'm sure," Bea said reassuringly.

A sudden clearing of a throat over to her left pulled Bea's

attention away from her conversation with Spicer. She pivoted around as a man exited the kitchen and headed towards her. Her stomach fell. It was not Rich.

Daisy, seeing a new person, rushed over to greet him, but he carried on walking, not even acknowledging the little dog. Bea frowned. *What sort of person ignores a dog who wants to say hello?* She lifted her chin and stiffened. Studying the stocky man in front of her, she realised he looked familiar. *Hold on, isn't he the surly sergeant who investigated the failure of the security system at The Dower House a couple of months before James died?* She remembered him because, after he'd left, she and James had joked that he looked more like a criminal than a PaIRS officer, with his very short hair, bulging muscles, and a menacing scowl on his face.

"Lady Beatrice, let me introduce you to Detective Chief Inspector Hayden Saunders from PaIRS," Mike said, gesturing towards the man who had now stopped in front of them. His Popeye-like arms straining against his shirt, indicating hours spent working out, along with his shaved head gave him an intimidating presence. *He looks more like a bouncer now.*

"DCI Saunders is here to head up the investigation into Vera Bolt's death," the inspector added.

Bea's stomach churned. *But what about Rich?* Bea glanced at Spicer. The detective sergeant simply shrugged, her eyes conveying sympathy but giving no clue as to what was happening. Bea's heart sank. They must have refused Rich's request to be assigned to the case. *He'll be so disappointed.*

Bea returned her attention to Saunders. His small blue eyes, on a level with hers, seemed to scrutinise her face. *Does he remember me?*

Mike coughed beside her. She hurriedly extended her hand towards Saunders. "We've met before, I believe, DCI Saunders." He raised an eyebrow. *Did he think I wouldn't remember?* "The security system at The Dower House was playing up, and you came to talk to my husband about it."

"Yes, we met briefly, Lady Rossex," he replied, shaking her hand with a firm grip.

Beside her, Daisy grumbled.

"And since then, of course, I've heard a lot about you," he continued, his thin lips spreading into a tight smile.

What exactly does that mean? An immediate dislike for the man bubbled inside her. Before Bea could respond, the door opened, and Rich strode in. Relief washed over her. Daisy darted towards him, swishing her tail enthusiastically. Rich bent down and gave the dog a good fuss, his face lighting up with genuine warmth.

"Fitz!" DS Tina Spicer beamed at Rich as she walked over to greet him.

"Fitzwilliam," Saunders said, his tone guarded as he turned to address him. "What are you doing here? You're supposed to be on sick leave."

Bea frowned. They clearly knew each other, but there was no handshake, no smiles. *What's going on?*

"True," Rich replied, his voice steady. "But I thought I might lend a hand by introducing you to the people here at Francis Court. It might help smooth your way, given my connections."

Bea smiled. *That's very gracious of him.* She looked at Saunders. His round face was pinched.

"Thanks," Saunders replied curtly, "but I don't need your help. I have the matter well in hand."

Bea's heart clenched at the brutal dismissal. *So disre-*

spectful. She glanced at Rich. His jaw tightened. He stared at Saunders for a second, then he nodded and stepped back. Bea's cheeks burned, and before she could stop herself, she blurted out, "Excuse me, chief inspector, but there's no need to be so rude."

Saunders fixed her with a steely gaze, silencing her with his icy blue eyes. "I don't know how things worked in the past with other members of PaIRS" —he glanced pointedly at Rich, suggesting that he knew *exactly* how things had worked between them—"but I'm here to do a job, and I will not tolerate any interference from anyone. Are we clear?"

The room went deathly quiet as tension crackled in the air. Bea's throat burned as she glanced at Rich. His face was now turning a deep shade of red, his hands balling into fists at his sides.

Who does this man think he is? Bea breathed in through her nose. *Don't let him see he's got to you.* "Crystal," she replied through gritted teeth, her heart racing.

Next to her, Rich mumbled, "Mike, Spicer," as he bobbed his head at them. Abruptly turning on his heels, he headed towards the door.

I need to talk to him. "I trust you'll keep me informed as a courtesy," she said, glaring at Saunders. *If it wasn't for me and my family, you wouldn't have a job,* she wanted to add.

"Of course, Lady Rossex," Saunders replied, although his eyes held a steely edge that suggested he was not one for courtesies.

She turned to a stunned-looking Mike and a shocked Spicer. "Mike, Spicer. Thank you." She gave them a brief smile, then calling, "Come on, Daisy," she hurried out of the office, her little terrier trailing close behind.

―――

"Rich, wait!" Bea called out as she caught up with him as he was just about to exit the Old Stable Block courtyard. He stopped and turned to face her, his shoulders tense and his jaw set firm.

"Are you alright?" she asked, looking up into his face as she and Daisy stopped in front of him.

"I just feel so useless right now," he said with a huff, his brown eyes meeting her gaze. "I want to be back at work." He let out a deep sigh, running a hand through his hair. "I just want things to go back to normal, Bea."

She swallowed. She'd been so concerned about his physical recovery these past few months that she'd completely forgotten to pay any attention to his mental wellbeing. *What can I say?* "Saunders is an idiot!"

He barked a laugh.

"And he's rude, disrespectful, and ridiculously muscular. He looks like Popeye!" she continued.

Fitzwilliam let out a full and long laugh as Daisy jumped around him.

That's better!

"And if he doesn't want your help, then good luck to him!" she said firmly.

Rich was smiling now. "And what about you? Are you going to investigate behind his back?"

Bea held a hand up to her chest in mock surprise. "As if I would!"

His eyes crinkled in amusement as he raised an eyebrow.

"I'm not getting involved. I promise," she assured him.

"Alright," he agreed. "We'll both stay out of it then."

"Deal! Now, I don't know about you, but I need a coffee. Care to join me?"

He tipped his head in a nod and followed her as she

turned towards the main house. As they followed the back of the Old Stable Block, Daisy trotting between them, Bea couldn't help think that despite their promises, staying out of this case might be easier said than done.

13

8 PM, MONDAY 19 APRIL

The comforting aroma of simmering Tuscan stew wafted towards Bea, mingling with the tantalising scent of freshly baked tomato and olive focaccia as Simon put the finishing touches to dinner in the kitchen in Rose Cottage. Her stomach grumbled.

"Here, try this," Perry said, pouring a generous amount of deep ruby-red wine into her waiting glass. "It's one Ryan brought over last week, so it should be good."

Bea swirled her glass. The rich bouquet hinted at notes of cherry and spice. She took a sip. "Um…that's good." She took another sip. "Where *is* Ryan?"

"He's gone back to London for the night. He has a meeting with the investors at Nonnina first thing tomorrow," Simon said as he handed her a deep bowl filled with home-made meatballs bobbing up and down in an orangey-red tomato sauce. Bea licked her lips.

"I'm surprised the police let him go," Perry said, leaning into the middle of the well-worn oak dining table and grabbing a chunk of bread. "I thought when there's been a murder, they keep everyone in the area."

Bea nodded as she took a scoop of the stew. It was delicious.

"Yes, normally they do," Simon said, helping himself to bread. "And he had to ask permission to go. But as the police have already interviewed him, and they have ruled him out as a suspect, they must have thought there was no risk in allowing him to go for just the one night."

Bea frowned. *They've ruled Ryan out as a suspect? How does Simon know that?* After her brief interview with Saunders late this afternoon, he'd not told her they'd ruled her out as a suspect, even though she and Perry had been together the whole morning. But then, from the little she knew of Saunders so far, he'd probably done that deliberately. She glanced up from her food and caught Simon's eye. He blushed. "Simon?" He looked down at his bowl. "How do you know they've ruled Ryan out as a suspect?"

"Er." Simon bit his lip. "I may have had a chat with Steve just before you arrived," he replied sheepishly. Steve Cox was an inspector who worked in Fenshire CID and a good friend of Simon's ever since they'd worked together as young police officers. He'd been a source of inside information for them in previous local cases. Bea had met him in person for the first time at Simon and Perry's wedding and had instantly liked the charming police officer with a wicked sense of humour and a cheeky smile.

"You've spoken to CID Steve about Vera Bolt's murder? Why?"

Simon shrugged. "Just having a catch up, you know."

Bea shook her head. Simon was a bad liar. Especially for an ex-CID detective. Her heartbeat slowed. "Are you investigating this case without me?" she asked the two men sitting opposite her.

"No. Of course not!" Perry cried, looking offended.

"Bea." Simon reached over and placed his hand on her arm. "It's nothing like that, I promise. Perry and I were just curious about where the police were with the case." He smiled tentatively at her.

She took a deep breath. Why did it matter if they wanted to know what was going on? She was the one who'd said she didn't want to investigate Vera Bolt's death. If they were keen to keep up-to-date with the case, that was up to them, wasn't it? She patted his hand and smiled as he withdrew it. "Sorry. I overreacted. It's none of my business if you want to talk to your friends."

Perry and Simon looked relieved as she took some bread from the bowl in the middle of the table. *I wonder who else they have ruled out as a suspect?* Bea took a bite of the savoury herb-flecked focaccia. *Stop it, Bea! You promised Rich you wouldn't get involved.* She took a sip of wine. *But it's not getting involved; it's just asking a few questions…* "So, er. Have they ruled Perry and me out as suspects too?" she asked casually.

Simon appeared to suppress a smile. "Yes. Nicky in the Breakfast Room confirmed you were both there until just after eleven."

"Well, that's good to know."

"Isn't it? Because from the way Saunders was talking to me earlier, I was worried! It was so uncomfortable." Perry sighed, swirling the red wine in his glass. "He questioned me as if I were the murderer," he said with a dry laugh.

Bea glanced over at Simon. He gave her a quick smile. *Oh!* That's why he'd contacted CID Steve — so he could put his husband's mind to rest that he wasn't a suspect. *Aw, that was sweet of him…*

"Well, it's not just you, Perry," she told him. Although she'd assumed the chief inspector's attitude towards her had resulted from their not so pleasant encounter earlier. "He definitely has quite the talent for making you feel like a criminal even when you've done nothing wrong. And he wasn't interested when I tried to tell him it seemed like the killer had just grabbed the nearest thing to hand, like the missing knife, as if it was a spur-of-the-moment thing. Or your theory about how the killer could have got out of the room without getting bloody footprints on the floor. He dismissed me." She shivered slightly, recalling the cold, calculated way he'd scrutinised her, as if searching for any hint of guilt.

"Well, I didn't like him at all," Perry said firmly. "Speaking of which…" He leaned forward conspiratorially. "I got the impression Fitzwilliam doesn't like him either. Did you notice how cagey he was about their relationship?"

Bea hadn't told Simon or Perry about what had gone on between Rich and Saunders at their first meeting in any detail, just that Rich had offered to help and Saunders had declined. But when she and Rich had arrived at the Breakfast Room straight afterwards and joined the others, it had been obvious he wasn't happy.

"Well, I've remembered something from way back," Simon said. "I recall hearing from Emma Adler at the time that Saunders should have been part of the PaIRS team investigating your husband's death, Bea. He missed out because he was on leave abroad. Fitzwilliam was the one who replaced him."

"Really?" Bea said, her curiosity piqued. *I wonder if that's got something to do with Saunders' hostility towards Rich?*

"So what else did CID Steve have to say? Have they narrowed down the time of death yet?"

"Yes, to between ten forty-five and five-past-eleven that morning," Simon replied.

"So a twenty-minute period then?"

Simon nodded.

"Okay. So who else has been—" There was a sharp knock on the door. Bea glanced at her mobile phone. It was late for someone to be visiting.

Perry shot up. "I'll get it if you'll get coffee," he said to Simon with a cheeky grin. Simon smiled slowly as he, too, rose from the table. He headed to the kitchen area, and a few seconds later, the rich aroma of freshly brewed coffee filled the room.

Perry returned with a tall distinguished-looking man. *Fred!* His brown eyes were shadowed with worry, and his usually upright posture seemed slightly hunched under the weight of whatever was on his mind. "Fred," Bea said, rising from her seat to greet him. "What brings you here?"

"Hello, Bea, Simon," he replied, forcing a smile as he walked across the room. "I'm sorry to disturb you so late."

"It's no problem," Simon assured him, gesturing for him to take a seat at the table. "We're just having coffee. Would you like one?"

"Thank you," he said, nodding. Simon brought over the coffeepot and four large cups as he sat down.

Fred's gaze flickered between his sister, Simon, and Perry before he took a deep breath. "I've just walked Summer back to her cottage in the village. I'm rather worried about her," he said, accepting a cup of steaming coffee from Simon.

"Summer? Why?" Bea asked.

Fred hesitated for a moment, swirling the coffee in his cup, then he said, "That new DCI from PaIRS, Saunders, interviewed her. Apparently, she has no alibi for the time someone killed Vera, and someone overheard her arguing with Vera around ten forty-five this morning in The Tent. She admits it was her. But she left just before ten-fifty, and Vera was still alive then."

So Summer could have been the last person to see Vera before she was killed...

"Saunders is treating her as if she's the killer," Fred continued, his voice strained. "She's been extremely upset since the interview."

"Where did Summer go after leaving The Tent?" Simon asked, concern etched on his features.

"She says she went for a walk around the grounds to calm down," Fred replied, rubbing a hand over his face. "But it seems Saunders isn't satisfied with that explanation."

Bea shared a worried glance with Simon. She didn't even need to ask him if CID Steve had told him that Summer was a suspect. It was written all over his face. She swallowed.

"Fred," Bea said softly, reaching out to place a comforting hand on her brother's arm. "I'm sure someone saw Summer and will come forward and confirm where she was."

"But what if they don't?" her brother asked, his voice thick with emotion. "The only person other than Summer who knows for sure that she didn't do it is the actual murderer."

Bea's mouth went dry. She took a sip of coffee. As the warm liquid slid down her throat, she gnawed at her bottom lip. No wonder Fred was concerned.

Fred took a deep breath. "So how are you getting on with your investigation?"

Bea choked on her coffee. "Investigation?" she sputtered, exchanging shocked glances with Perry and Simon. "Fred, we're not investigating anything."

"Bea's right," Perry chimed in, shifting uneasily in his seat. "We're all quite busy, and as sad as Vera's death is, we didn't really know her."

Fred's brow furrowed. "I just assumed that was what you were doing here." His voice grew urgent. "But you must get involved. Saunders is trying to pin the murder on Summer, and I know she couldn't kill anyone." He leaned forward, worry etched on his face. "Please can you help her by finding out who the killer is?"

Bea's head was pounding. She wanted to help her brother and Summer, but she'd promised Rich that she wouldn't investigate the case. And then there was Saunders. There was no way he would tolerate any interference from them. *But poor Summer...* She glanced at Perry, who raised an eyebrow. *I know what you're thinking...*

Just then, Fred's phone rang. He sprang from his seat and answered it. He pointed to the room next door as he moved away.

As soon as he was out of earshot, Perry spoke up. "I say we do it. We can't just sit back while that...that....*idiot* accuses Summer of murder."

Simon frowned, rubbing the back of his neck. "I hate to be the one to say it," he whispered. "But we don't know for sure she didn't do it."

Bea put down her coffee, her mind racing. She stifled a groan. Of course, Simon was right. But she also trusted her brother's judgement. *If he's saying Summer isn't a killer, then I believe him.* The sound of Fred's hushed voice drifted from the sitting room, spurring Bea to decide. "Alright," she said, determination steeling her resolve. "Then we'll have to *prove* that she didn't!"

Perry's face lit up. "Yes!" He clapped his hands together.

They both looked at Simon. He hesitated, then gave a deep sigh. "Okay, we'll help. But we have to be careful not to draw attention to ourselves." Bea and Perry nodded eagerly in agreement.

Fred re-entered the room, his face etched with concern. "That was Summer," he said, running a hand through his short brown hair. "The police want to speak with her again first thing in the morning." He picked up his coffee and drained it in one go. "Right. I need to organise a lawyer for her."

He looked imploringly at the others. "Is there anything you can do? I'm afraid they'll arrest her."

"Alright, Fred," Bea said, her voice laced with determination. "We'll help."

"And remember," Simon added. "She might not have an alibi, but they need to have some proof that links her to the crime before they can charge her. So get her an excellent lawyer and try not to worry."

Fred smiled, his eyes filled with gratitude. "Thanks. I'll catch up with you later." He hurried across the kitchen and out of the door.

"Okay, so what's the plan?" Perry asked, rubbing his hands together in anticipation as they heard the outside door slam closed.

"Well, I'll talk to Adrian Breen in the morning and see if I can find out who was on-site at the time of Vera's murder."

"And as a double check, I'll talk to Steve and get a definitive list of suspects," Simon said. "I'll also ask Roisin if there's anything interesting coming out of Forensics."

Bea smiled. They were lucky that Simon's best friend worked at Fenshire Police in the forensics department.

"What about me?" Perry asked, his eyes shining with excitement.

"Why don't you talk to that runner, Ana? She might have heard something useful."

"Perfect," Perry grinned. "Let's meet for coffee mid-morning to share our findings."

"And let's not forget the rules," Simon cautioned, looking at each of them. "No interviewing suspects before they've talked to the police. Be discreet. We can't let Saunders find out we're involved, but if someone shares something important, then you must advise them to tell the police. Okay?" Bea and Perry nodded.

"Should we tell Fitzwilliam?" Perry asked.

"No," Bea replied quickly, feeling a flush of embarrassment creep up her neck. "I mean…he's on sick leave and needs his rest. I don't think we should bother him about it right now."

Simon tilted his head to one side. "He might want to help too, Bea."

And then he'll know I've broken my promise! "Or he might feel obliged to warn us off *and* tell Saunders what we're up to," she pointed out. She nervously fiddled with the rings on her right hand. He wouldn't really do that, would he? She mentally shook her head. *I don't think so.* But guilt at breaking her promise to him nagged at her. They could tell him later if it became necessary. Right now, she couldn't let her brother down. They needed to help Summer.

14

THE NEXT DAY, 8 AM, TUESDAY 20 APRIL

The Society Page online article:

Vera Bolt, Queen of Bakes, dies unexpectedly aged 66

The Bake Off Wars *judge and national treasure Vera Bolt CMPC died yesterday, her agent has announced. She was sixty-six years old. No cause of death was included in the statement.*

Austin Matthews, director of Bake Off Wars, *led the tributes to the late judge, describing her as "a magnificent cook, and an inspiration for all bakers everywhere". TV chef Ryan Hawley, her fellow judge in the new series of* Bake Off Wars, *currently filming at Francis Court in Fenshire, said, "We're all in shock to hear of Vera's sudden death. She was a unique character, and* Bake Off Wars *will not be the same without her."*

Born in Oxford, the renowned pastry chef began her career in Paris, where she worked under the chocolatier Marcel Lebonne. In a recent interview, she described her time with Lebonne as "pivotal to the person and chef I later became. His attention to detail, where only perfection was good enough, instilled in me the high standards that I now demand of myself and others". After leaving Paris, she returned to London, where she took up the role of head chocolatier at the renowned Chocolate Bar at the Charlton Hotel in Mayfair. In 1992, she won the coveted Association of Bakers and Pastry Chefs' 'Pastry Chef of the World' award.

Shortly after, she became a Certified Master Pastry Chef and moved to The Grand Hotel in London as executive pastry chef. She became highly in demand as a judge in pastry competitions all around the world, and ten years ago, she made her television debut in her own show, Vera Bolt Bakes. It was a great hit with the public, and two years later, she was announced as the senior judge on the first series of Bake Off Wars. She has produced many baking cookbooks, and four years ago, saw the mass production of her now famous VB Hazelnut and Chocolate Sauce, which sold out in stores within two days of its launch. Six months ago, the rights to produce the popular sauce were purchased by Orel Foods for a reported £3.4 million. Vera never married and lived in the Cotswolds.

Popular chef Mark Jacobs, who was a fellow judge of Vera's for seven series of Bake Off Wars, was unavailable for comment. A source close to the show's production reports that Jacobs was seen yesterday in Windstanton, a seaside town close to Francis Court. Rumours already circulate that he will be asked to return as a judge so that the series currently being filmed can be completed. A spokesperson for Eat Cake Productions, who makes Bake Off Wars, commented that everyone was still reeling from Vera's death and that there were no plans to find a replacement at this time.

15

8:30 AM, TUESDAY 20 APRIL

Perry sat in Tappin's Teas, a quaint and old-fashioned tea shop on the coast road that ran through the heart of Francis-next-the-Sea, drumming his fingers on the worn wooden table. His gaze wandered over the floral wallpaper and lace-edged tablecloths towards where Peter Tappin, the owner of the tea shop, bustled around the room, attending to two elderly ladies who lived in the village. *He's still ignoring me!* Although it was an open secret that the tall and tanned owner harboured a crush on Simon, Perry's husband, he'd never admitted to being gay. This unspoken truth had led to an affected way of speaking and a disapproval of Perry, whom he continued to pointedly ignore as he fussed over his other customers.

Perry gritted his teeth as Peter's balding head nodded up and down as he listened to the two women talking as he fiddled with a pair of clear glasses dangling around his neck on a chain. *Why do I keep coming here?* Well, the food for one. There was no question in Perry's mind that Peter's breakfast was the best for miles around. Then there was the other reason. Perry suppressed a grin. He liked forcing Peter to *have* to acknowledge him eventually. He and Simon had even started to make a game of it when they came in together. Simon would specifically mention Perry to Peter, and they would watch with glee as Peter would try his best to ignore the reference without being rude to Simon.

Stifling a sigh as Peter continued to pretend to be engrossed in the wittering of the two women, Perry admitted to himself that it was less fun needling Peter when he was on his own. *If he doesn't come and take my order soon, I'll—*

The door opened, and Ana entered. Her brown eyes lit up when she spotted Perry. She smiled, revealing white teeth framed by a large mouth as she hurried over.

"Morning, Perry," Ana said, sliding onto the seat opposite him. "Thanks for inviting me. I'm starving!"

And you may well starve if that man doesn't acknowledge me soon!

Picking up the plastic-covered menu that Perry now knew by heart, she studied it, licking her lips as she did so.

It's no good... "Excuse me, Peter, could we place an order, please?" Perry called out, doing his best to sound polite and patient even though he felt like being neither.

Peter sighed dramatically, mumbled something to the ladies, then made his way over. "Yes?" he barked, grabbing the pencil from behind his ear. He took their orders for breakfast and tea with a distinct lack of enthusiasm before retreating to the kitchen.

"Sorry about him," Perry said, rubbing the back of his neck. "Anyway, how have you been holding up?"

Ana's smile disappeared. "It's been hard. I've had nothing like that happen to me before." She scowled. "And that policeman who looks like Stretch Armstrong was so intimidating."

Perry slapped his hand to his mouth as he stifled a laugh. *What a perfect description of Saunders.*

"From the way he was talking, anyone would think I'd killed her myself!" She threw her open hands out to the sides and shrugged.

Seems like Saunders isn't making any friends...

"But I'm feeling better today." She took a steadying breath. "They've told us we can now have access to the offices and kitchens but not The Tent." She gave a slow smile. "I'll be glad to get back to work."

"I can imagine," Perry said, sipping his tea. "So what's going to happen now?"

"Well," Ana said hesitantly. "They've decided to carry on with filming this weekend."

Really? That felt almost distastefully too soon after the show's head judge's death.

"I know it seems a bit soon, but according to Austin we're on such a tight schedule, he has no choice."

I imagine all the staff and equipment are only available for the original planned duration of the show. Any delay would cost a fortune.

Peter returned to the table, expertly balancing a tray laden with their food and drinks. The powerful aroma of freshly brewed coffee wafted through the air as the owner set down the steaming coffee pot and a pair of mismatched, yet charming china cups. "Here you are," Peter announced, his voice carrying a hint of forced cheeriness as he placed their plates of food in front of them. "Enjoy."

"Thank you," Ana replied, her smile genuine as she eagerly picked up her fork. Perry nodded his thanks, already salivating at the sight of the perfectly cooked scrambled eggs and crispy bacon before him.

"So who will they get to replace Vera?" Perry asked, buttering a slice of toast.

Ana paused, adding milk from a pretty bone china jug to her coffee. "They haven't decided yet, as far as I know. From what's been said, it's likely they'll bring in a guest judge." She blushed as her eyes met his, then looked back down at her plate as she speared first a mushroom, then half a sausage and raised the fork to her mouth. "While they look for a permanent replacement for Vera," she added as she popped the food into her mouth.

"Will it be Mark Jacobs?"

Ana shook her head, then swallowed. "I don't know."

They continued to eat in a comfortable silence. *It will make sense for Mark to rejoin the show*, Perry thought. At least he was experienced and knew the format. And from what people had told him, it had only been Vera who'd wanted him off the show. Perry started. *That gives Mark a strong motive to want Vera dead. Just as well he wasn't on-site that morning, or he would be the prime suspect!*

Perry finished his food and pushed his plate to one side. *Delicious.* Taking a sip of coffee, he recalled Ryan telling them how tense the meeting on the morning of Vera's death had been. *It will be useful to get Ana's take on it.* "So what was the meeting like yesterday morning?" he asked, trying to sound casual despite his burning curiosity.

Ana hesitated, taking a sip of her coffee before answering, "Well, Vera was in a foul mood. She snapped at me and Cleo for no apparent reason." She shook her head. "Oh, and she really tore into poor Summer, criticising her for being too friendly with the contestants. As if that's a thing. It was so unfair. It's the presenter's job to make the contestants feel at home and relaxed."

"And how did Summer take it?"

"She was furious and embarrassed, especially as Vera did it in front of everyone."

Perry frowned, taking another sip of coffee, then placing his cup down. So Vera *had* humiliated Summer. He swallowed. *Humiliated enough to stab her?* "That seems out of line. Was Vera like that with the previous presenters?"

Ana shook her head. "She liked working with Claudia and Kit. I think mainly because they'd all worked together for so long. Vera doesn't... Sorry, I mean *didn't* like change. So she was gutted when they resigned because Mark had left. I think she thought they were on her side."

Perry topped up his coffee cup. So had Vera just been hard on Summer because she wasn't Claudia? "What about Hamilton Moore? Was Vera tough on him too?"

Ana tilted her head to one side and gave a wry smile. "Oh, yes! He'd fluffed his lines quite a few times over the weekend. Vera took great pains to point it out. She told him he was as wooden as a tree. He seemed so upset that Austin had to have a quiet word with him after the meeting."

"Upset as in angry?"

Ana looked pensive. "No. More as in disappointed in himself."

"So it wasn't just Summer that Vera was unhappy with at the meeting then?"

"Oh no." Ana shook her head. "She also accused Leah and Shelly of trying to sabotage the skills challenge." Her voice grew quieter as she leaned in. "She complained that they'd convinced her and Austin to give the contestants more time, which made the round less intense and resulted in bad television. Austin disagreed though. He said he thought the timing for the first skills test was just right. Vera didn't like that either."

"It sounds like quite the bun fight," Perry observed, fiddling with his teaspoon.

Ana nodded. "More than usual. Vera had no filter that day. It wasn't like our production meetings last series." She paused, her brow furrowing. "You know, I've only just realised how much Mark used to keep Vera in check."

Interesting... Had someone become fed up with an unfiltered Vera without him there to keep her under control? "So what happened after the meeting?"

"Most of the crew went back to the hotel since they weren't needed until later," Ana replied. "I stayed behind with Hamilton to help him with his lines; he asked for my help after Vera had a comment about him being wooden. We went to his trailer, and I rehearsed there with him." She frowned. "Ryan went off. He said he had an appointment locally. I'm not too sure about Austin and Harvey."

"And Vera?"

"She said she was going to The Tent to check on the bakes Leah and Shelly had made the day before, and they went with her."

So Leah and Shelly had been with Vera straight after the meeting. But they must have left not long after if someone had caught Summer and Vera arguing at quarter to eleven. *Who overheard them? Was it Ana?*

"Ana," Perry asked, hesitating. "How did you end up finding Vera?"

Ana's eyes darkened, and she stared down at her empty plate. "Well, just before eleven-fifteen, I left Hamilton to get my copy of the production notes so we could discuss his timings for the week. I'd last had them in The Tent." Her voice wavered, and she took a deep breath. "When I went inside, I saw her lying there..." Her hand shook, causing the teaspoon to rattle against her cup.

Perry reached across the table, gently patting her hand. "I'm sorry, Ana," he said softly. "You don't have to talk about it any more if it's too painful."

"Thank you," she whispered, swallowing hard. The clink of china and silverware filled the air as Perry and Ana sat in silence for a few minutes.

Perry changed the subject. "How's everyone else doing?" he asked.

"Mostly, they're just carrying on," Ana replied, finishing her coffee and dabbing at the corners of her mouth with a napkin. "Leah and Shelly are quite upset, obviously; they've worked with Vera for years. But everyone else...they don't seem all that bothered. All they're talking about is who will replace Vera as the new judge and how soon they can get back to work."

Perry suppressed a sigh. *How sad when the people you've worked with for over seven years aren't that bothered by your death. I hope if anything ever happens to me, everyone will be too devastated to go back to work for weeks. Months maybe...*

"Anyway," Ana said, glancing at her watch. "I'd best leave and head over to Francis Court. Austin has called a meeting at ten. Thanks so much for inviting me to breakfast. It was fabulous. How much do I—"

Perry held up his hand. "My treat." He knew TV show runners earned next to no money.

"Thank you." Ana smiled gratefully. She stood, then she paused and added, "There's one other person who seems to be taking Vera's death quite badly, and that's Cleo. She's even quieter and more withdrawn than before, and when I saw her yesterday, she looked like she'd been crying."

Perry frowned. "Were she and Vera close?"

"No, not at all. Vera seemed to ignore Cleo when she wasn't complaining about her not doing things quick enough," Ana replied. "Cleo's quite laid back, you know, like most nineteen year olds are," she added with a grin, then, with a quick, "Thanks again," she picked up her mobile and left the teashop.

Perry caught Peter's eye as the owner chatted with some locals. With an exaggerated sigh, Peter left them and approached Perry's table. He tore a page off his pad and slapped the bill down in front of Perry. Perry offered a tight-lipped smile, which Peter returned with a disdainful sniff.

"Thank you, Peter," Perry said, giving him a forced beaming smile as he watched the man flounce back to his other customers.

As Perry examined the piece of paper, his thoughts returned to his conversation with Ana. Her account of the meeting matched Ryan's, but there was new information to consider. For a start it turns out Hamilton hadn't left the site after the meeting. *Rats! I should have asked Ana if she and Hamilton had been together the entire time between the end of the meeting and her finding Vera's body.* After all, they had both been on-site when someone had murdered Vera; either could have conceivably found time to commit the crime.

And then there were Leah and Shelly, who had accompanied Vera to The Tent. Could there have been trouble brewing between the three of them? And lastly, Summer had been furious, according to Ana. Could they really rule her out just because Fred said she wasn't the killing type?

He took out his wallet and retrieved his payment card. *Hopefully I can get Peter's attention so I can pay and get out of here!*

16

MID-MORNING, TUESDAY 20 APRIL

Bea absentmindedly stirred her coffee, her thoughts preoccupied with how Summer was getting on with the police. She glanced down at her phone. Nothing from Fred yet. *Is Summer still being interviewed?* Bea picked up her cup and took a sip of coffee. The dark liquid warmed her throat. Some of the tension left her shoulders, and she scanned the room as she leaned back in her chair. The Breakfast Room at Francis Court had a pleasant mid-morning air about it. Sunlight streamed in through the large windows, casting patterns on the polished wooden floor. It was that quiet hour after breakfast had been cleared away but before lunch preparations began, so there were only a few other tables occupied.

Seated opposite her at the elegantly set table, Perry and Simon sipped their coffees and exchanged hushed words. Bea smiled at the sight of them together. *They're such a contrast, and yet at the same time, they're a perfect match.* Perry, tall and slim with his spiky blond hair and fashionable attire, complemented Simon's slightly unkempt appeal. Shorter than Perry, Simon was stockier, with light-brown hair and a well-trimmed beard framing his round face. As always, he wore his usual ensemble of T-shirt and jeans, giving off an air of casual confidence. Perry looked like a model in his white shirt, unbuttoned at the neck, and his blue-and-pink chequered waistcoat with matching suit trousers.

Underneath the table, a soft *woof* came from Daisy, who lay on the floor, her head resting on her paws as she dozed peacefully, occasionally twitching in response to a dream. A smile tugged at the corner of Bea's mouth. *Aw, bless her. I hope it's a good one!*

"What are you smiling at?" Perry asked jovially.

"I was just wondering if Daisy will finally catch that squirrel."

Perry chuckled as he bent down to peer under the table at the sleeping dog. They liked to play a game of guess what Daisy was dreaming about. "That's way too tame. I think she's chasing a van that's loaded with stolen bacon—"

"Or sausages…" Bea jumped in.

"And only she can save it!" Perry added with a flourish.

They laughed as Simon looked up from his tablet. "Alright," he said, adjusting his reading glasses as he scanned the screen in front of him. "Following my call to Steve this morning, I've made a list of all the potential suspects who were on-site that morning. I've split it between those with an alibi and those without. So in the first half, we have Ana Halsall, Hamilton Moore, Leah Goldrich, and Shelly Black—"

"Ana and Hamilton were together," Perry interjected. He told them about Ana's account of what she'd been doing that morning after the meeting and before she had found the body. "Oh, and Ana also told me that Leah and Shelly had gone with Vera into The Tent after the meeting to discuss the practice bake they'd done the afternoon before."

"Are they the ones who do the baking challenge run throughs?" Bea asked. Perry nodded.

"They were together in the practice kitchen, according to what they told the police. Okay, so next I have the list of those without alibis, according to the police. They are Summer York, which we already know, Harvey Jury — the food producer who said he was in his office, Austin Matthews — the director, also in his office, and finally Cleo Barrington — the runner who was in the compound clearing up inside the storage container."

Perry frowned. "And none of them saw each other?"

Simon shook his head. "Not according to Steve. What he has confirmed is that Summer is the prime suspect at this stage since she was the last person to see Vera alive, that they know of."

Poor Summer. Bea glanced at her blank screen. *I hope Saunders isn't harassing her.*

"Do we know who overheard Summer arguing with Vera?" Bea asked, her brow furrowing as she tried to piece together the puzzle before them.

Simon glanced at his list. "Er…Cleo. She told the police about the argument."

Perry leaned forward. "So that means Cleo must have been around too," he pointed out. "And Vera was tough on her in the meeting, according to what Ana and Ryan have said."

"True," Simon nodded as he lifted his coffee cup to his mouth.

"And what about Harvey and Austin?" Perry continued. "Either of them could have gone into The Tent after Summer left."

"Yes, I know," Simon said with a sigh. "*And* they have no evidence to link Summer to the murder. But at the moment, Saunders is apparently fixated on the fact that Summer was angry and upset with Vera and was heard arguing with her just before she was found dead. Saunders thinks it's one of those murders where someone just snapped and, grabbing a knife that was lying around, stabbed her."

Bea took another sip of coffee. *Isn't that what I suggested to him?*

Perry touched his chest with his hand. "A crime of passion!"

That made sense. Then maybe they'd panicked and taken the knife and disposed of it somewhere? "Have they found the knife yet?"

Simon shook his head. "SOCO searched the area but found nothing."

I wonder where it is?

"Summer wasn't the only one Vera had upset. Ryan told us Vera called Austin out in front of everyone too," Perry pointed out.

Bea's brow creased. *What had she supposedly said? Oh, yes.* "She said to him something along the lines of, 'Don't think I don't know what you two are up to,' and pointed to him and Harvey. So they could both have a motive to kill her."

"Exactly," Perry cried.

Bea sat back. She mentally ticked off the names Simon had listed against the names of those known to be on-site that morning, which Adrian Breen had given her. *Oh, hold on. There's a name missing from the list of suspects.* "Mark Jacobs!" Her friends stared at her with wide eyes. "He was on-site that morning. He went in via the public entrance when it opened at ten. The police identified him, according to Adrian, because he paid by debit card."

"He isn't on my list," Simon said, frowning. "I'll check with Steve." He picked up his phone and began to text.

"Oh, there are also two others Adrian said the police wanted to identify — a man in his thirties and a teenage girl. They were picked up by the gate CCTV. They both paid in cash," Bea added.

"Were they together?" Simon asked.

Bea shook her head. "It doesn't appear so. They came in a few minutes apart."

"I'll see if Steve knows anything about them too, then."

As they waited for a response, Perry told them how Ana had said that Leah, Shelly, and Cleo seemed to be the only people upset about Vera's death.

Bea could understand why Leah and Shelly were upset. Hadn't someone said they'd worked with Vera for a long time? But Cleo? It was her first series, and they'd only been here for a few months. *Why is she so upset that Vera's dead? Is she the—* Bea checked herself. Cleo was only very young, and this was her first series. *She's probably just feeling over-whelmed.*

Simon's phone buzzed on the table, drawing their attention. "Steve's just got back to me," Simon said as he scanned the message. "They've now interviewed Mark Jacobs. He claims he was walking in the grounds that morning."

"Could he have slipped past security to get closer to the filming area?" Perry asked, his fingers drumming on the table.

"From the road, it's controlled by security," Bea said. "But the way in on foot via the Long Drive isn't." She turned to Perry. "Remember how we walked around that closed sign just after eleven on Monday morning and didn't see anyone? Mark could have done the same."

"Steve also mentioned that CID is trying to identify the

other man and the young woman who paid cash," Simon added. "Everyone else is local and used season tickets or membership cards to get in, which is normal for this time of year, apparently."

Perry nodded. "Until the house and State Rooms are opened to the public in May, it's mostly locals with their dogs who visit the gardens during the week."

Bea tapped a finger on her chin, her mind working through the possibilities. "So based on what we know now, we have at least three other people who could be viable suspects, as well as Summer. Mark, Harvey, and Austin. They all have possible motives and no alibis."

"And Cleo," Simon added.

"But she's only nineteen," Perry cried.

Simon sighed. "I know, but we can't discount her purely on age. We know she had opportunity, and we know Vera was very critical of her." He shrugged. "Teenagers are full of hormones and can be very unpredictable, according to my friends with children that age…"

Perry shook his head. "Well, I just don't believe she would kill anyone. I'll talk to her next and see if I can find out more about her whereabouts during the crucial time."

Simon patted his husband's arm. "Okay. Well, Austin asked to speak with me this afternoon. I'll see what I can find out from him. If I get a chance while I'm there, I'll try to talk to Harvey as well. Meanwhile, Bea, can you have a chat with Summer?"

"Indeed. As long as she's up for it. If she's been at the station all morning, she might not want to talk about it anymore." Bea glance at her phone again. Still no message from Fred.

"Of course," Simon said. "Just see how—" His phone buzzed, and he studied the screen. His eyebrows furrowed ever so slightly as he read the message. "I've got to pop back to the village," he said, pushing his chair away from the table. "That's Dylan. The young girl who was looking for me has turned up again."

"Do you want me to come too, love?" Perry asked, jumping up and grabbing Simon's arm. "If she's a stalker—"

"No, no," Simon said, a hint of a smile on his face. "I'm sure she's just a fan or something. I'll be fine. We'll be in the pub. It's a public place." He patted Perry's hand. "I think I'll be safe. I'll see you both later." With a quick wave, he walked across to the outside door and left the restaurant.

Perry remained standing. "I'm going to head over to the office and check on the paint order we need for the kitchen at The Dower House. After that, I'll wander over to the *Bake Off Wars* site and try to find Cleo."

"Talking of The Dower House, I'll pop over there now and check on those kitchen work surfaces. But can I meet you after at the site? I'd like to have a look around the TV compound and get the layout of the place clear in my head. It might help us work out where the killer exited the room after stabbing Vera and where they might have gone next."

"Good idea," Perry said as he bent down to pat a still sleepy Daisy on the head. He straightened up. "I'll see you later."

She drank the last of her coffee, then glanced down at her phone. *Where are you, Fred?* With a huff, she picked it up, her thumbs flying across the screen as she texted Fred to ask how Summer had fared with the police and if they could meet.

She hit send. *Beep.* A message came through. *Rich.* Her pulse quickened.

. . .

Fitzwilliam: *Do you fancy a walk?*

Bea hesitated, guilt prickling at the edges of her conscience. Would she be able to keep it from him that they were investigating Vera Bolt's death? Would he be able to tell? It was his job to read people, after all. *But I want to see him…*

Bea: *How about this afternoon? Meet you outside your cottage at 2:30?*

Fitzwilliam: *Great. See you then.*

Well, she was committed now. *Beep.*

Fred: *Summer's good. The lawyer did a great job. How about lunch at my apartment? I'll pick up sandwiches for the three of us xx*

A smiled cracked Bea's face as she rose from her chair and grabbed her jacket from the back of it. Daisy got up and stretched, a low grunt coming from the little white dog.

Bea: *Great idea. Tuna for me, please. See you soon xx*

17

12:30 PM TUESDAY 20 APRIL

Bea strolled into her brother's apartment, Daisy trotting at her heels. Having navigated the narrow entrance hall, she entered the large sitting room that was bathed in the light pouring through the large windows that lined one wall.

"Hey, sis. Hope you're hungry," Fred greeted her with a peck on the cheek, his brown eyes twinkling as he smiled.

"Always!" she said, moving over to the windows while Fred bent down to give Daisy, her tail wagging furiously, an affectionate pat on the head.

Bea sighed as she took in the breathtaking vista of the front of the Francis Court estate before her. *I never tire of this view.* To the left, the Long Drive stretched out, flanked by trees that concealed the *Bake Off Wars* compound. The sun glistened off The Cascade water feature, the silver liquid running down the twenty-two steps into the pool below. To the right, in the distance, she could just make out the back of The Dower House beyond The Lodge where her sister, Lady Sarah, and her family lived. Bea smiled. The kitchen work surfaces had been delivered this morning, and nothing was damaged. *Only a few more days now and I'll be living there...*

Fred cleared his throat, and Bea turned her back on the windows and moved through the elegant and inviting seating area, which was furnished with plush armchairs and bright cushions, to the grand dining table over on the other side.

"Beatrice, thanks for offering to help us." Summer walked in from the butler's pantry, carrying a coffeepot, her grey-blue eyes lighting up as Bea approached. She placed the pot on the table and leaned down to pet Daisy.

"Let's eat, shall we?" Fred said, gesturing towards the table, where an array of sandwiches and rolls was laid out. Bea's stomach rumbled. *I really should eat breakfast...* The warm sunlight filtered through the large windows, casting a golden hue on the room as they all settled in their seats. Daisy, sensing the opportunity for food, hovered around the table, her hopeful eyes darting from one person to the next.

"So how did it go?" Bea asked as she helped herself to a tuna and cucumber roll.

"It's all been a little overwhelming," Summer said, toying with the edge of her cheese sandwich. "I'm just so grateful for the lawyer Fred organised. She's been incredibly supportive and stopped that horrible would-be Arnold Schwarzenegger from hassling me. I really don't know how I would have coped without her." She ran her free hands through her long brown hair. "I'd have probably confessed to killing Vera just to get him off my case." She gave a wry smile.

"Don't even joke about it, hun," Fred said, slipping a small piece of ham to Daisy, who eagerly gobbled it up. He turned to Bea. "Everything they have is circumstantial, according to our lawyer. She thinks they're fishing for anything they can get."

Bea nodded. Saunders was probably hoping Summer would say something to incriminate herself. She looked across the table and studied Summer's oval face. Even her signature black eye make-up couldn't hide the dark circles under her eyes. A nervous energy was radiating from her. Part of Bea wanted to leave Summer alone, knowing she'd had a tough morning already, but then, if they were going to help her, Bea needed to ask some questions.

Leaning over, Bea grabbed the pot and poured herself a large mug of black coffee. *Here goes…* "Summer, could you tell me about your argument with Vera just before someone killed her? I know it must be difficult to discuss, but any information might help us understand what happened after you left."

Summer sighed, her gaze drifting to the window for a moment before returning to Bea. "It wasn't really an argument, as such. I was upset after the meeting." She raised her hand and shook her head. "And not because of what Vera said about my presenting skills. I can take criticism. It comes with the job." She shrugged. "And anyway, Austin had told me just before the meeting that he thought I'd done a great job over the weekend, so I wasn't really bothered by what Vera thought. It was the fact that she said it in front of everyone. It was humiliating." Her fingers tightened around the glass of orange juice she was holding. "I confronted her about it. I told her if she had an issue with my presenting in the future, she should talk to me in private about it."

"And did she apologise?" Bea asked, leaning forward slightly.

"Sort of," Summer replied, pulling a face. "She seemed surprised that I'd called her out on her behaviour, but she said she wouldn't do it again." She frowned. "There wasn't much shouting, really, so I'm confused about why someone reported it as an argument."

"Do you know who reported it?" Bea asked, knowing it

was Cleo but keen to find out if Summer knew or had guessed.

"The police won't tell me," Summer replied, the frustration clear in her voice. "But I think it was Cleo. She's the only person I saw after I left Vera. She was in the compound heading towards the stores, and she looked very furtive to me." Summer's eyes narrowed. "Why don't they think Cleo did it? She had the opportunity too, and Vera was often mean to her."

Bea's thoughts swirled. She sympathised with Summer's predicament, but in her heart, she couldn't see Cleo as the culprit. The girl was too young, and from what Ana had said to Perry, she hadn't taken Vera's comments that seriously. *And*, she reminded herself, *you're only hearing Summer's version of events*. Cleo might tell Perry something completely different.

Bea chose her words carefully. "I'm sure they're exploring all the options, Summer." She took a sip of coffee. "So after your conversation with Vera, what did you do next?"

Summer sighed, her eyes drifting towards the window again. It was clear she was growing weary of rehashing the same events over and over. "She was fine when I left," Summer said, her voice taking on a mechanical quality. "I went for a walk around the grounds just to regain my composure, you know?"

"Did you see anyone while you were out there?" Bea asked.

"No," Summer replied. Bea caught a slight hesitation in her voice. *Is Summer holding something back? There must have been a few members of the public wandering around, probably with their dogs.* "Are you sure?" Bea pressed gently.

Summer's eyes flashed with defensiveness, but she maintained her politeness. "Yes, I'm certain," she replied firmly.

Next to her, Fred bristled. "Have you finished interrogating her now, sis?"

Not wanting to risk alienating Fred and Summer so early in the process, Bea said, "I'm so sorry," offering Summer an apologetic smile.

Fred leaned back in his chair, a thoughtful expression on his face. "You know Saunders is inexperienced and ill-equipped to handle a high-profile case like this."

Bea raised an eyebrow. "Why do you say that?" She didn't like the man, but she couldn't imagine the senior management at PaIRS would have given him the job if they didn't think he could handle it.

"Did you know he only got his promotion to chief inspector a month ago, and he's never dealt with a murder investigation before; he's mostly worked on cyber-related cases from what I've found out."

Ah, so Fred has been doing some digging…

"Then why assign him to this case?" Bea asked.

Fred shrugged. "I hear that they're short of experienced senior police officers at the moment. Everyone is assigned to other things." Hadn't Rich said that Em was busy in Wales?

"They should have given it to Fitzwilliam," Fred continued, taking a swig of coffee.

"But he's on sick leave at the moment," Bea pointed out.

"I'm sure he could have managed with Spicer's help. You know, I've half a mind to report Saunders to PaIRS. He shouldn't be allowed to harass Summer like he did. This investigation needs someone more experienced at the helm." His eyes narrowed, and he fell silent. Abruptly, he stood up from the table. "Excuse me. I need to make a call."

Bea sighed. She wasn't convinced Fred could get Saunders removed from the case, however much she might want the man gone. She glanced over at Summer, who seemed lost in her own thoughts. There were faint lines of tension around her dark eyes. "Are you alright?" Bea asked gently.

"I'm fine, just tired of the same questions," Summer replied, forcing a small smile.

"Of course." Bea nodded. She glanced at the door to the hallway where Fred had disappeared a few minutes ago. Did she have time to ask Summer a question that had occurred to her earlier? She took a deep breath. *May as well try...* "Summer. Why did you stay on-site at Francis Court after speaking with Vera? Why didn't you just go back to your cottage?" The walk back to Francis-next-the-Sea would have given her plenty of time to calm down.

Summer glanced at the door, her cheeks flushed a deep pink. "Er, I just... As I've already said I wanted to walk around the grounds to clear my head," she stammered, her gaze darting away from Bea.

Really? Something's not adding up. As Bea opened her mouth to press further, Summer looked her squarely in the eye and said, "I promise you, Beatrice, I had nothing to do with Vera's death."

The earnestness in Summer's voice was convincing. Bea wanted to trust her instincts, and they told her that Summer was innocent.

Just then, Fred returned to the room, a sly grin playing on his lips.

"Everything alright?" Bea asked.

"Yes, thanks," he replied, resuming his seat. He picked up a sandwich, still smiling, but offered no further explanation.

Has he really got Saunders removed from the case?

As they resumed their lunch, Bea's thoughts remained

preoccupied with what Summer wasn't telling her. Whatever it was, Bea was sure it was something Summer didn't want Fred to know.

18

MEANWHILE, TUESDAY 20 APRIL

Simon pushed open the huge oak door of The Ship and Seal, feeling a rush of warm air greet him as he entered. He stood at the entrance and paused for a moment. He took a deep breath. *She's probably just a fan. It's not a big deal.*

The pub was quiet, which wasn't surprising given the time of day. A few tourists were dotted around at the tables in the dining room on his left, sipping coffee and chatting quietly after their morning strolls along the picturesque coast-line or browsing the quaint seaside shops of Francis-next-the-Sea. The low hum of conversation and clinking of cups provided a soothing backdrop as Simon spotted Dylan Milton, the landlord, behind the bar of the snug to the right. Dylan caught Simon's eye and tilted his head subtly towards a young woman wearing an oversized blue jumper and baggy jeans sitting at a table in the corner. Her long ginger hair had fallen over her face like a curtain as she sat slightly hunched over her phone. A half-empty glass of Coke rested on the wooden table beside her.

Simon nodded at Dylan as he slowly made his way across the worn floorboards towards her, the familiar smell of wood polish with just a hint of stale beer lingering in the air. She looked like a student to him — probably studying creative writing or something similar — and he recalled past encounters with eager young minds seeking advice or interviews about his books. He relaxed. *She looks harmless enough.*

As he neared, she tucked her hair behind her ears. Her blue eyes flicked up from her phone, meeting his gaze for just a moment. She seemed nervous, almost vulnerable, and Simon couldn't help but feel an odd sense of protectiveness towards her. He smiled. "Hello, I'm Simon Lattimore," he said as he stopped in front of her. "Dylan said you've been looking for me."

"O-oh!" She stuttered, her eyes widening as she stood up. "Yes, I—I am. Hi," she said with a lilting Scottish accent. She gave him a weak smile, her fingers fidgeting with the edge of the phone clutched in her hand.

The girl seemed anxious, yet there was a glimmer of excitement in her eyes — the kind that came with meeting someone she admired. *Oh no...* Perhaps she *was* one of those fans with an unhealthy fixation? It wouldn't be the first time he'd encountered doe-eyed admirers. He'd just make this quick and be on his way.

"Thank you for coming," she stammered, seeming to regain some composure.

"Of course," Simon replied, still smiling. "Shall we sit?"

She bobbed her head, and he lowered himself into the chair opposite her. Sitting, she smoothed down her jumper as if trying to settle her nerves.

Simon waited for her to introduce herself, but she simply stared at him, her mouth slightly open. "So you know who I am, but..." He trailed off, hoping he had hinted strongly enough that it was her turn.

She blushed, her fingers twitching against her phone. "Oh, sorry. I'm Isla. Isla Scott."

He smiled and held out his hand. "It's nice to meet you, Isla."

She hesitated before taking his hand, her grip faint and uncertain. "Um, I'm sorry to just show up like this," she said as she dropped his hand, her cheeks flushing. "I'm a student studying creative arts, and I wondered if…if I could interview you for a project I'm doing on crime writers? I'm staying nearby and thought it would be easier than emailing."

He found her candidness endearing. *So just as I thought; she's a student, not a crazed fan.* He suppressed a grin. *Perry will be relieved!* "I'd be happy to help."

"Really?" Her face brightened, relief washing over her features. "Thank you so much!"

"Would you like to do the interview now?" Simon asked.

Isla's eyes sparkled. "Yes, if you have the time."

"Of course. I'll just get a drink if that's okay?" She nodded, and Simon stood. He made his way to the bar, and Dylan met him with a raised eyebrow.

"She's just a student who's in the area wanting an interview," Simon told him as he ordered a pint. Dylan smiled, his curiosity seemly satisfied, and handed over a beer.

Returning to Isla, Simon found her scrolling through what looked to him like a list of questions on her phone. She glanced up. "Do you mind if I record this? It'll make it quicker."

He agreed, and taking a deep breath, she began. "So tell me about your characters. Where do they come from?"

Simon scratched his beard as he answered. "Well, some are inspired by real-life people I've met, while others are purely fictional. It's a mix, really."

"And are you a planner, or do you let the story unfold as you write?"

"A bit of both, actually," Simon said, taking a sip of his pint. "I usually begin with a rough idea and then form it into an outline. But apart from a few lines of what I want to reveal in each chapter, I just write and see where it goes. I try to give my characters the freedom to take the story forward however they want to."

They continued discussing story structure and the intricacies of crime writing, their conversation flowing more easily than before. Halfway through, Isla excused herself to go to the bathroom. Simon leaned back in his chair and sipped his drink. She seemed genuinely nice, but there was something familiar about her piercing blue eyes that nagged at him.

When Isla returned, she sat down, then hesitated before asking, "Can I ask you some background questions?"

"Er, yes," Simon said, intrigued and nervous in equal measures. He much preferred to talk about his writing and his characters than he did about himself.

"Why write crime novels?" she asked, her eyes focused intently on him.

"Ah, well," Simon said, swirling the last bit of his pint. "I was in the police. So I suppose it was a matter of writing what I knew and then cranking it up a notch."

"And why did you leave CID?" *So she already knows that then?*

He hesitated, feeling an unexpected vulnerability. "Er, I got a six-book publishing deal and wanted to focus on my writing career." *That's sort of true…*

Isla's gaze didn't waver. "There's more to it than that, isn't there?"

Simon swallowed, surprised by her perception. "In all

honesty, I always felt like a square peg in a round hole in the police. It could be because I'm gay."

"But you were married to a woman, weren't you?"

She really has done her homework.

"Yes. It was a different time in my life. We were both very young and grew apart over the years."

"And now you're married to Perry Juke? I read about your wedding in the papers; it sounded amazing. And your honeymoon in Italy. You've got family there?" she asked, her eyes softening with curiosity.

A warm smile spread across Simon's face at the mention of his husband. "Yes, it was truly magical. I've never been happier. And yes, I have family in the Abruzzo region of southern Italy."

"On your mother's side?"

Simon hesitated. Why did he get the impression that she knew all this already? He nodded.

"Ah, I see," Isla murmured, looking down at her phone..

I'm not saying any more about me... "So where in Scotland are you from?"

"Uh, a small town on the east coast," she replied looking up, hesitation creeping into her voice. She shifted in her seat, her fingers fidgeting with the edge of her phone.

"And where are you studying?" Simon asked, curious to know more about this young woman.

"*Universitat de Barcelona.* Sorry…I mean the University of Barcelona."

That was unexpected. And her pronunciation had been perfect.

"So how does a girl from Scotland end up studying in Spain?"

"Well, I have family in Spain, and I speak Spanish," she

said, her voice still unsteady. "Plus, the university has an incredible creative arts course."

Simon's brow furrowed as he sensed her unease, and he chastised himself for pushing too many personal questions. A tension settled between them. *Well, this is awkward…and it's my fault.* "Look, I'm sorry if I've made you uncomfortable," he said, rubbing the back of his neck. "I have a meeting soon, so I should probably get going if you've got everything you need?"

Disappointment flashed across Isla's face, but she dipped her chin in understanding. "Of course. I appreciate the time you've given me today. Thank you, Mr Lattimore."

"Simon please." He smiled as he stood to leave. She stared at him for a few seconds, then hesitantly returned his smile.

With a wave, he turned towards the door, unable to shake the feeling that those wide blue eyes had seen straight into his soul. A shiver ran down his spine. *Thank goodness I won't have to see her again.*

19

_____

2:35 PM, TUESDAY 20 APRIL

Bea's thoughts were troubled as the light cast a golden blaze on the lush greenery of the formal gardens at Francis Court. Despite the sunshine, a crisp chill lingered in the air, and she tucked a stray strand of her thick hair behind her ear, before pulling her coat tighter around her as she walked in step with Rich. As much as she enjoyed his company, guilt gnawed away at her for hiding from him her ongoing investigation into Vera's death. *You promised him you wouldn't get involved.* Yet here she was, working behind his back with Perry and Simon to prove Summer's innocence.

As she walked alongside him with Daisy trotting happily at their heels, occasionally sniffing at the various flowers that lined their way, she couldn't help but worry that she was risking ruining their burgeoning friendship. She stole a glance at him, admiring his ruggedly handsome features and enjoying the way she felt so at ease with him. *I would hate to lose this now…*

"How did your interview with Saunders go?" Rich asked, dragging Bea back from her internal musings.

She hesitated, unsure of how much to reveal about her

distaste for the man. "It went... all right, I suppose," she said vaguely, kicking at a small pebble on the path.

He chuckled. "Come on, Bea. It's not like you to hold back. I got the impression you didn't take to him yesterday when he appeared."

"Alright, I'll be honest with you," she said, looking around the garden to make sure no one was within earshot. "I don't like Saunders at all. He's rude and dismissive."

"Isn't that what you used to say about me?" A grin slowly spread across his face.

Touché! Bea smiled sweetly. "Used to say? How do you know I don't still say that?"

Rich threw his head back and laughed.

Bea's heart fluttered. *I've made him laugh!*

"Anyway," she continued. "There didn't seem to be much love lost between the two of you yesterday either."

"Ah, Saunders and I... Our relationship is complicated," Rich admitted, rubbing the back of his neck. "He's always been a bit off with me since I replaced him on the investigation into your husband's death. He was originally a DS in Reed's team along with Em but was away climbing a mountain when the accident happened. By the time he returned, I'd been moved onto Reed's investigations team permanently, and Saunders got shifted into a security and protection team. He's never quite forgiven me for that even though it wasn't my decision."

So she'd been right the other night about the source of Saunders' hostility. "But that was fifteen years ago!"

He nodded. "I know. But his career stagnated after that, and instead of acknowledging his own choices—he was always taking time off to climb a mountain or compete in an Iron Man challenge while the rest of us worked our guts out —he blamed the situation."

No wonder he's only just been promoted to chief inspector... "He sounds like he's one of those entitled types who feel they should have everything everyone else has but without putting in the same amount of effort."

Rich stopped walking and turned to face her. "I think that sums him up perfectly."

He flashed her one of his rare, genuine smiles that transformed his face entirely, causing her heart to flutter. *He really does have a lovely smile...*

Suddenly Daisy dived off into a bush, emerging a few seconds later with what remained of a yellow flower on her nose. They both laughed as Bea bent down and brushed it off. "But seriously," she said as she straightened up. "I'm worried that he's going to pin Vera's murder on Summer without doing a thorough investigation."

He raised an eyebrow. "Why Summer?" he asked, his voice tinged with suspicion.

Oh no! Have I given away too much? She hesitated before mumbling, "Fred's been so upset about the whole thing... Anyway, enough about that. How are you feeling? Are you doing your exercises?"

Fitzwilliam tilted his head to one side, then let out a small chuckle and nodded. "Yes, Bea, I am. Thanks for your concern."

She suppressed a sigh. She hated keeping things from him. But what choice did she have? She had to help Fred. As they continued their stroll through the gardens, heading back towards Rich's cottage, Bea spotted a tall well-built man wandering in an area usually closed off to the public. He was moving towards the *Bake Off Wars* compound. *What's he up to?*

She stopped. "Isn't that Mark Jacobs?" she asked, nudging Fitzwilliam and pointing in his direction. "Why's he on-site?" Could he be the real killer, lingering to cover his tracks?

Fitzwilliam squinted at the lofty figure as it disappeared around a Portakabin, his expression thoughtful. "I'm not sure." Then he mumbled something that Bea strained to hear.

Did he just say, "Maybe he's trying to cover his tracks?" What the… Oh my goodness, is he… "Wait! Are you unofficially investigating this case?" she blurted out, her eyes wide.

Rich's face turned red. He stammered, "No, no, it's just… I had Spicer over for dinner last night, and she might have mentioned something."

Did she now?

He didn't meet her eye. "Er, so do you think Mark will be asked back as a judge on *Bake Off Wars*?"

He's changing the subject! "I didn't know you were a fan."

"Fan might be too strong a word," he replied, looking up and grinning sheepishly. "But Perry talks about it non-stop, so I can't help but be a little invested."

She grinned back, and the tension between them seemed to dissipate. They started walking again.

Does Spicer think Mark's a credible suspect? If he was, then maybe they would leave Summer alone. "He had a pretty good motive to kill Vera, you know."

Fitzwilliam's expression immediately sobered. "Why would you care? You're not investigating the murder, remember?"

"But does Spicer think Mark did it?" Bea pressed, unable to let it go.

"Why do you want to know?" Fitzwilliam asked, his eyes narrowing.

Don't push it, Bea, or he'll know…

"Um, no reason. Just curious,"

"Curiosity killed the cat, you know, Bea," he warned her with a slight smile.

But the ex-judge had no alibi, and now it seemed that Spicer was seriously considering him as the prime suspect. She would talk to Perry and Simon about— *Perry!* She glanced at her watch. *Rats!* Perry would be waiting for her at the *Bake Off Wars* site. "Anyway, I should be off," Bea told him. "I'm meeting Perry at—" She stopped herself just in time. "I mean, now. Have a good afternoon, Rich. Come on, Daisy."

Bea stifled a huff as the little terrier stopped and looked from her to Rich and back. *Sorry, Daisy, but you'll have to leave him now…*

Fitzwilliam bent down and patted Daisy on the head. "See you later, Daisy." Then he smiled briefly at Bea. "Thanks for your company," he said before continuing on towards his cottage.

I'd best look like I'm heading to The Dower House, then I'll double back to the compound. She gave a deep sigh. She hated this deception.

———

Rich looked over his shoulder and watched Bea's retreating figure, a mix of admiration and worry churning within him. Had he successfully distracted her enough so she hadn't realised he was getting involved in the murder investigation? He shook his head. He wasn't convinced. *Bea has great instincts.* It was hard to hide anything from her.

He sighed. He really hadn't wanted to get dragged into it all anyway.

When Spicer had appeared on his doorstep last night with a takeaway and had talked about the case, he'd listened but not said much. Even when she'd told him that Saunders was fixated on Summer being the murderer and wasn't showing much interest in exploring other options, he'd kept his opinion that Saunders was showing his inexperience of dealing with a murder case to himself. But when Fred had called at lunchtime today and had begged him to help, Rich had wavered. Fred had talked about reporting Saunders, and as much as Rich didn't particularly like the man, he was a fellow PaIRS officer, and Rich had always felt a little responsible for Saunders' sideways move to accommodate him. A direct report of harassment from a member of the royal family really would kill Saunders' future in PaIRS.

Rich had reasoned in his head that maybe if he could help Spicer, who in turn could steer Saunders in the right direction, then they might solve the case with no one realising Saunders was out of his depth. And if they were lucky, Saunders would learn something from the experience that would make him a better investigator in the future.

But in order to placate Fred, Rich had had to agree to step in and investigate Vera's death. He'd made it very clear to Fred that he would have to go wherever the evidence took him and that that could ultimately lead to Summer. Fred had accepted the deal.

When Rich had called Spicer, she had been relieved too, even when he'd warned her she would have to be careful so Saunders didn't find out about his involvement.

So now he was committed to help.

But could he keep it from Bea? *And what is she up to?* For someone who wasn't investigating the case, she seemed to be especially interested in Mark as a suspect.

Fitzwilliam sighed, running a hand through his greying hair. Recalling their past adventures solving cases together, he knew Bea was stubborn and fiercely independent. It was one of the many qualities he admired in her. Even if it made his job more challenging. But if history was any sign, danger had a way of finding her when she least expected it. Was she putting herself in the line of fire again?

"Blast it, Bea," he whispered under his breath, a hint of affection lacing his frustration. "Why do you always have to be so curious?"

And of course she's right. The chef was a strong suspect, with an obvious motive and no alibi.

Fitzwilliam walked down the path leading to his cottage, his hands in his pockets, and his eyes taking in the vibrant colours of the flowers in the surrounding borders. *Is he really lurking around to cover his tracks?* He chided himself; he knew jumping to conclusions without evidence wasn't productive. If only he could focus solely on the investigation without worrying about Bea getting involved — or worse, finding herself in harm's way once again.

For now, he had to trust that she would respect their agreement and keep her distance from the investigation. But deep down, he knew that with Bea, nothing was ever quite that simple.

20

3:15 PM, TUESDAY 20 APRIL

Bea peered cautiously from behind the hedgerow, her gaze tracking Rich as he ambled up the lane towards his cottage. *Right, he's gone now.* Bea bit her lip, glancing over her shoulder at the empty lane. Did he have a suspicion she was looking into Vera's death? She would have to be careful. Very careful. She crept out from behind the bushes. "Alright, Daisy, let's go," she whispered as she emerged from her hiding spot, her breath forming a small cloud in the cool air. Brushing dirt and stray leaves off her dark jeans, she scanned her surroundings before she and Daisy legged it towards the *Bake Off Wars* compound on the other side.

As they hurried across the Long Drive, Bea mulled over what Rich might be doing. Was he secretly assisting Spicer with the investigation? Surely not; not only was he supposed to be resting after his injury, but both he and Spicer would face serious consequences if Saunders' or Rich's superiors discovered their collaboration.

Bea stepped onto the *Bake Off Wars* site, scanning the area for any sign of Perry. *He's probably given up waiting and gone inside the building.* Her boots made a soft thud against the gravel path as she entered the Old Barn.

The faint aroma of vanilla and cinnamon wafted through the air as she approached the end of the hallway and followed it around to the right. Daisy's tail wagged excitedly while the sound of clattering pans grew louder. A door stood ajar, revealing a brightly lit room bustling with activity. Bea scooped Daisy up in her arms, then poked her head inside, finding herself peering into a spacious kitchen. Stainless steel countertops gleamed under the warm glow of pendant lights, while an array of colourful ingredients and baking tools covered every available surface.

Voices drifted towards her, and Bea straightened, plastering a polite smile on her face as she entered the room. Two women Bea didn't recognise were working diligently at their respective stations — one kneading dough with a focused expression and the other carefully piping cream on the top of dainty cupcakes.

They looked up as Bea entered. "Excuse me," she called out over the noise of what sounded like a discussion on different types of flour coming from a speaker sitting next to a phone on the work surface between them. "I'm looking for Perry Juke. Have either of you seen him?"

The curvaceous woman with the piping bag shook her head, her eyes wide with surprise. "Er, no...my lady. I'm afraid not," she replied, placing the bag down on the counter and leaning over to turn off the discussion programme. She shot a look at the other woman and hissed, "Shelly, it's Lady Beatrice!"

"Oh, heck!" The other woman plopped a handful of sticky white dough into a bowl and dropped a cloth over the top of it.

Bea coloured slightly. "I'm so sorry to disturb you. Please don't let me stop you."

The woman smiled, a stray black curl poking out from under her head covering. "It's okay, my lady. I'm Lilian Livingston, but please call me Leah, and this is Shelly Black." Leah's warm voice carried a hint of a Birmingham accent, adding to her friendly demeanour.

Bea smiled at them. "It's nice to meet you both." Daisy wriggled in her arms, desperate to say hello.

"Oh, and who is this?" Leah asked as she and Shelly moved closer.

"This is Daisy. Who, given half a chance, will eat just about everything in here," Bea said, smiling.

The two women cooed over Daisy, who welcomed the attention with a flickering tongue.

"Would you like a cup of tea, Lady Beatrice?" Leah offered, removing her blue food prep gloves and reaching for a kettle.

"Thank you, but no," Bea replied, shifting Daisy in her arms. *Well, now I'm here, I may as well ask a few questions…* "You worked with Vera Bolt, didn't you? I'm so sorry for your loss. How are you both holding up?"

"Thank you," Shelly said quietly, her blue eyes clouding over. "It's still hard to believe she's gone."

"I keep expecting her to come in and…" Leah's voice cracked as she trailed off.

Bea nodded sympathetically. "I've heard that she could be quite the taskmaster."

Leah's brown eyes narrowed. "Her bark was worse than her bite, really."

She looked over at Shelly, who sucked her cheeks in. "You got used to it after a while."

After everything Bea had heard about Vera, their defence seemed odd. Misplaced even. She tilted her head, watching them closely. Leah had crossed her arms and was leaning against the large steel work bench. Shelly darted a glance at Leah, then stepped back and returned to her dough. *Oh dear, they seem to have shut down.* Clearly saying anything bad about Vera would not go down well with these two. *I need a different tack...* "Poor Vera. With Mark no longer part of the team, she must have been under immense pressure to make this series a success."

Shelly and Leah exchanged a glance before nodding in agreement.

"She had such high standards, you see." Leah unfolded her arms and sighed. "The pressure of the show and Mark leaving...it was getting to her, making her sharp with people. She just wanted everything to be perfect."

Bea dipped her head, then quickly moved her face away as Daisy's tongue appeared from nowhere. Unsuccessful at licking her mistress, the little dog sighed and rested her head back on Bea's arm.

"Vera was definitely feeling the pressure," Shelly agreed, busying herself with measuring out flour. "But we were all doing our best to help her."

"You must have been a great support to her." The two women smiled. They seemed to have relaxed again. *Tread carefully...* "Was she disappointed about how the first weekend of filming had gone then?"

Shelly shook more flour onto the work surface, then shrugged before darting a look at Leah.

"As I said, she had high standards," Leah chimed in, her voice filled with conviction. "She expected nothing less than excellence from everyone on the show."

"Did you see her after the morning meeting yesterday?"

Bea asked, knowing they had but not wanting them to know she knew.

Leah hesitated for a moment before speaking up. "Vera gave us feedback on the bake we'd done the day before. We agreed to make some changes and then left after about ten minutes." She glanced at Shelly, who nodded in confirmation. "We came back here together and were redoing the skills challenge bakes until we took a breather to grab a coffee at around ten past eleven."

"Did you see anyone else during that time?" Bea asked, noticing their eyes darting towards each other again before answering.

"Nobody," Shelly replied, her blue eyes flickering between Bea and Leah.

What's going on between them? Why do they feel the need to validate what each other is saying? "Would you have seen anyone who went past?" Bea asked, recalling the open door she herself had come in through.

"It's unlikely," Shelly responded, shaking her head. "The door here in the practice kitchen was closed. We wouldn't have noticed anything unless someone had knocked on the door and come inside."

Bea studied Leah's and Shelly's faces, noting the subtle tension in their expressions. *What do they know?* "Is there anyone you think would have wanted to harm Vera?" she asked, her voice gentle but probing.

Shelly hesitated before saying, "Well, Vera was trying to get Harvey Jury sacked after he openly supported Mark at the end of last season."

She looked pointedly at Leah, who dipped her head in agreement. "He was removed from doing her cooking — that's how I got involved— because Vera refused to work with him. She was telling everyone she'd have him off the show by the end of the third episode."

Bea hid a knowing smile. It seemed Vera's assistants could be rather loose-lipped for all their earlier caution. *This could prove useful.*

Shelly, her blue eyes wide, added, "I've heard that the police have questioned Summer. Is she the prime suspect?"

"No. Why would she be?" Bea replied. *Oh no! Do they know something that could support Saunders' conviction that Summer is the killer?* Bea held her breath.

"Only that she was very upset at the meeting that morning about the way Vera spoke to her," Shelly said, wringing her hands nervously. Bea's shoulders relaxed. *So nothing new then...* In fact, maybe they could help. "Did you see Summer after the meeting?"

Both women shook their heads, saying in unison, "No."

Oh well, it was worth a try. "What about Mark? It's no secret that he and Vera parted on bad terms," Bea continued, watching their faces closely for any reaction.

Shelly and Leah exchanged glances, clearly confused. "But he isn't here on-site anymore, so how could he have attacked her?" Shelly asked, her brow furrowing.

"Indeed." It was best not to disclose that he'd been in the grounds yesterday. She shifted Daisy in her arms. The terrier was getting heavy now. *It's all that bacon Perry has been feeding her!* "Well, it was nice to meet you both. I'd best find my friend now."

The two women smiled and said goodbye.

As Bea and Daisy left the practice kitchen, a nagging feeling settled in the pit of Bea's stomach. Something about the two women's demeanour set off alarm bells in her mind. She couldn't shake the feeling that there was more to their story than they were letting on.

21

A SHORT WHILE BEFORE, TUESDAY
20 APRIL

"Come on, Bea," Perry muttered under his breath as he leaned against a sturdy oak tree, his arms crossed, casting a glance around the deserted compound. The area was eerily quiet, almost as though the entire place had taken a collective breath, waiting for something to happen. He checked his watch for the third time and sighed. *She's taking her time! Is she still with Fitzwilliam?* He shook his head, a smile tugging at the corners of his lips. Those two were like the last two pieces of a puzzle that just needed a gentle nudge to fall into place. If only they'd realise what a good match they made. He imagined Bea finally letting someone into her life who could handle her unique blend of royalty and stubborn independence. His heart swelled at the thought of his best friend finding happiness after everything she'd been through.

He pushed off from the tree and paced, the crunch of gravel underfoot punctuating his frustration. *Alright, I've waited long enough!* He wouldn't hang around while Bea and Fitzwilliam made eyes at each other. He took one last look in the direction Bea might appear from before turning on his heels and setting off to find Cleo. *Now where will she be?* He scanned the compound, searching for a familiar face. Just as he was about to give up, he spotted Cleo heading towards a small Portakabin tucked behind one of the larger ones. He quickened his pace to catch up with her.

"Hey, Cleo!" Perry called out, stepping into the dimly lit cabin. Papers were strewn across a wobbly table. A laptop lay open by a pile of scripts. The smell of stale coffee hung in the air.

Cleo spun around, clearly startled. Her blue eyes peered at him through black glasses. "Oh, hi, Perry. Are you looking for Ana?" Petite and all dressed in black, she looked like a character from one of the online fantasy games Ana had told Perry Cleo loved to play.

"She's not here. She's gone back to the hotel to pick up some paperwork," Cleo continued, her voice quiet but warm.

"Oh, okay, thanks." It served his purpose for her to think he was there to see Ana. Maybe she wouldn't notice so much when he started asking questions. "So how are you holding up, Cleo?" Perry asked, his concern genuine. He remembered Ana mentioning how upset Cleo had been about Vera's death.

Her eyes clouded over, and she bit her lip. "It's all been a bit of a shock, you know? And I wasn't sure if I would lose my job and have to go home… Well that is until they told us filming would carry on as planned."

"Is this job important to you?"

"No, not anymore," she replied hesitantly.

Perry's eyebrows shot up. *What does that mean?*

Sensing his confusion, Cleo stammered, "I mean, not for much longer. I start university in September where I'm studying media studies. I deferred for a year to get some work experience; that's why I applied for this runner's job. But now…" She let her voice trail off, worry etched on her pale face.

Perry studied the young girl in front of him, noting her nervous energy. *Why did she volunteer all that extra information? Was it just nerves? Or was she over-explaining to hide the truth?* He needed to gain her trust so he could find out more. *Subtle, Perry. You can do subtle…* "So Vera must have been a handful to work with."

Cleo's face transformed into an impassive mask. "She was okay, I guess. She mostly ignored me and dealt with Ana, what with her being more senior."

There was a subtle tension in Cleo's posture as she spoke of the late judge.

"But wasn't she quite rude to you and Ana?" he pressed on, trying to sound casual. "I heard she could be snappy about her coffee."

Cleo shrugged. "That's just part of the job — us runners are the general dogsbodies. Everyone bosses us around." A hint of warmth crept into her voice as she added, "Except for Ryan; he's nice and kind."

Perry nodded. He needed to find out more about Cleo's movements around the time of Vera's death. "So what were you up to after the meeting yesterday morning?"

Cleo hesitated, her fingers twisting the hem of her T-shirt. "Er, Ana asked me to clean out the storage container," she finally said, avoiding eye contact. "I went straight there and didn't leave until Ana came to find me later. That's when I found out Vera was dead."

Really? He knew she'd told the police that she'd overheard Summer having an argument with Vera. Why wasn't she telling him the truth? Was she just being discreet in front of someone who didn't work for the company, or was she hiding something more sinister?

Forget subtly. He needed to confront her directly. "Cleo, I know you heard Summer arguing with Vera not long before she was found dead."

A flicker of panic flashed across her face, then it was quickly replaced by curiosity. "How do you know that?" she asked, her voice shaky.

"Er, my husband's an ex-policeman. He's helping them with the case." *Well, that's sort of true...*

Cleo's shoulders relaxed slightly. "Alright," she murmured. "I heard them arguing. But the police told me not to say anything about it." She fiddled with a strand of her curly brown hair. Her blue eyes were filled with uncertainty. *Aw, bless her. She's so young.*

"Tell me what happened," Perry urged gently.

Cleo took a deep breath. "Well, I was looking for a stepladder to reach something high in the storage room. I remembered seeing some steps in The Tent at the weekend. One of the cameramen was using it to get some higher angles. So I went to the Old Barn."

"What time was this?"

"About twenty to eleven."

"Did you see anyone on your way there?"

"No. When I got close to The Tent, the door was open, and I could hear voices coming from inside."

"Were they shouting?"

Cleo frowned. "No, not at first. I couldn't make out what they were saying, but their voices were raised. It definitely seemed like an argument or a heated discussion. I heard Vera raise her voice, and then I recognised Summer's voice too." She hesitated.

"Go on," Perry said, his voice low.

"I didn't know what to do. I didn't want to disturb them,

but I wanted the ladder. So I thought I'd just wait until they finished, then I'd go in and get it. So I just hung around outside the entrance in the corridor. Then it seemed like they moved away from the door," Cleo continued, her voice barely more than a whisper. "I couldn't hear anything for a few minutes. I even wondered if they'd gone out the other way. Then I thought I heard a clatter, like something being knocked over."

Perry leaned in, his eyes fixed on Cleo's face. Had things got physical between Vera and Summer?

"Then suddenly I heard footsteps hurrying towards the door, and I panicked." She swallowed noisily while looking down at her hands. "So I turned to leave, and I knocked into a table in the corridor. After that I just ran. But as I fled, I heard Summer shout, 'And don't think you've heard the last of this!'"

"Did Vera reply?" Perry asked, trying to hide the urgency in his voice. If Vera had responded, then at least it would prove Vera had still been alive after Summer had left.

Cleo shook her head. "I didn't hear her say anything in reply."

Perry's mind raced with possibilities. "Did you turn around and see Summer?" he asked gently. If Summer had killed Vera, she might have still been holding the murder weapon.

"No, I didn't," Cleo said, her voice trembling slightly. "I just wanted to get out of there before she saw me." Her eyes filled with tears. She sniffed, wiping them away with the back of her hand. "I really like Summer. I never meant to get her into trouble." Her lips quivered. "Why do the police think she killed Vera when I heard Summer talking to her as she left?"

Or that's what Summer wanted you to think. He kept the

thought to himself, not wanting to upset her further. His heart ached for Cleo as she stood there, distraught and confused.

Suddenly, the sound of tiny paws tapping on the stairs to the Portakabin caught his attention. Both he and Cleo started as a small white dog bounded into the room, her tongue lolling out of her mouth in a joyful grin. *Daisy!*

Cleo wiped her face with her hand and smiled down at the terrier dancing around her feet.

A moment later, Bea appeared in the doorway, her red hair streaming behind her. "Ah, there you are!" she said. Then she stopped and cast a concerned glance at Cleo. "I hope I'm not interrupting?"

"No, not at all," Perry reassured her, trying to subtly convey that now was not the best time for further questions. He sensed Bea understood; she had always been good at reading people.

"Come on, Daisy," Bea said, gesturing towards the door.

"I need to head back to the office," Perry said, giving Cleo a soft smile. "Take care, Cleo. And remember, I'm here if you need to talk."

Cleo returned a weak smile and nodded.

As he left the cabin, Perry fell into step beside Bea, Daisy trotting happily at their heels. The sun cast long shadows across the grounds, and the air held the faint scent of baked goods, momentarily lifting the sombre atmosphere.

"Is she alright?" Bea asked, her voice low and concerned, her green eyes searching Perry's face for answers.

Perry hesitated. What Cleo had just told him could be the reason Saunders was so sure Summer was the prime candidate to be Vera's killer. He had to tell Bea what she'd said. But it was going to make it difficult to help Fred if everything pointed to Summer being guilty. They reached the Long

Drive, and Daisy ran ahead, burying her head in the under-growth of the trees lining the driveway.

"Perry?" Bea sounded concerned.

I've got to tell her…

Perry took a deep breath. "Er, Bea…"

22

7 PM, TUESDAY 20 APRIL

Bea squiggled back into the leather seats of the booth in The Ship and Seal, Francis-next-the-Sea's only pub. The hum of conversation from the other diners filled the air, mingling with the enticing aroma of freshly cooked food. A crackling fire danced in the hearth over the other side of the dining area, casting flickering shadows on the oak-panelled walls adorned with framed black and white photographs documenting the village's history back to the fifteenth century.

Daisy, who was nestled next to her, snored gently, while across the table, Perry's blue eyes sparkled with excitement, his blond hair catching the glow of the pub's dim lighting. *What's he so giddy about?*

Simon, ever the picture of laid-back comfort, slouched beside his husband in his usual attire of jeans and a T-shirt.

Suddenly, Perry clapped his hands together, barely able to contain his enthusiasm. "Simon, you must tell Bea your news!"

Simon grinned, holding up a hand in surrender. "Alright, but let's order food first. I'm famished."

"Okay, I suppose," Perry pouted as Bea picked up her

menu. Her mind raced with possibilities. What could Simon have discovered that warranted such eagerness from Perry? She hoped it would be something that might exonerate Summer within the time of death window.

Perry drummed his fingers on the table, casting a glance at Simon. Simon smiled and signalled to the server, who came over and took their order.

The booth creaked as Simon shifted his weight and leaned forward. Bea's heart skipped a beat as she almost held her breath.

"Alright," Simon said, his voice low and conspiratorial. "I've heard from CID Steve and Roisin about the autopsy and forensics results. Unfortunately, no fingerprints were found at the scene, which suggests the killer wore gloves."

Bea's heart sank. This complicated matters. A gloved killer implied premeditation rather than a crime of passion, which would also mean they would have had a plan to dispose of any incriminating evidence, making it more difficult to find.

"Have they narrowed down the time of death any further?" Bea asked. If they could pinpoint the exact time of Vera's death, then perhaps they could clear Summer's name.

"Sadly, no," Simon replied, meeting her gaze with sympathy. Disappointment washed over Bea like a tidal wave. The evidence seemed to point more and more towards Summer being the culprit. Bea couldn't bring herself to believe it, but the thought nagged at her like a splinter under her skin.

"Wait!" Perry interrupted, his excitement bubbling over. "That's not the news I meant, Simon. The other news!"

Other news? Bea's curiosity piqued as she looked at her friends. She'd been so focused on the implications of the forensics report that she'd assumed Perry's enthusiasm for whatever this news was of Simon's was about the case.

"What news?" Simon asked, a grin playing across his lips.

"Oh, for goodness' sake!" Perry couldn't contain himself any longer. "Austin has asked Simon to be a guest judge on *Bake Off Wars* for a couple of weeks while they find a replacement for Vera!"

Wow! Bea grinned. "Congratulations."

"Thank you," Simon replied modestly, a hint of pride in his brown eyes. "I'm very flattered that they asked me, although I can't help think that Ryan had something to do with it."

That would make sense. Ryan would be pleased to have his friend by his side as he faced his first weekend of filming without the more experienced Vera supporting him. *But what about Mark? Why isn't he being asked back as a judge?*

Their food arrived, steaming and aromatic. As they tucked into their meals, Bea's thoughts returned to the subject of the ex-judge. "Rich and I saw Mark Jacobs heading towards the *Bake Off Wars* compound this afternoon. What do you think he's up to? Is he hoping to come back to the show now, do you think?" In her mind, he still had the strongest motive of all to get rid of Vera.

Simon took a bite of his shepherd's pie before answering, "Well, when I spoke with Austin, I asked if he would ultimately replace Vera. He was evasive at first, but eventually he admitted they hoped so. He also said he'd just been talking to Mark earlier that afternoon. It appears they're in negotiations for his return."

Perry raised an eyebrow. "I wonder if he knew this would happen if Vera was out of the way. It gives him an obvious motive to—"

"Hold on," Simon stopped him. "Before you get carried away, Nancy Drew. He has an alibi for Monday morning when someone killed Vera."

What?

"Go on," Perry urged, his eyes wide with interest.

"Austin told me he and Mark met on Monday morning at ten-thirty and walked around the gardens together. It turns out he has backing to front a new baking competition show to rival *Bake Off Wars* and wanted Austin to direct it. That's also why he was meeting Harvey in Windstanton last week. He wants him to join the show too. Of course, now that Vera's dead, things have changed. But before that, Mark was trying to poach Austin and Harvey for his own show."

"How long were they together for?" Perry asked through a mouthful of fish.

"About an hour, apparently."

Bea's fork paused mid-air, disappointment settling like a stone in her stomach. If neither Mark nor Austin were suspects any longer, then that left only three: Cleo, Harvey, and Summer.

Perry toyed with the crispy chips on his plate, his brow furrowing as he said, "I wonder who stands to inherit Vera's estate? She must have been worth quite a bit with all her cookbooks and that chocolate sauce that she's famous for." He plucked a chip off his plate and handed it across the table to Daisy, who gobbled it up in seconds.

"Perry!" Bea hissed. He gave her a sweet smile and went back to eating his food.

"That's a good question," Simon said, wiping gravy from the corner of his mouth. He looked at Bea. "Why don't we ask Fred to do some digging?"

"Great idea," Bea said, putting down her fork and pulling out her mobile. She swiftly texted Fred their request. She knew they could trust him to discreetly uncover the information they needed. How he got it, she had no idea, but it was probably something to do with his contacts at MI6.

When they'd finished their food, Bea told them of her chat with Shelly and Leah, including their thoughts that Harvey might have had a good reason to want Vera dead.

"Harvey? Really?" Perry asked, surprise clear in his voice.

"If Vera really was trying to get him sacked, then I suppose that could give him a motive," she pointed out.

Simon shook his head slowly. "Except we now know that Mark was offering him a job on his new show. And I think it was a promotion. So would he really care if Vera tried to get rid of him?"

Probably not. Bea sighed. So that was potentially Harvey without a strong motive, and Cleo with no motive at all that they knew of. "I hate to admit it, but Summer is still our most likely suspect at the moment," she said with a heavy heart. What on earth would she say to Fred when the time came?

"Let's not forget Cleo either," Simon added, tapping his fingers on the table. He turned to Perry. "I know she's young, and you say she's very sweet, but she's still in the mix. Even you weren't convinced she was being completely honest with you when you spoke to her this afternoon."

"I suppose so," Perry agreed reluctantly. "I just don't see her as a killer."

"And we should still speak with Harvey before we completely rule him out too," Simon said.

Bea nodded. Maybe she shouldn't give up just yet on proving Summer innocent of Vera's murder.

———

Rich sat in his cosy cottage, the soft glow of the fire casting shadows on the walls as he nursed a large cup of black coffee. His mind was a whirl of thoughts and images. The lack of credible suspects in this case was bugging him. Motives were thin at best, and the time of death window of only twenty minutes had narrowed down the opportunity even more. Then there was the unidentified man and the girl in the grounds yesterday morning. They'd still had no luck finding out who they were. Could one of them have known Vera and had a motive to kill her?

Someone, somewhere did. *But who?*

He sighed and took a sip of the hot black liquid. And on top of all of that, Bea kept popping up in his mind. Her soothing voice. Her beautiful smile. Her slightly citrusy smell. Her flowing red locks. And those green eyes that seemed to see into his soul. *What am I going to do about Bea?*

His mobile buzzed on the table beside him, jolting him from his musings. He glanced at the screen: DS Tina Spicer. Rich grabbed the phone and stabbed at the green button to accept the call. "Spicer, what have you got for me?"

"And good evening to you too, Fitz," Spicer said, the hint of amusement coming through in her voice reminding him that he wasn't actually her boss on this case, so a smidgen of politeness wouldn't go amiss.

"Sorry, Tina. How are you?"

"A little suspicious, if I'm honest. We've just received an anonymous tip. Apparently, Summer York was seen leaving The Tent in bloodied kitchen overalls at ten-fifty yesterday morning."

"What?" Fitzwilliam's heart skipped a beat. Could this be the break they needed? *But*, he checked himself, *not the break he wanted.* He'd been convinced, like Fred, that Summer was innocent. But if this was real, then it didn't look good for her. "Are you certain about the time?" he asked, struggling to keep his voice steady.

"Our informant certainly is. Saunders is ecstatic. He's ready to throw the book at her."

"What do we know about the tipster?"

"Not much. The message was pre-recorded. The voice has been run through some app to make it sound different. CID are analysing it now. They may get something eventually, but it's unlikely."

If the tip was true, it placed Summer squarely in the frame for Vera's murder. But why would someone wait until now to come forward with such damning evidence?

"Be careful, Tina," he said, his thoughts racing. "This could be an attempt to mislead us or even to frame Summer."

"I've pointed that out to the chief inspector," she replied with a sigh. "I'm not sure he's open to that idea at the moment, but I'll keep you updated."

"Thanks, Tina." Fitzwilliam ended the call, his mind churning with questions. Was Summer truly capable of murder? Or was someone else trying to set her up? And who had made the anonymous call?

He leaned back in his chair, gazing at the fire once more. He just hoped Saunders wouldn't overreact and do something silly…

23

THE NEXT DAY, 8:30 AM, WEDNESDAY 21 APRIL

The Society Page online article:

TV Presenter Summer York Arrested in Connection With the Murder of Vera Bolt

The Daily Post *is this morning reporting that Summer York (35), presenter of* Bake Off Wars, *was last night arrested by Fenshire CID in connection with the death of* Bake Off Wars *judge Vera Bolt, who died on Monday, aged 66.*

Fenshire CID refused to comment on the report but issued the following statement a short while ago: 'A 35-year-old woman has been arrested and is helping us with our inquires into the death of Vera Bolt. No further information will be released at this time.'

Social media has been awash with support for the comedian and presenter, with her friends stating that there must have been some mistake. Fans also posted their disbelief that

Summer could be involved in anything nefarious. One supporter wrote: 'It's like a very weak plot line in a terrible book. Who could possibly believe that Summer was involved in Vera's death?'

Miss York's agent was unavailable for comment at the time of publication.

In a further bombshell, The Daily Post *has also reported that Lord Frederick Astley (39), Earl of Tilling, has been secretly dating Miss York for the past month. According to the paper,* Bake Off Wars *staff have observed Miss York and the earl together frequently around the set and in the nearby village of Francis-next-the-Sea. One source claims the couple "have been an item for a while now" and say that it's common knowledge among the cast and crew that they are in a relationship. Adding fuel to the fire, according to local sources, ex-Army intelligence officer Lord Fred, who is the future Duke of Arnwall, was seen arriving at the police station in King's Town late last night, accompanied by lawyer Charlotte Mansell (42) from the firm Bowstreet, Mansell, and Tuft, who has represented the royal family in several libel cases against various publications, including* The Daily Post *and* The Sunday Post.

The news of a possible romance between the king's nephew and the TV star has sent the popular press scrambling to Francis Court in Fenshire, where they are now camped out at the main gates of the Astley's stately home.

A press relations officer from Francis Court, who speaks on behalf of the Astley family, said that they do not comment on private matters relating to the family.

———

"Can't you do anything, Ma?" Bea begged, pacing up and down in front of the large windows in her parents' apartment at Francis Court. "Can't you get these articles stopped?" The early morning sun was already high in the sky, its beams of light bouncing off the water, running down The Cascade at the head of the Long Drive and bubbling into the large basin at its base. Bea huffed as she turned away from the familiar view.

Her Royal Highness Princess Helen sighed deeply. "You know that's not how it works, darling. I have no—"

"Well, what's the point of you owning *The Society Page* if you can't stop this…this drivel from being published?" Bea cried, running her hands through her long red hair.

"It's not up to me—"

"But why can't you—"

"Because none of it is untrue, Beatrice!" her mother snapped. Bea stopped pacing. She turned to face her mother, her eyes wide. *Surely she isn't defending the behaviour of the gutter press?*

"Well, is it?" Princess Helen's green eyes challenged Bea. "Summer *has* been arrested by the police in connection with that chef woman's death. Fred *did* go to the police station with Mrs Mansell from BMT last night. Against my advice, I might add. She could have gone on her own; she's a grown woman, after all…" The princess trailed off for a moment. She shook her head slowly. "And let's be honest, Fred and Summer have hardly been discreet about their relationship. They've been wandering around the estate like a couple of lovesick teenagers. Holding hands. Staring lovingly into each other's eyes. So of course everyone here has noticed. Fred's been a regular visitor to Summer's cottage in the village, *and* he's had her stay overnight in his apartment here." She let out a short, loud breath. "Did they really think no one would talk?

I can't believe they've managed to keep it under wraps for as long as they have."

Bea raised a hand to rub at her temples, where a dull ache had begun. Her mother was right. Fred and Summer had done little to hide their budding romance, so it had only been a matter of time before someone had gone to the press with the juicy gossip that the king's nephew was romancing the *Bake Off Wars* presenter.

"So what can I do? Nothing they've said isn't true. All *TSP* is doing is reporting what the rest of the press are saying."

Right again! Bea's stomach dropped. She hated when her mother was right.

After Princess Helen had revealed to a shocked Bea last year that she'd owned *TSP* since she'd been in her twenties as a way of having some control over how the royal family was reported in the UK press ("if you can't beat them, join them") Bea knew that although her mother had a final veto over what *TSP* reported, she also had to give her editors the freedom to do their jobs without too much interference. So unless something was untrue, Princess Helen restricted her involvement to correcting falsehoods, encouraging positive articles about the family, and dropping in information that gave good publicity for Francis Courts and its events. After all, she had her husband's family's business to run.

But even so, that's no excuse for the press to descend on Francis Court like a pack of hungry hyenas ready to devour everyone who comes near them. Bea's chest tightened. *What happens if they get a whiff of my friendship with Rich?*

"So I'm sorry, darling, but there isn't much I can do. It's not illegal for the press to—"

"Well, it should be! It's chaos outside, according to Adrian Breen. They found two members of the press trying to scale the wall at The Dower House at six this morning. I'm moving in this weekend. How can I—"

Her mother stood. "Beatrice Rose!"

Bea stopped mid-sentence. *Oh dear. I've really pushed her buttons this time.*

"Listen to me," Princess Helen barked, her elegant grey-white bob shimmering in the sunlight. She gave a deep sigh. "I appreciate the situation is less than ideal, but this is not about you right now, darling," she said, her voice lower and softer now. "Poor Fred is in bits. His girlfriend could be a murderer! What he needs right now is our support."

So did her mother think Summer had done it? Bea opened her mouth—

"Not, I might add, that I believe for one minute that Summer killed that woman. Why on earth would she?" The princess raised a perfectly sculpted eyebrow at Bea. Bea looked away and swallowed. What could she say?

Her phone beeped. *Saved by the bell!* She whipped her mobile from her pocket.

Fred: *Vera worth about £7m. She had a daughter now dead and a granddaughter who was adopted. Trying to get more details. xx*

Interesting. Seven million was a *lot* of money. Could that be the motive, after all? If so, then unless Summer somehow inherited Vera's money, maybe there was hope yet.

Bea: *Thanks. Will pass it on to the others. How are you bearing up? xx*

. . .

Fred: *Just sitting around waiting. Charlotte is in with Summer and the police now. xx*

"Beatrice?"

Bea turned to her mother. "That was Fred."

The princess' face softened. "Is he alright? Does he need anything?"

Yes. He needs me to prove that Summer's innocent!

24

AT THE SAME TIME, WEDNESDAY 21 APRIL

Spicer? Rich looked at the screen of his phone, his brain still foggy with sleep. *What's she doing ringing so—* He looked at his watch. *Blast!* He really must start setting an alarm, or when it came time to go back to work, he would struggle to get up and into the office on time. He hit the accept button.

"Good morning, Fitz. Sorry, did I wake you?"

"Er, no." He cleared his throat. "Is everything okay?"

"Sort of. I don't know if you've seen the papers yet? We arrested Summer York last night."

Really? "So the anonymous tip off was good?"

"We found a bloodied chef's coat in the back of her car in a plastic bag."

Well, that seems fairly conclusive…

"We're waiting for Forensics to match the blood to Vera's."

"And what did Summer have to say about it?"

"That it's not hers and that she's no idea where it came from. Her lawyer is saying that someone else must have put it there."

Rich frowned. *Why hasn't Summer disposed of it by now*

149

if it belonged to her? She'd had two days to wash it and remove all traces of blood, or she could have burned it or even thrown it in the sea. *Why keep it in her car?* "Does anyone else have access to Summer's car?"

Spicer sighed. "She leaves her car in the car park at the *Bake Off Wars* compound because there's no parking at the cottage she's renting in the village. The keys are hung up in the production office so the car can be moved if the production staff need to."

"And don't tell me, the office isn't kept locked." In his experience, security within a site like that was all concentrated on stopping anyone from getting in. Subsequently, inside it was pretty lax.

"No. Not when everyone's on-site."

"CCTV?"

"Only on the outside perimeter of the compound."

So anyone could have borrowed the keys… "So unless Summer's fingerprints are also on the coat, then it will be hard to prove a solid link to her."

"Yes, exactly." Spicer sounded confident. "Unfortunately, DCI Saunders doesn't agree. He thinks that he's now got the proof he's been looking for. He's already told Summer's lawyer he will apply for an extension to hold her beyond the normal twenty-four hours until the blood test results come in, which is when he expects to charge her."

Fitzwilliam shook his head. That was a bold statement for Saunders to make at this early stage of the arrest. "And what do you think, Tina?"

"I think we should still explore other options."

"I agree. What can I do to help?"

25

10:15 AM, WEDNESDAY 21 APRIL

Bea sauntered through the meticulously kept private gardens of Francis Court, the morning sun casting a golden sheen over Daisy's white fur as she pranced ahead, her tail wagging as she occasionally stopped to sniff the bases of the bushes lining the walkway. Rich strolled beside her, his brown eyes reflecting the blue sky above them. Bea shot a glance at his profile, noting how the sunlight softened the grey at his temples, giving him an almost boyish charm that belied the ruggedness of his features. He turned and caught her staring. *Blast!* She glanced away.

Daisy darted off ahead of them towards a sculpted hedge, her nose twitching with curiosity, and they walked on, the silence between them like a comfortable blanket, punctuated only by the occasional chirp of birds.

Bea's mind was churning over what Simon had told her earlier when he'd rung. *Why would Summer keep such incriminating evidence as a bloodied chef's jacket? Was it a desperate oversight or something more insidious?* Using gloves suggested that Vera's murder had been premeditated, so surely the killer would have had time to plan the disposal of any incriminating evidence. *They wouldn't have just left them lying around near the murder scene, would they?* Her thoughts twisted further, snaking around the question of the inheritance. Vera's granddaughter would surely have a size-able claim on the estate. If Vera had been sixty-six, then the granddaughter would be…about Cleo's age. Cleo had no alibi to speak of *and* was the person who'd implicated Summer. The pieces of the puzzle seemed to align. A surge of adren-aline shot through her. She squeaked softly. *Have I cracked the case?*

Rich turned to her, a puzzled look etched on his face. "What's the matter?"

Rats! Did I make that sound out loud? "Er, nothing. I was just...startled by a bee," she lied poorly, her eyes darting to the side, where no bee buzzed. A twinge of guilt shot through her. She hated to deceive Rich, but she couldn't risk exposing her sleuthing to him. *He'll be disappointed that I broke my promise.* She wasn't fully prepared to admit she didn't want to disappoint the man walking next to her.

"Right…" Rich replied, not sounding entirely convinced.

Bea took a deep breath, preparing to change the subject when Daisy's barking distracted her. The little dog had spotted a figure approaching and charged off with a burst of energy.

"Fred!" Bea called out as her brother came into view. She noted the dishevelled state of his clothes and the weary slump of his shoulders. As he got closer, Fred's normally composed and clean-shaven face bore the evidence of a sleepless night; stubble darkened his jawline, and there were shadows beneath his bloodshot eyes.

"Rough night?" Rich said, clapping him gently on the back as they converged.

"You could say that," Fred grumbled, running a hand

through his unkept hair, which stood at odd angles, as if he'd been pulling at it in frustration. "I've only just left the police station. I needed to come home, have a shower and get changed." He sighed. "They won't let me see Summer at the moment anyway." He raised his head, squinting against the sun. "They're waiting on some forensic tests." He rubbed the bridge of his nose. "I think someone's trying to set her up."

Bea felt a tingle at the base of her spine. *Cleo?*

"So how are you getting on with the investigation?" Fred asked, his gaze darting between her and Rich.

What the…? Her mind raced, thoughts tumbling over one another. Why was Fred asking her now, in front of Rich? *Of all the irresponsible—* "W-what investigation?" she said, her heart thudding erratically. "I'm not—"

"Looking into anything," Rich interjected simultaneously, his voice a shade too casual.

Bea stared at him.

Their shared denial hung awkwardly over them like a poorly constructed tent. *So is he investigating behind my back?*

The same uncertainty was mirrored in his face.

They blurted out in unison, "But you said you weren't!"

Fred's lips twitched into a knowing smile, and he stepped forward. "Er…I might have asked both of you to help me," he admitted, sheepishly rubbing the back of his neck.

Both of us?

The buzzing of Fred's phone sliced through the tension. He glanced at the screen, then cast an apologetic look towards them. "It's Charlotte, Summer's lawyer. She's heading back to the station. I need to go." He turned away.

Wait! "You have some explaining to do, big brother!" she called after him, but Fred was already charging towards the house.

"Sorry, sis," he hollered over his shoulder. "But maybe you two should pool your resources and work together on this? Summer needs your help."

"You'll be the one needing help when I get my hands on you," Bea murmured at Fred's retreating figure.

Beside her, Rich fidgeted. She turned back to look at him.

His hands in the pockets of his jeans, his gaze was fixed on Daisy, who currently had her head in a bed of pansies. "Look, Bea," he began, his voice roughened by an uncharacteristic sheepishness. "I'm sorry for not being forthright about my…er, activities."

She grinned, the tension between them dissipating like morning mist. "And I'm sorry for sneaking around behind your back. It seems we're both terrible at keeping our noses out of a murder investigation."

He grinned back. "I think that would be a fair comment." He quirked an eyebrow. "You know, Fred might have a point. I assume Simon and Perry are involved too?" She nodded. "And Spicer has the inside track. If the five of us work together, we might stand more chance of success."

Warmth spread through her chest. They would work together again. Just like they had back at Drew Castle earlier in the year…

"Unless, of course, you've already figured it out," he said, a teasing quality to his voice.

Had she? *Should I tell him of my theory that Cleo is the killer? No!* She berated herself. She had no proof to back it up, and Rich would want evidence, not wild suppositions. She didn't even know for sure that Cleo *was* Vera's granddaughter. Bea smiled. "If I told you, I would have to kill you."

He threw his head back and laughed. Her heart skipped a beat.

He was still grinning when his phone beeped in his jacket pocket. He pulled it out and glanced down at the message. "Spicer's on-site."

"Perfect timing," Bea said. "How about we get everyone together for coffee? The Breakfast Room in, say, fifteen minutes?"

"Like a council of war," he said, a glint in his eye. "I'm in. I'll let Spicer know."

"Great. I'll gather Perry and Simon up." Her lips curled into a smile, feeling the thrill of the chase reignite. "See you there shortly."

26

11:45 AM, WEDNESDAY 21 APRIL

Bea gazed around the familiar surroundings of the Breakfast Room at Francis Court. The morning light cascaded through the tall windows, painting the room in a warm golden hue. The air held a subtle scent of beeswax polish mingled with the comforting aroma of freshly brewed coffee. A small smile tugged at the corners of her mouth as she stole a glance through the corner of her eye at Rich sitting next to her. *Thank goodness he knows now!* Her shoulders dropped a little. Excitement fluttered inside her. They could now work together rather than at cross purposes. Daisy, curled up on the floor under the table between her and Rich's feet, gave a gentle snore. Rich turned to Bea, and meeting her gaze, he winked. Bea felt heat rise up her neck and glanced away.

Opposite her, Simon was scanning the restaurant. "It's quiet in here today, isn't it?" he murmured, his brown eyes moving over the handful of tables that were occupied.

"It's the lull before lunchtime." Perry, sitting next to him, extended a well-manicured hand and adjusted the cuff of his suit jacket.

"Well, let's order our drinks now then before the place

fills up," Simon replied, twisting around to catch the attention of Nicky, the server.

"Oh, here's Spicer," Perry said as the pretty, fresh-faced woman in her early thirties hurried across the room to join them.

"Sorry I'm late," she said, taking the seat at the head of the table. She placed her mobile phone in front of her and removed her black suit jacket, hooking it over the back of the chair.

Nicky arrived and took their order. As she disappeared into the kitchen, Spicer said, "Shall we dive in?"

"Indeed," Bea said, her voice steady despite the fluttering in her chest. She knew that every piece of information exchanged here could be a stepping stone or a stumbling block on the road to finding out what had happened to Vera.

"I'll start, shall I?" Simon offered. Spicer and Rich nodded. Simon told the two PaIRS officers what the three of them had uncovered so far.

Spicer's fingers danced over her phone screen as she made notes. She paused at the mention of Mark and Harvey's meeting on Monday morning. "Well, that's news to me," she admitted, surprise fleeting across her features. "That means they both have alibis." She looked over at Rich and raised an eyebrow. He bobbed his head in response.

After Simon finished, with a quick glance at her and Perry, he said, "I think that's everything we have." Spicer smiled.

Next to Bea, Rich shifted in his seat. "You seem to know an awful lot," he said, a slightly accusatory tone in his voice as he folded his arms across his chest.

Blast! Maybe they'd shared too much. Bea met Simon's eyes. Had Rich guessed that they had an inside informant at Fenshire Police? The weight of unspoken knowledge nipped at her conscience. They had to protect CID Steve. "It's remarkable what people will share when they find a sympathetic ear. You'd be amazed at how much everyone talks to us." The statement hung in the air as their drinks arrived. *Did that work?*

Bea smiled gratefully at Perry when he steered the conversation towards Vera's estate. "We know her financial legacy is rather sizeable," he said, raising his cup to his lips. "But we haven't been able to find out who gets what."

"Perhaps I can shed some light on that," Spicer offered as she flicked through the notes on her phone. "According to Vera's will, Shelly Black receives a lump sum of seven hundred and fifty thousand pounds plus all the royalties from Vera's books, amounting to about two hundred and fifty thousand a year."

How much? Admittedly, Vera had worked with Shelly for several years, but even so…

"There's also a considerable trust for an unnamed granddaughter valued at about two million—"

Crikey! The granddaughter was going to be rich.

"—and Lilian Goldrich inherits the house and what remains of the estate, estimated at approximately three million."

"Oh my giddy aunt!" Perry dropped his cup on the table, his blue eyes wide with shock. Bea's mind churned at the implications, the pieces of the puzzle shifting and resettling in new configurations. Shelly and Leah had a powerful motive to want Vera dead. Assuming they'd known the contents of her will…

"Neither Leah nor Shelly claimed any knowledge of being beneficiaries when I interviewed them just now," Spicer continued.

Bea started. There was a noticeable scepticism in Spicer's manner. "But you don't believe them?"

Spicer took a sip of her tea, then said, "It's more that they seemed wary about talking to me."

Yes! That's exactly how I felt when I spoke to them. "I agree. When I spoke to them yesterday, their nervousness was palpable. They kept darting looks at each other as if they had to be sure what they were saying was what they'd agreed. They even pointed fingers at Harvey Jury when I asked them who they thought might want Vera dead. Vera was trying to get him sacked from the show, according to them."

Rich cleared his throat. "But that seems unlikely if, as you said, Simon, Harvey was planning on leaving the show and joining Mark and Austin in their new venture. Why would he be worried about being sacked, even if Vera had that sort of sway?"

Perry's fingers, which had been drumming an absent rhythm on the white linen tablecloth, stopped. "Could they be in it together?"

"What, Mark, Harvey, and Austin?" Rich asked, sounding confused.

"No. Shelly and Leah. After all, we only have their word about where they were at the time someone killed Vera. Maybe they *were* together. Killing her." He waved his cup in the air rather dramatically, and a drop of coffee dripped down onto the white tablecloth. He swore under his breath and grabbed a napkin, dabbing it at the stain.

Bea sipped her drink. *Perry has a point.* If Shelly and Leah *had* known about the will, then they could've set the whole thing up together to get their hands on the money.

"It's possible, I suppose," Spicer said, a hint of frustration in her voice. "But Saunders is utterly convinced that Summer is our killer and won't contemplate an alternative theory at the moment. I'll try and find out if they knew about their legacies."

"So until the results on the bloodied jacket come back, Saunders is sticking with Summer as the killer?" Bea asked, her voice tinged with disbelief. She wrapped her hands around her coffee cup.

"We know the killer wore gloves, so I think it's unlikely that we will find anything on the jacket that points the finger either way," Spicer replied.

"And how does Saunders feel about the idea that someone might be framing Summer?" Simon asked.

Spicer shook her head. "He's not having any of it."

Bea chewed on her lip, her mind racing with theories and possibilities. Should she tell them about her theory that Cleo could be Vera's granddaughter and was the one trying to frame Summer? She glanced at Rich beside her. He was tracing the rim of his cup with a thoughtful expression. *Will he think it's a silly idea?* She took a deep breath. *May as well give it a go…* "May I suggest…" Her voice sounded hesitant to her own ears. Spicer gave her an encouraging smile. "What if Cleo Barrington is Vera's granddaughter? Could she be the killer?" Bea said with growing conviction.

Rich turned around to face her. "Funny you should say that. I've been wondering if the granddaughter is someone we know. Although I'll be honest, my money was on the unidentified girl seen wandering the grounds on Monday. But Cleo sounds like a more likely candidate."

"Interesting," Spicer said, nodding at Bea. "That would certainly cast doubt on Cleo's account of things. Summer denied she and Vera argued. Cleo's story about their noisy altercation could be a ruse to set Summer up."

Perry interjected with a shake of his head. "I'm sorry, but I just can't picture Cleo as a killer. When I spoke to her yesterday, she seemed truly distressed, regretful even, that by having reported overhearing them together, she'd implicated Summer."

"Appearances can deceive," Rich pointed out. "She could be a talented actress."

Bea's thoughts were clouded with uncertainty. Perry normally had good instincts about people, but there lingered within her a niggling suspicion that Perry's faith in Cleo might be misplaced.

"Leave it with me," Spicer said decisively. "I'll dig deeper into Cleo's background. We need to know more about her connection to Vera if there is one."

A low growl emanated from Perry's stomach, breaking the silence that had settled over the group like a thick fog. He stretched his tall frame and cast an apologetic grin at the others. "Sorry, all this sleuthing has worked up my appetite. How about we adjourn to The Ship and Seal for lunch? We can hash out more of this over some tasty pub grub?"

Spicer glanced at her watch, frowning. "I'd love to, but I ought to be scooting back to King's Town. Saunders will have my head if he clocks I'm not back yet." She rose from her seat and retrieved her jacket from the back of the chair.

"Sounds like a good idea to me," Simon said, pushing his chair back as he stood. "But let's make it snappy. I need to be back at the *Bake Off Wars* set by two. Run-throughs start a day early for the weekend's filming as I'm new…"

"Of course," Bea said as she rose. "How are you feeling about it?"

"Nervous!" Simon said, pulling a face.

"Well, I'm in," Rich said, getting up slowly, then moving out of the way as Daisy uncurled herself from under the table by his feet and performed a downward dog stretch.

27

12:30 PM, WEDNESDAY 21 APRIL

The Ship and Seal pub teemed with the gentle murmur of conversation and clinking glasses as Bea pushed her half-empty plate away and leaned back into the leather-clad booth. She had little appetite today for the crispy cod and golden brown chips. It felt wrong to be enjoying a hearty lunch while Fred was in such a state over Summer's arrest. *Poor Summer. I bet she's not getting beer-battered fish and triple-cooked chips for lunch.*

Next to her, Rich was tucking into his fish and chips. As always, she was acutely aware of his presence, their bodies almost touching. His familiar musky smell caught in her nostrils. She took a shallow breath in through her nose. She closed her eyes. *Goodness, he smells good.* A sudden urge to lean over slightly to her left and bury her head in his neck washed over her. *Get a grip, Bea! He'll think you're off your rocker if you throw yourself at him like that!* She opened her eyes and cleared her throat as she shifted slightly away from him. She looked up to see Perry, who sat across from her, staring. There was an amused look on his face. *Busted!* Heat burned in her cheeks.

With a smile tugging at a corner of his mouth, Perry plucked a small piece of sausage off his plate and dropped it into the waiting mouth of an ever expectant Daisy, who was sitting by his side. *Perry!* But like a naughty school child caught writing a rude word on the classroom chalkboard, he looked more proud of himself than sorry. *You wait…*

Beside him, Simon shovelled another hearty spoonful of stew into his mouth. He paused, a contemplative frown briefly knitting his brow. "You know, I think I might do something like this for the restaurant. We'll fancy it up a bit but keep the basic comforting feel to it. A 'pub classics' section, perhaps?"

"Brilliant! And you can call it 'Daisy's Lots of Sausages Stew'," Perry quipped, winking at Bea as he offered Daisy another piece of sausage.

Bea gave him a look. "I think Daisy's had more than enough sausages now, don't you?" Perry grinned at her.

Beside her, Rich chuckled. Bea turned to watch the laughter lines around his eyes deepen in a way she found both endearing and slightly worrying; he looked like he needed more rest. *Is he sleeping okay?*

"I suspect there's no such thing as too many sausages in Daisy's book, is there, little girl?" He picked up a small bit of fish from the side of his plate. "How about some fish for a change?" he asked as Daisy shot under the table and reappeared by Rich's side just in time to gently take his offering.

Are they all trying to make her the chunkiest dog in town? Opposite her, Perry snorted. "Right, everyone, can we stop feeding Daisy, please?" She looked sternly around the table. *Did Rich just wink at Perry?*

Under the table, Daisy let out a soft whine, her tail thumping against the wooden floor in a rhythmic plea for attention. Bea reached down and stroked the dog's head, feeling the coarse fur under her fingers. "I'm sorry, Daisy-doo, but you know what the vet said."

"Poor Daisy," Perry whispered, a cheeky grin on his face. Bea rolled her eyes at him.

Rich pushed his plate away with a satisfied expression. "That was very good."

"So was that," Simon declared, wiping his beard with his napkin. "Right, so let's briefly recap where we stand, shall we?" He leaned forward and planted his elbows firmly on the wood of the booth's table. "Only Harvey, Cleo, and Summer lack solid alibis. Harvey's motive is thin—"

"Summer's too," Perry chimed in.

"Then there's Cleo," Bea continued. "If she *is* Vera's granddaughter... Well, that could change everything."

"Spicer's digging into that as we speak," Rich added, his voice carrying the authority that came naturally even though he was off duty.

"I'll have a chat with Cleo," Perry announced with an air of casual determination. "See if I can subtly tease anything out of her?"

Bea eyed him doubtfully. Perry did many things very well, but subtlety wasn't one of them. "Do you want me to come with you?"

"Er, no thank you," Perry said with a knowing smile. "I'll be the model of delicacy, I promise. And besides, I'll be with Simon on the *Bake Off Wars* set. So two birds, one stone, you know."

"Just remember, Spicer might want to talk to Cleo herself," Rich cautioned Perry. "So don't get too carried away."

"My middle name is discretion, Fitzwilliam," Perry told him.

Bea coughed, but before she could formulate any further

argument against Perry talking to Cleo on his own, a young woman appeared in the dining area entrance, a glass clutched in her hand. She scanned the room.

"It's Isla," Simon said as he stood up and waved over to her.

"Your stalker?" Perry asked, sounding alarmed.

Simon let out a scant breath. "She's *not* my stalker." He turned to a confused-looking Rich. "She's just a university student who interviewed me for a project she's doing."

So why is she still here? Bea hunched her shoulders as she studied Isla moving towards their booth. Dressed in a green oversized jumper, skinny grey jeans, and pixie boots, she looked elf-like as she wafted across the floor. *You could blow her down with one puff*, Bea thought as the young woman stopped in front of them. Under the table, Daisy gave a low *woof* and crawled out to sit by Bea's legs, her tail sweeping the floor like a windscreen wiper.

"Hello," Isla said, looking up at Simon, her Scottish accent soft as she stood awkwardly in front of him, her glass now clasped in both hands.

"Everyone, this is Isla Scott," Simon introduced her, gesturing around the table. "Isla, this is my husband, Perry, and my good friends Lady Beatrice and Fitzwilliam."

"Hello," Isla said, her voice betraying a hint of unease. Daisy nudged the young woman's leg. She looked down, a large smile splitting her face. She placed her drink on the edge of the table, then bent down to fuss Daisy.

The tension in Bea's shoulders eased. *She likes dogs. That's a good sign.*

"And this is Daisy," Simon added as Isla continued to pet the little dog.

"She's cute," Isla said, giggling as Daisy tried to lick her face.

"Would you like to join us?" Perry asked.

Isla looked up at Simon, her hand still on Daisy's head.

"Yes, please do," Simon added as he leaned over to the table next to them and grabbed a spare chair that he plonked down at the end of the booth.

"Okay, thanks." She straightened up and sat down. As if sensing Isla's nerves, Daisy sat herself down close to her. Isla reached a hand out to rest it on the little terrier.

As Isla stole another glance at Simon, Bea's concerns resurfaced. *Could she be more than just a conscientious student?*

"We were just talking about the recent murder of Vera Bolt. It happened near here, you know," Perry told her.

"Hasn't the TV presenter Summer York been arrested?" Isla asked, her discomfort palpable as her eyes darted around the table.

"She has, but we don't think it was her," Perry said, leaning back against the plush seat. "We think she's been framed."

Moving her hand off Daisy, Isla picked up her drink and took a gulp, her ginger hair falling over her face as she did so.

Next to Bea, Rich shuffled forward on the bench seat and leaned over the table. "So, Isla, what part of Scotland are you from?"

She looked up, and her blue eyes widened. "Er, my family is from a small town on the east coast just up from, um... Aberdeen." Her response lacked commitment.

She's clearly nervous. Bea suddenly felt sorry for the young woman. "It's lovely up in that part of Scotland, isn't it?"

Isla gave her a little smile as she tucked her long hair behind her ear.

"So what brings you to these parts?" Fitzwilliam seemed

intent on finding out more about her. Does he think she's up to no good?

"Er, well, I…I just thought I'd explore a bit of the country before I went back to uni…and, well, when I heard that Mr Lattimore lived here, and I have this project…so I thought if I could talk to him in person, then…" She trailed off, her slightly freckled cheeks now turning crimson.

"And how much longer will you be in town?" Rich continued, appearing to be oblivious to her discomfort.

"Er, well… I'm not sure," Isla hesitated, her fingers fidgeting with the bottom of her jumper before she stood abruptly. "It was nice to meet you all. I should really be going."

Simon jumped up, giving Rich a look as he did so. "If you're sure."

She nodded, and reaching down, she patted Daisy on the head before pivoting on her heels and heading to the exit.

Simon turned to Rich. "Was it really necessary to give her the third degree?"

Rich, whose gaze had followed Isla's back as she'd left, swung around in his chair to face Simon. "Do you realise who she is?"

He knows her?

Simon frowned. "She's just a student who—"

Rich interrupted him. "She's the girl from the morning Vera was killed."

What girl?

He reached for his phone. "The one we couldn't identify who entered the grounds of Francis Court around ten and paid cash." Bea leaned across as Rich pulled up image on his screen—a grainy figure of a man captured on camera. He flicked past it, then stopped and held up a similar screen capture but this time of a young woman. *A young woman like the one we've just been talking to…*

"Blimey, you're right," Perry said, cocking his head to one side as he looked across the table at Rich's phone. "That's definitely her."

Simon frowned, idly twisting his wedding ring around his finger, his brow furrowed in thought. "So she was here before…"

Bea tapped her lips thoughtfully. *Hold on!* Hadn't Rich said earlier that he thought maybe the unidentified girl could be Vera's granddaughter? "Could she be…? Rich, you mentioned Vera's granddaughter—"

"Exactly." He tilted his head to one side and smiled. "She fits the bill too."

Perry shifted, turning to his husband. "We should let CID St—"

"Spicer," Bea interjected swiftly, exchanging a knowing glance with Simon. "We should contact Spicer about this." She glanced sideways at Rich. Did he realise Perry had nearly revealed their informant at Fenshire CID? He was closing down his photos on his mobile and didn't seem to have noticed.

"Yes, of course, Spicer will need to know," Simon answered smoothly, hiding Perry's near slip with practiced ease.

Rich looked up from his phone. "I'll inform her we've identified the mystery girl, shall I?"

Simon nodded, and gently grabbing Perry's arm, he said, "Right, we need to be off, Perry."

Perry, at first looking rather startled at the swiftness of their departure, stood and straightened his suit jacket, recovering quickly. "Yes. We don't want you to be late on your first day of filming, my love."

"Good luck. I'll check in later to see how it's going if I get a chance after I see how they are getting on with the kitchen installation at The Dower House."

"Yes, I hope it goes well," Rich added, smiling.

"Thanks," Simon said. "See you later."

Bea watched Perry and Simon depart, then turned to Rich. He was tapping out a text message, presumably to Spicer. His rugged features were set in determination as his two thumbs did most of the work.

"Right, that's done," he said as he placed his phone down on the table.

"Do you really think Isla could have something to do with Vera's death?"

"Well, we know she was on-site at the time Vera was killed. And I'm sorry, but I don't buy the whole student doing a project thing. Did you see the way she watched Simon all the time?" He gave her a wry smile. "There's certainly more to her than meets the eye."

28

2:15 PM, WEDNESDAY 21 APRIL

The golden afternoon sun dappled the cobbled path leading up to Francis Court from the village as Bea and Rich ambled back from the pub. Zigzagging along the path in front of them, Daisy had her nose only centimetres above the ground as she sniffed every scent the walkway offered.

As they neared the foot gate to Francis Court, Bea paused. "Rich," she hissed and pointed to half a dozen people loitering near the entrance, equipment clutched in their hands or slung carelessly over their shoulders. The telltale glint of camera lenses proved them to be members of the press.

"What are they doing there? I thought they couldn't get access to this entrance?" Rich murmured, his brow furrowing slightly as he took in the scene.

"Indeed." He was right. Hidden from the main roads and nestled within the hedgerows that ran along the stone wall of the estate, the side gate could only be accessed from the village via the private walkway that was used by staff who lived locally. Her gaze swept over the assembled group until it landed on a familiar face. Jeff, the lead security officer, whose presence was as much a part of Francis Court as the ancient oaks lining the Long Drive, was in the thick of it all. His posture was rigid, the set of his jaw firm. When his eyes met Bea's, there was a flicker of recognition, followed by a swift, deliberate motion—his hand subtly guiding her gaze towards a bush blooming with delicate white flowers to her left.

"Rich," Bea whispered urgently, nodding towards Jeff's signal. "We should…"

"Hide? Yes, I think you're right." Without missing a beat, he scooped Daisy up in his arms, and holding her close to his chest, he and Bea ducked behind the lush foliage. The leaves brushed against Bea's cheek as she peered out from their leafy haven. She could see Jeff's lips moving quickly, his intentions clear as he and the two police officers herded the insistent paparazzi away from the gate. Each step the press took seemed reluctant as they dragged their tripods and cameras behind them.

All Bea could feel was the thrum of her heartbeat as she waited for the all clear. Perhaps it was the thrill of evading unwanted attention, or maybe it was the closeness to Rich as they shared their makeshift hideaway. She glanced out of the corner of her eye and studied his profile as he watched what was happening ahead of them. Daisy was still clasped in his arms. His jaw was tensed with concentration, but he looked calm and in control. The flecks of grey at his temples caught the sun, and she wanted to reach out and touch them. *Bea!*

The murmur of voices finally dissipated, and the coast was clear. With a shared nod, Bea and Rich emerged from their hideout. Rich gently dropped Daisy to the floor, and she went bounding ahead as they made a swift beeline for the entrance.

Jeff rounded the corner just as they approached, his expression apologetic. "I'm so sorry about all that, my lady," he said, tipping his hat slightly. "They're trying to get quotes from the staff about Lord Fred and Summer York. We had to remind them this isn't public property." He unlocked the gate and held it open as Daisy ran through.

"Well, thank you, Jeff," Bea replied as she and Rich followed the small white dog into the sanctuary of Francis Court.

"Are you alright?" Rich asked, his brown eyes searching hers as they rounded the corner, the magnificent all-glass Orangery looming head of them.

Aw. That's sweet of him to ask…

"Yes, I'm fine," she said, although her thoughts were anything but calm. She remembered all too well the relentless attention she'd got last year when her short-lived love life had become tabloid fodder. *Could I ever willingly step into that maelstrom again?* She stole a glance at Rich, who seemed unfazed by it all, his demeanour as steady as his protective stance. Was it simply his experience in PaIRS that afforded him such composure? A tiny spark of curiosity flickered within her. What would it be like, having someone like Rich by her side, facing the world together? She could almost picture them, united against the prying eyes and vicious tongues…

"Bea?" Rich's voice broke into her reverie, and she shook her head, dispelling the foolish notion.

Well, that's never going to happen, is it?

"Spicer and Saunders have just arrived on-site," Rich told her as he glanced down at his phone. His thumb moved swiftly over the screen, sending a quick reply before slipping the device back into his pocket.

Suddenly Daisy's excited barking pierced the calm. Bea recognised that alarm bark. *What's she found now?* Over by the wall just beyond the Orangery, Daisy had her head buried deep within a large Chaenomeles bush bursting with white blooms. All that was visible was her tail, which was wagging vigorously. Bea turned to Rich with a smile. "It's either a squirrel, or she's found us a clue."

Rich chuckled as they approached the bush. He reached out, parting the dense foliage, then he gently coaxed Daisy away. "Can you take her, please, Bea?" he asked calmly. Bea ran forward and glanced quickly into the mass of leaves. The sight of something half wrapped in blue kitchen roll sent a chill down Bea's spine. She grabbed Daisy and lifted her out of the way.

Rich drew out his phone once more. "Spicer, it's Fitzwilliam. We're over by the Orangery. We've found something that you might want to see," he said into the phone, his eyes never leaving the object in the bush.

Bea's heart raced, each beat thudding louder in her ears. She held Daisy close, feeling the dog's warm breath against the side of her face. She'd been joking when she'd suggested Daisy might have found a clue. But this was no joke.

A gruff voice heralded Saunders' arrival as he barked, "What are you two doing here? Were you looking for clues?"

"Of course not," Bea replied, hardly able to disguise the irritation in her voice. "We were just walking back from the village, and Daisy found it."

"Well done, Daisy." Spicer moved over to where Bea was standing with Daisy in her arms and patted the little dog on the head before withdrawing a pair of gloves and a large plastic evidence bag from her coat pocket.

"Be careful, Tina. The bush's spiky," Rich murmured to her as she passed them. "It's on the ground. You'll see it's wrapped in kitchen roll."

"I'm sure my sergeant knows what to do. Thank you,

Fitzwilliam," Saunders sniped, the light reflecting off his shaved head, making it look like a shiny beach ball.

Bea felt Rich bristle beside her. She turned and gave him a sympathetic smile. *He's an idiot who feels threatened by you. Take no notice…*

Rich stood tall despite his recent injury, meeting Saunders' glare unflinchingly. "Hayden, we're just trying to help. You know I've got a lot of experience with this sort of thing." His voice remained steady, but Bea caught the flicker of defiance in his brown eyes.

Saunders snorted, his broad shoulders heaving in barely contained frustration. "Help? More like hinder…" He trailed off as Spicer's top half disappeared into the bush.

She emerged a few seconds later, gingerly holding something in her hand. She unfurled the rest of the kitchen towel, revealing in full the ominous glint of a knife, its blade marred by a dark stain that Bea knew all too well was blood.

29

SHORTLY AFTER, WEDNESDAY 21
APRIL

"Is that the knife used to kill Vera, do you think?" Bea asked
Spicer as she lowered Daisy to the floor.

The sergeant re-wrapped the knife and dropped it into the
evidence bag. "Well, it could—"

Saunders cut Spicer off sharply. "This isn't something
we're prepared to discuss with you, Lady Rossex."

But we found it! And he'd not even said thank you. *What
an obnoxious man!*

Saunders turned back to Spicer. "Get someone to come
and pick that up. We need to concentrate on finding this
mystery woman." As Spicer moved to the side and typed a
message, Saunders eyed Fitzwilliam. "So I hear you think
you've identified the woman seen on the CCTV in the
grounds here on the morning someone killed Vera Bolt?" he
asked curtly. Bea watched the tension ripple across his
powerful shoulders as he stood with a posture so rigid, he
looked like a soldier stood to attention. She could almost hear
the creak of his muscles, he was wound so tightly as he faced
off with Rich. She shivered with dislike.

Rich nodded. "Her name is Isla Scott."

"And where do we find this Isla Scott?"

"I don't know," Rich replied, scratching at the grey at his temples. "She disappeared before I had a chance to ask."

"No doubt because you were questioning her when you shouldn't have been!"

That's not fair! Okay, so Rich might have asked her a few questions, but he'd only been trying to help.

Rich ignored the accusation. "She's probably staying somewhere local, if I had to guess."

"Local? Well, that's not very helpful, is it?" Saunders said, his voice dripping with disdain. "Thanks to you, she's likely been scared off." He huffed. "So how do you suggest we find her now then?"

Rich stared at him for a moment.

Tell him it's his problem, Bea urged Rich in her head. *After all, he's told us more than once that he doesn't want our help…*

"Well, if it was me," Rich said, a gleam in his eye. "I would talk to the landlord of the pub The Ship and Seal. I noticed she said goodbye to him as she left, so I don't think that's the first time she's been in there."

"Right. Well, thank you for passing the information on to us," Saunders said through a pinched mouth. "But don't think this means that you're now in any way helping us with our investigation. Please stay out of this case. Just let us do our job. Come on, Spicer."

Bea locked her eyes with Saunders' smaller blue ones, ready to defend their actions, but before she could speak, Saunders spun on his heels and marched away, his heavy boots thudding against the gravel path.

"Sorry," Spicer mouthed, her face creased with embarrassment as she hurried after Saunders, who was already storming towards a black BMW parked by the side of the outbuildings just behind the Orangery.

Bea turned to Rich, her thoughts racing. They'd only tried to help, but Saunders, with his pointy ears practically steaming, was too wrapped up in his own insecurities to see it. She reached out and gave Rich's arm a reassuring squeeze. "If it helps, he's a million times worse than you ever were."

Rich threw his head back and laughed.

That's better!

They made their way towards the manor house, then skirted around the front, heading towards The Dower House and Rich's cottage. Daisy scampered ahead of them, stopping every now and again to poke her head into a flower bed or a bush.

"Seriously, Rich. Why are you bothering to help Saunders?" Bea asked, her voice betraying her exasperation. "He's incredibly rude and has no respect for your experience at all."

Rich shrugged, his gaze following Daisy as she jumped over a low bed of spring bedding plants and disappeared behind them. "Well, for a start, I'm doing this to help Fred, not Saunders. But either way, the man is way out of his depth. Murder investigations aren't his area, so he's probably feeling the pressure and lashing out."

Is he really defending him? Bea checked herself. *Maybe he's just willing to make allowances for a fellow PaIRS officer who is in over his head. Even so...* "But why not ask for help then? He's completely sidelining Spicer, and she's got lots of valuable experience that could assist him."

"Ah, I expect it's a macho thing," Rich said, the corners of his mouth twitching into a smirk. "Saunders is all about manly competition. He bench presses problems rather than solves them."

Daisy suddenly barked and raced ahead. Through a break

in the hedges, Isla Scott appeared, her slight figure framed by the large trees of the Long Drive just behind her. Daisy was already greeting the young woman with eager sniffs and a wagging tail.

"Sorry about her," Bea apologised as they caught up, noting Isla's startled expression.

Isla bent down and fussed over Daisy. "It's okay," she said, brushing a stray lock of hair behind her ear. "I find the gardens...relaxing. They're perfect for clearing your head. I just wasn't expecting to see anyone I knew…" She trailed off as she straightened.

"Speaking of the gardens," Rich said, his tone casual but his eyes sharp. "Were you here on Monday morning?"

"Er, yes, I was," Isla replied, shifting slightly, her hands nervously clasping together. "It was a lovely morning, and someone had recommended coming here to me the night before."

Bea leaned in, her instincts tingling. "Did you see anyone else while you were walking around then? Perhaps someone out of place?"

A flicker of hesitation crossed Isla's face, then she frowned. "I won't say out of place exactly. But I was surprised to see Summer York walking around the grounds." She shrugged. "But, of course, that was before I knew *Bake Off Wars* was being filmed here."

Bea's heart skipped a beat. *Summer has an alibi!*

"Was she on her own?" Rich asked.

"No. She was with a man."

Bea started. *She was with Fred? So why haven't either of them mentioned it? Hold on… Fred was in London that morning.* Bea remembered he'd gone up the day after the family dinner when he'd introduced Summer to their parents. Hair lifted on the back of Bea's neck. So who *was* this man that Summer was with? And why hadn't she said anything to anyone about it?

30

AT ABOUT THE SAME TIME,
WEDNESDAY 21 APRIL

Perry stood at the edge of the bustling Old Barn, his blue eyes dancing with a mix of pride and amusement as he watched his husband, Simon, practice his segues and intros on the *Bake Off Wars* set. Although referred to as The Tent, the only connection to previous seasons, which really *had* been filmed in a tent, was the fluttering bunting that hung from the ceiling.

In the centre of it all, Simon and Ryan stood side by side, their presence commanding even amidst the whirlwind of activity. Ryan, dressed in a blue shirt and jeans, was a beacon of energy; his laughter punctuated the air as he cracked a joke, the crew responding with a chorus of chuckles. Simon, in jeans and a polo shirt, was more reserved but no less captivating, offering a wry smile as he listened to the direction Austin was giving them. Simon's square jaw tensed with concentration, then relaxed as he nailed his lines with the ease of a professional. A camera operator weaved through the maze of stainless-steel workstations, capturing close-ups of Simon and Ryan as they talked about the challenges of this week's skills test.

"Simon's a natural, isn't he?" Perry said to Ana, his words laced with pride, a soft smile playing on his lips.

"Absolutely," the senior runner agreed, her attention momentarily drifting to the monitor displaying the practice feed. "And Ryan's energy is infectious. They're quite the pair."

Simon glanced over, meeting Perry's gaze from across the room. A silent conversation passed between them. Perry offered a subtle thumbs up, and Simon's responding beam made him smile back.

Hamilton, alone before an unused camera in the back of the area, was practicing his lines.

"Odd, isn't it?" Ana said, her voice low, almost lost amidst the clatter of equipment and hushed directives. "Without Summer here, it's like the tent's lost a bit of its sparkle."

Perry's gaze lingered on the space beside Hamilton where Summer had stood last weekend, her laughter echoing off the walls.

"Hopefully she'll be back soon," Ana said, her clipboard clutched to her chest like a shield against the controlled chaos.

"Let's hope so," Perry replied, trying to keep the doubt out of his voice. *Will they eventually have to replace Summer too?* His shoulders were heavy. If only they could crack the case. Then she would be back where she belonged in time for the weekend. But if they didn't and the police charged her with murder, then… He sighed heavily, then straightened. *Well, come on, Perry, do something about it then! Talk to Cleo rather than standing here admiring your husband…*

"Have you seen Cleo, Ana?"

Ana leaned against a trestle table laden with various baking accoutrements, her gaze fixed on the monitor to her side. "Cleo?" she said vaguely. "I think she's in the production office printing the new scripts."

"She's a funny little thing, isn't she?" Perry fished. "She doesn't say much, but I expect she's a keen observer."

"You're right," Ana said, turning to face him. "But if she's going to do well on her media studies course, she's got to come out of her shell a bit, you know. Be more open and friendly."

Perry bobbed his head sagely. "So she doesn't talk much about herself then?"

Ana shook her head. "All I know is that she's going to uni in Brighton, and her folks live in Surrey."

Parents? Perry frowned. *Isn't Vera's daughter dead?*

"No juicy titbits of anything," Ana continued. "Well, actually—" She hesitated, then lowered her voice. "I've seen her personnel file, and guess what?"

"She's really a man?" Perry said flippantly, trying to mask the intensity of his interest.

Ana giggled. "No, silly." She glanced around them before leaning in closer. "But she changed her surname about eight years ago."

"Changed it from what?" Perry's heart raced with anticipation.

"Bolton, I think," Ana said, then nodded. "Yes, that's right. It struck me because it sounded so close to Bolt, Vera's surname, you know?"

Perry feigned nonchalance, though inside, his mind was alight with connections.

"Oh, and her first name is really Emily. Cleo is her middle name."

So she was Emily Bolton before she changed her surname?

"Do you think she and her family are in some sort of witness protection program?" Ana asked conspiratorially.

"Er, maybe," Perry replied, Ana's suggestion seeming no more ridiculous than his supposition that she was Vera's granddaughter and the heir to her millions.

The director's voice cut through their exchange, calling for quiet on set. Perry watched as Simon, alongside Ryan, delivered an intro to the camera, their chemistry effortless and engaging. When they finished, Ana rushed over to talk to Austin, and Simon ambled over, tugging his hand through his short brown hair.

"Thoughts?" Simon asked, a crinkle of concern etching his brow.

"You were spot on, love," Perry said, smiling, his eyes still blazing with excitement.

"And what have you been up to?" Simon asked.

Oh, he knows me so well…

"Well…" He relayed Ana's revelation. Understanding dawned in Simon's eyes.

"That's definitely interesting," Simon murmured, his face serious. "But tread lightly, Perry. If she *is* Vera's granddaughter, then you don't want to scare her off."

"You know me. Subtlety is my middle name."

"Hmm."

What does that mean?

Simon patted him on the arm. "Just be careful."

———

Perry slid into the *Bake Off Wars'* production office, a space cluttered with papers and the warm hum of printers churning out more. Cleo was over in the far corner arranging a stack of freshly printed pages.

Here goes! Perry approached, his heart tapping an uneven beat against his ribs. "It's quite the paper jungle in here," he said with a friendly smile.

Cleo glanced up, a flicker of annoyance crossing her face before it disappeared, and she gave him a shy smile. "The scriptwriters have been busy," she replied, batting a loose strand of hair away from her face.

"Your parents must be proud of you, handling all this," Perry said, steering the conversation towards the personal as nonchalantly as he could muster. "Are they in the media business?"

A shadow passed over Cleo's petite features, her response measured. "Er, no. My dad's a GP, and mum's a hairdresser." She shrugged, then a small smile crept over her face. "But, yes, you're right. They *are* proud of me." She looked up at him. The shutter came down again.

She's not giving much away. "Only child?" Perry prodded, his palms beginning to sweat.

"Yep. Just me." Her voice held a note of finality.

Well, this is going well! He'd seen the way Bea prised information out of people. She made it look so easy. *What am I doing wrong?* He swallowed, his mind fighting with the urge to dive into the heart of the matter.

The weight of silence hung between them until it became unbearable, and then, like a dam breaking, he blurted out, "You're Vera's granddaughter, aren't you?"

The colour drained from Cleo's cheeks, her eyes widening. The papers crumpled in her grip as she stepped back.

I can't believe I just said that!

They stared at each other for a moment. Then she opened her mouth. "How—"

"Look, I didn't mean to upset you," Perry rushed to say,

his pulse hammering in his ears. He watched, powerless, as a single tear tracked down her cheek. "I'm so sorry," he mumbled.

"Nobody was supposed to know," Cleo whispered as she brushed her wet face with the back of her hand.

Perry reached out, hesitating inches from her shoulder before pulling back. Instead, he gave her a reassuring smile. "Do you want to tell me about it?"

She nodded slowly, then took a deep breath. "My birth-mother, Michelle Bolton, was Vera's daughter," she said, her gaze anchored to something distant and unseen over Perry's shoulder. "Bolton was Vera's name before she changed it to Bolt. I don't know why. My mum... Well, she was an addict by the time she was my age. She tried to get clean, but she just couldn't break her bad habits. Eventually Vera cut ties with her."

She paused and swallowed before continuing in a trembling voice, "Social Services tried to take me away when I was three. Mum attempted to clean up her act one last time so she could keep me. She contacted Vera and begged her to take me temporarily while she was in rehab. Vera refused."

Perry stifled a cry. *How awful for Michelle and Vera. And poor Cleo...*

"Later, after they took me away, I bounced between foster homes and got kicked out of school," she said, the words spilling out faster now. "Then finally the Barringtons adopted me. They...they saved me. I owe them everything. They're my *proper* parents, you know."

"Is that why you changed your surname eight years ago?" Perry asked gently.

Cleo sighed sadly. "From Bolton to Barrington. And I used my middle name rather than my first name. I wanted a fresh start when I went to secondary school." She paused and swallowed noisily. "I found my mother again when I was twelve, but she was still fighting her demons. She died two years later but not before telling me her side of the story."

Perry's heart ached for the girl.

"I'm so sorry for everything you've been through, Cleo," he said, his own emotions threatening to breach the surface. "No wonder your parents are proud of you."

Cleo's composure was seemingly hanging by a thread. "The Barringtons are everything I could've asked for in a family." She offered a small smile, but it didn't quite reach her eyes. "But there was always this...curiosity about Vera. So when the opportunity came up to work on *Bake Off Wars*, I thought maybe it was fate."

Perry smiled at her, squashing his desire to ask more questions. *She's opening up now. Just let her talk.*

"So I deferred my uni place in media studies," she continued, "thinking that would give me the chance to meet her, get to know her, and decide if I should tell her who I really was."

Silence fell between them for a few heartbeats. Perry searched for the right words. "And did you? Get the chance, I mean," he asked softly.

Cleo's gaze dropped to the floor, her shoulders slumped. "No," she said, a tremor in her voice. "I wanted to wait until I'd been around longer. So she would get used to me. Maybe even begin to like me." She let out a ragged sigh. "I left it too late in the end."

The air seemed to grow heavier. Perry reached out, his hand hovering just shy of her arm. "I'm so—"

"I tried that morning, you know. I wasn't really looking for a ladder," Cleo blurted out, raising her blue eyes to his face. "I heard Summer and Vera in the tent. I thought I'd wait and then when they'd finished I'd go in and talk to Vera. But then they started arguing…" Cleo whispered, almost to herself. "Then I heard Summer sounding like she was leaving. And I didn't want to get caught eavesdropping, so I fled." She dropped his gaze. "I went back five minutes later, hoping—" She paused and swallowed hard.

She went back? Perry leaned in, hanging on her every word.

"But someone was in the corridor," she finally finished. "I saw the back of them and panicked again. I ran without looking back."

Oh my goodness!

"Did you recognise who it was?" he asked tentatively, barely daring to breathe.

Cleo shook her head, her face a mask of cool indifference. She shrugged. "I've no idea. It was a bit of a blur. They were moving. I'm fairly sure they were wearing a white chef's jacket, you know, but that's all I saw. I can't even be sure if it was a man or a woman. Sorry."

Disappointment flooded Perry's mind. *Who did she see? A witness or a killer?*

"Did you see anyone else?" he asked.

She shook her head. "No, but it might be worth asking Shelly and Leah. The light was on in the practice kitchen, and I could hear the mixer and them talking, so I know they were in there."

"Did you hear what they were saying?"

"No, sorry." She sighed sadly and looked down at the floor.

Rats! There goes my earlier theory they might've killed her together.

As he studied the flickering shadows created from the overhead strip lights that danced across Cleo's pale face, framed by her black glasses, he felt sure that the youngster hadn't killed Vera. It was clear she was bereft at losing her grandmother, as well as their chance of ever having a relationship. But there was one more test he could try to be *absolutely* sure of her innocence. "Did you know," he began gently, his voice barely rising above the steady hum of idling printers, "that you're one of the principal beneficiaries of your grandmother's will?"

Cleo's eyes widened, the colour once more draining from her cheeks as quickly as if someone had pulled the plug in her veins. "But why?" Her voice trembled. "Why would she leave me anything if she loathed my mother...if she loathed us?"

"Loathe is a strong a word," he said cautiously. "Maybe she just felt powerless to change what your mother had become."

"I always dreamed of speaking with her properly. Just once." Her voice cracked, and she took a deep breath. "To hear her side, you know, to try to understand…" Cleo balled her hands into tight fists, her knuckles white. A single tear trailed a path down her cheek before she hastily swiped it away.

Perry thought his heart would break.

With a deep breath, he braced himself. "You'll need to tell the police about all this," he said, the words heavy on his tongue. "They'll find out who you are soon enough, but if you tell them first, then it will be much better for you. But don't worry," he added quickly, seeing panic flit across the young woman's face. "I know the sergeant who's handling the investigation. She's lovely and has an open mind. She'll guide you through it step by step."

"Thank you," Cleo said, her voice barely above a whisper. The gratitude in her eyes washed through him like a warm coffee. "Will you ring her now?"

"Of course," Perry said, taking out his mobile phone. As he called Spicer's number, he gave himself a virtual pat on the back. It might not have gone as smoothly as he'd planned, but he'd identified Vera's granddaughter and, through her, possibly discovered a new sighting of the killer. *Not bad at all if I say so myself!*

31

MEANWHILE, BACK OVER HERE, WEDNESDAY 21 APRIL

"Can you describe the man you saw with Summer?" Rich's stance was relaxed, yet his gaze bore into Isla with quiet intensity.

Isla hesitated, her eyes darting to the gravel path beneath their feet before meeting Rich's steady gaze. "He was about this tall" —she indicated with a hand just above her head— "in his thirties, I suppose. Dark hair, clean shaven..."

Bea's heart quickened, each detail painting a familiar picture. It was as if Isla had plucked the description straight from the grainy photo of the man Rich had shown them at lunch earlier. It was the other unidentified member of the public who had entered the grounds on that Monday morning. She glanced over at Rich. A small smile was playing on his lips. *He's made the connection too.*

"And how did they seem?" Rich asked.

"Comfortable, I'd say. Relaxed. Like good friends," Isla said confidently. "I couldn't hear what they were saying, but they were quite animated. Not a fully blown argument, more like a disagreement."

Interesting... Bea's mind whirred with possibilities. *Is he a lover? Oh, gosh...is he an accomplice? Or perhaps the real culprit?*

Isla added, almost as an afterthought, "Summer didn't look like a woman who'd just committed murder—or was about to."

"Do you remember what time it was that you saw them?" Rich asked.

"Yes. It was eleven."

That's precise...

Isla shrugged. "My phone beeped to remind me to call my aunt for her birthday."

"And where in the gardens did this encounter take place?" Rich pressed on.

"Er, over by the rose garden at the back of the house." Isla pointed behind her with fingers that trembled ever so slightly.

Bea's gaze lingered on Isla, and once again, she was torn between whether Isla's reticence was nerves or if she was holding something back. Bea tucked a strand of hair behind her ear and suppressed a sigh. The unease in Isla's darting eyes was almost unmistakable, like a skittish deer surrounded by hunters. "You're not telling us everything, are you, Isla?" Bea said, her voice gentle and steady.

Isla wrapped her arms around herself. "What would I be hiding?" she retorted, raising her chin, but there was a tremor in her words.

"I'm not sure." Bea's eyes narrowed as she watched Isla's reaction with the precision of a hawk. *I'm getting close; I know I am.* "Family ties, perhaps? To someone involved in all of this?"

The colour drained from Isla's face.

Bingo!

"That's absurd. Why would you think that?" A note of panic threaded through Isla's voice.

"Because I believe you may be related to Vera Bolt." The name hung in the air between them for a few seconds, then Isla's surprise morphed into confusion.

She shook her head vehemently. "What? The old woman from *Bake Off Wars* who was killed?" she stammered out, her confusion melting into what appeared to be relief. "No way. I didn't even know her."

Bea's heart sank. *Have I got it wrong?* Isla's denial seemed genuine.

Bea glanced at Rich. He gave her a slight shrug, then cleared his throat. "The police will want to have a word with you about seeing Summer on Monday morning, Isla. My friend is one of the people investigating the case. She's very nice and will help you through giving a statement. If you give me your address and mobile number, I'll pass it on to her and make sure she's the one who talks to you. Is that okay?" His request was gentle, but the authority behind it was unmistakable. He unlocked his phone, tapped the screen, and handed it to her.

"Fine." Isla typed her details into the app he'd opened, her hand quivering ever so slightly, then handed it back to him. "Can I go now?"

Rich nodded, and with a quizzical look at Bea, the young woman walked past them and headed off around the side of the manor house.

Once Isla had vanished from sight, Bea turned to Rich. "That went well, don't you think?" she said with a wry smile.

He met her gaze, his brown eyes twinkling. "Finding out Summer was with a man that morning went well. Accusing Isla of being Vera's granddaughter? Not so well."

"Indeed," Bea replied, raking her fingers through her hair, a thoughtful frown creasing her forehead. "She really seemed shocked at the suggestion. And it felt real. Not practiced."

"Then I think we can agree that she's not Vera's grand-daughter," Rich said with a brief nod.

"Was I too harsh?" A twinge of guilt tugged at Bea's conscience. Isla's fragility had been unexpectedly disarming.

"No, I just think you caught her by surprise."

"But she is rather delicate, and Saunders isn't the most tactful of men…"

"Don't worry. I'll ask Spicer to talk to her. Tina's good with people," Rich reassured her, already tapping out a message on his phone.

As his thumbs moved swiftly over the screen, they began to walk again, their footsteps a rhythmic crunch on the gravel path that wound its way towards The Dower House and beyond it, to the cottages where Rich was staying. Daisy, scampering ahead of them, sniffed at the flowering bedding plants that lined their route.

"Done," Rich declared, slipping his phone back into his pocket.

"So who do you think this mysterious man was with Summer?" Bea asked as she glanced sideways at Rich.

"Well, clearly from Isla's description, it's the man who was caught on CCTV. He came in with the public that morning, so it's unlikely he's someone connected to Francis Court or the show. But apart from that, he could be anyone," Rich replied. "An old friend. A new lover. A confidant. Family…"

"Or an accomplice?" Bea suggested, unable to keep her concerns from him.

"Let's not get ahead of ourselves." Rich's words were a gentle reminder to ground her speculations in fact rather than conjecture.

They paused at the fork in the path. Daisy stopped to look back at them, her head cocked to one side as if deciding which one to follow.

"Right, I'm off to see how the kitchen installation is coming along," Bea said, holding up her right hand and crossing her fingers.

"I'm sure it'll be fine. And I've got my exercises to do. Doctor's orders, you know."

"Good," she replied, the corners of her mouth lifting in a soft smile. His commitment to his recovery was reassuring. "We've walked a lot today, so no overdoing it."

"Yes, ma'am!" He gave her a mock salute.

Rats! I've done it again. But when she looked at his face, he was grinning. The tension eased from her shoulders. "Alright. Well, I'll see you later. Come on, Daisy."

Her little dog changed direction and ran ahead of her as they made their way towards the secure back gate to her new home. Her mind was still a kaleidoscope of possibilities, each more colourful and unlikely than the last. She was fairly sure of one thing though. Whoever this man was, Summer had deliberately not told anyone about meeting him. Not the police and not Fred. *So what's she hiding?*

32

5 PM, WEDNESDAY 21 APRIL

The Society Page online article:

Summer York Released After Arrest Over the Murder of Vera Bolt

Summer York (35), the comedian and a presenter on Bake Off Wars, *has been released following her arrest last night by Fenshire CID in connection with the death of renowned pastry chef Vera Bolt, who died on Monday.*

Fenshire CID issued the following statement a short while ago: 'A thirty-five-year-old woman, who was arrested yesterday, has been released without charge. The investigation into the death of Vera Bolt continues.'

Lord Frederick Astley (39), the future Duke of Arnwall, was seen escorting Summer York and royal lawyer Charlotte Mansell from the police station in King's Town to his parent's stately home, Francis Court, just before news of Miss York's release was made public.

Reports of a potential romance between the king's nephew and the TV star remains the subject of much speculation in the popular press. Francis Court is described by one local as "overrun with paparazzi".

———

SPB Group Chat:

Bea: *Just seen Fred. He's still not clear why Summer was suddenly released. All they told Charlotte was that they had insufficient evidence at the present to charge her. He's not sure if that means they know she's innocent or if they have let her go because the 24 hrs were expiring and they didn't have a strong enough reason to get an extension.*

Simon: *CID Steve says they confirmed Vera's blood on the chef's coat, but they haven't found any prints. Saunders is not a happy bunny!*

Perry: *Loads to tell you. We need a pow-wow. Can you come over for dinner at 7pm?*

Bea: *Things to tell you too. Dinner sounds good. Are you going to invite Rich? He may have more from Spicer.*

. . .

Perry*: Doing it now…*

Bea: *Simon, how did filming for BOW go?*

Simon: *Okay, I think.*

Perry: *He was magnificent!*

Simon: *You're biased!*

Perry: *Okay, Fitzwilliam says yes to dinner.*

Bea: *This place is teeming with press so will get Ward to drive. Will pick Rich up on the way. See you at 7 x*

33

6:55 PM, WEDNESDAY 21 APRIL

Bea peered through the tinted windows of the sleek black Daimler with a sense of foreboding. Ward had suggested they leave Francis Court through the trades entrance rather than out of the main gates because of the hoard of press still camped out there. But she knew from her and Rich's almost-encounter with a handful of paparazzi at lunchtime that they were a resourceful bunch who would do anything to get a picture or a story. However more difficult it was to gain access to the tradesmen's road, it was likely that some of them would have found a way through and stationed themselves at the alternative exit just in case. She drew in a breath, willing calm into her nerves.

"We'll be through in a jiffy, my lady," Ward assured her in his deep, unruffled voice. His eyes met hers briefly in the rearview mirror before returning to the road.

"Thank you, Ward," she replied, attempting to match his even tone. But the flutter in her chest betrayed her anxiety.

"Are you okay?" Beside her Rich shifted, unsettling Daisy, who was curled contentedly on his lap.

Bea nodded, grateful for his reassuring presence. Her

gaze lingered for a moment on her little dog's wiry coat, then on Rich's hands—strong and capable—as they stroked Daisy soothingly. She felt an unwelcome warmth spread through her at the sight. *I wish I was Daisy...* She swallowed hard, forcing her attention back to the window. *Get a grip, Bea!*

The car glided forward, the engine purring discreetly as they approached the exit. Only a handful of press lingered there, their cameras poised like hunters' rifles. As Ward manoeuvred through the gates, the air inside the car seemed to thicken, charged with the anticipation of what was to come. Bea caught her breath.

Click, click, click!

Flashes erupted, momentarily illuminating the interior of the car with stark white light. Bea braced herself, focusing on the steady rhythm of her own breath. The cameras clicked and whirred, an invasive cacophony that she endured with practiced stoicism.

"Alright?" Rich's voice broke through the clamour, low and concerned.

"Of course," she responded, her voice betraying none of the turmoil swirling beneath her composed exterior. "I'm used to it," she lied. Would she ever get used to that sudden and unwelcome exposure?

"You handle it with grace, as always," Rich said, his gaze lingering on her profile.

Her heart skipped a beat. *Really? Is that what he thinks?* A smile tugged at the corners of her mouth. *Grace, heh?*

As the car sped up, leaving the persistent journalists behind, Bea allowed herself a small sigh of relief. But her heart was still beating fast. Was it the delayed reaction to their encounter with the press or the proximity of the man beside her?

———

The evening light cast a soft glow on the ivy-covered façade of Rose Cottage as Ward brought the car to a stop outside the iron gate. Daisy's tail thumped eagerly against Rich's lap as she whined in excitement. Bea suppressed a smile as Rich tried to calm the bundle of fur long enough to get his seat belt undone. She looked down at his hands as he finally reached the red button and depressed it. What would it be like to arrive with him for dinner as more than just friends or joint-investigators in a murder case but hand in hand like a proper couple? A tingle ran down her spine, and she shivered.

Rich looked over at her and gave her a lazy smile. *Oh my goodness…*

The car door opened, and Daisy bounded off his lap and out onto the cobblestone walkway with a soft *woof*. Rich followed her. As Bea slid over the back seat, he turned and offered her his hand. Bea's heart stopped as she hesitated, her breath caught in her throat. The invitation was clear in his eyes, drawing her towards him like a magnetic force. The warm evening breeze whispered through the trees, carrying the scent of the rosemary that lay along the pathway to the cottage. It seemed as if time had paused, allowing this moment between them to stretch infinitely. With trembling fingers, she reached out and accepted his hand. His touch sent an electric wave coursing through her body, igniting a fire that burned deep within her. The pressure of his hand holding hers as he gently pulled her towards him was both comforting and exhilarating.

She wasn't sure her legs would hold her as she tentatively placed first one, then the other on the cobbles. As they stood there hand in hand, a sense of belonging washed over her like a gentle tide, pulling her closer to him with an irresistible force.

"Will that be all, my lady?" Ward, who was standing behind the car door, asked as he closed it behind her. She dropped Rich's hand, her own suddenly feeling empty and cold. "Er, yes. Thank you, Ward."

He gave her a short bow. "Ring me when you're ready to leave, my lady."

She smiled in agreement. Turning to Rich, she was keen to recapture the connection she'd felt with the warmth of his touch, but he'd already followed Daisy up the path to the sage-green door of the cottage. She stifled a groan of frustration. *Maybe it's for the best*, she told herself as she drifted up the path. *Nothing can come of it anyway.*

———

Daisy made a beeline for Perry as Bea and Rich entered the cottage and headed straight to the kitchen. Perry greeted the little dog with open arms and laughed as she attempted to lick his nose.

"I'll get the wine when this little monster leaves me alone," he said, his blue eyes twinkling. "You sit down."

I need a bucketful, Bea thought as she tried to steady the fluttering thoughts about Rich flying around in her head.

Daisy claimed her usual throne — the large armchair in front of the French doors that overlooked the garden and curled up with a contented sigh. Bea made her way towards the oversized wooden dining table in the far corner of the open-plan kitchen-diner.

"Food's almost ready," Simon called out as he opened the door of the cooking range along the kitchen wall. The aroma of rosemary and thyme wafted over towards Bea. She licked her lips. *Food!* She stole a glance at Rich as he joined her at the table and took the seat opposite her. *Food will have to do for now.*

"Malbec okay?" Perry said, arriving at the table bearing a bottle of red wine. She nodded as he uncorked it and poured the rich red liquid into glasses. When he handed one to Bea with a flourish, she grabbed it gratefully, taking a gulp before he'd even said his usual, "Cheers!"

Simon arrived carrying dishes of roasted chicken, herb potatoes, and vegetables glistening in butter. He placed them on the table and sat down next to Rich.

"This looks delightful," Bea said, her stomach backing up her words with a timely grumble.

"And smells delicious," Rich added, unfolding his napkin with an appreciative nod towards Simon.

"Well, tuck in then," Simon said, reaching over for the vegetables. "So how did you get on today, Bea?" he asked, scooping up a spoonful of orange carrots. "Is the kitchen at The Dower House coming along alright?"

She picked up her knife and fork. "Yes, it's looking good. They hope to have it finished on time." She shifted in her seat as she leaned over and speared a roasted potato. "But I have much more exciting news. On our way back from the pub, and thanks to Daisy's sniffing prowess, we found a knife hidden beneath a bush near the Orangery. It looked like the murder weapon."

Perry, his fork momentarily suspended in the air, said, "Oh, maybe it will have fingerprints on it and then—"

"Sorry, Perry, but before you go down that route," Rich said, a piece of chicken halfway to his mouth. "I have an update on the knife."

Bea put down her cutlery in anticipation. *Will this give us the answer we need?*

"It came back clean."

Deflated, Bea picked up her glass and took a sip of wine. They just couldn't catch a break with this case.

"Well, no fingerprints at least," Rich continued. "They confirmed Vera's blood on the blade, and it was the one missing from the kitchen set. So we know it was the murder weapon."

So nothing new…

"But I do have something else."

They all stopped what they were doing. Bea's stomach fluttered. *Come on; please be good!*

"Additional test results from the autopsy suggest that Vera died closer to eleven than originally thought. Maybe only five minutes either way." He raised an eyebrow. "That's why they had to release Summer. Cleo saw Summer leaving the Old Barn earlier, at ten-fifty."

Simon frowned. "But couldn't she have simply doubled back and—"

"No!" Perry, Bea, and Rich cried at the same time. They all looked at each other.

Bea glanced at Rich, then said, "You go," to Perry.

He smiled. "Thanks. I was just going to say Cleo told me she went back to talk to Vera after Summer had left, but she fled when she saw someone in chef's whites moving in the corridor outside the tent."

"She saw the killer?" Bea asked, her eyes wide. "Who was it?"

Perry shook his head. "Sorry. She didn't recognise them; she only briefly saw them from the back."

Simon cleared his throat. "So it could have been Summer if she'd got hold of—"

"No!" Bea and Rich cried in unison. The others looked at them expectantly. Rich tipped his head at Bea.

"Rich and I bumped into Isla at Francis Court this afternoon. She admitted she was in the grounds Monday morning, and she saw Summer with a man in the rose garden. That was at eleven o'clock," Bea said.

"Ah…" Perry nodded. "So Summer couldn't have killed Vera."

"Not if what Isla told us was true."

"So is she Vera's granddaughter?" Simon asked.

"No!" Bea and Perry cried in sync. They looked at each other and grinned.

"You go this time," Perry said to her.

"Isla insists she's not related to Vera. Yet something feels…off about her."

Rich dipped his chin. "So it's possible she *is*—"

"Cleo is Vera's granddaughter!" Perry, practically buzzing with excitement, blurted out.

They all turned to look at him.

"I've been dying to tell you all evening," he said with a grin.

Bea grinned back as she picked up her wineglass. She'd underestimated Perry's ability to subtly question a witness without them shutting down. "Good job, Perry," she said, raising her glass to him. "That must have taken some serious finesse to find that out without scaring her away."

Perry blushed and rubbed his nose. "Er, yes," he murmured, burying his head in his wineglass.

"Come on then; tell us all about it," Simon said, a hint of amusement in his voice.

Perry gave a subdued account of his conversation with Cleo, telling them about her mother's addiction and Vera's subsequent rejection of her daughter and granddaughter.

Bea's heart ached when he told them how Cleo had finally plucked up the courage to attempt to talk to her grandmother on the day Vera had died but had been thwarted by first Summer and then the unknown figure in the corridor. Bea stared down into her wineglass. *She never got to tell her...*

"I've told Spicer. She'll be interviewing Cleo tomorrow morning," he concluded.

"I wonder who this figure was she saw in the corridor," Simon said.

Bea frowned. "Perry, which way did Cleo go in?"

"She was in the store Portakabin beforehand, so she went in from the back door. She told me she walked down the corridor past the practice kitchen—"

"Did she see Shelly and Leah?"

"No. She said the light was on, and she could hear a mixer and them talking—"

That makes sense. The women had told her they'd been busy remaking their skills test bakes after their meeting with Vera.

"Then she carried on along the corridor, turned the corner, and that's when she got a fleeting look at the back of someone moving near the entrance to the tent. She turned and fled."

"Well," Rich replied, leaning over the table and refilling his glass. "We're running out of options of who it could be if we believe what Cleo—"

"Surely you can't think Cleo did it?" Perry's voice held a defensive edge, his brows knitting together as he glanced between Bea and Rich.

"If it wasn't her and it wasn't Summer, then all we're left with is Harvey," Rich said, taking a sip of his wine.

Bea put down her glass. *Goodness, he's right.* Harvey's

the only one left. Bea twirled the rings on her right hand. *But*... "He has no motive…"

"That we know of," Rich pointed out. "I talked to Spicer just before I left. She's digging into Harvey's past as we speak. There might be a connection we've missed."

Bea stifled a sigh. So Harvey seemed like their only option at the moment, however unlikely.

The conversation lulled for a few minutes, then Perry, his eyes wide with a mixture of concern and intrigue, leaned forward in his chair. "What do we know about the man seen with Summer? Could he be in on this?" he asked, glancing towards Bea.

"Isla puts him with Summer and nowhere near the tent when Vera was killed, so I don't see how he could be," she replied.

"Does Fred know?" Simon asked.

"I don't think so," Bea admitted, a heaviness in her chest. "He told us Summer left the Old Barn and went for a walk to cool off, remember? I don't think she's told him or the police she was meeting someone." In her mind's eye, she saw Fred — his jovial demeanour, his easy laughter, and she shuddered to think how this revelation might fracture his world. Her gaze drifted over to Rich, seeking reassurance in his steady presence.

"Hold on," Rich said, giving her a quick smile. "We don't know who this man is. He could be a friend or a relation. We shouldn't assume Summer is up to something behind Fred's back."

She smiled back at him. *Of course! There must be a perfectly reasonable explanation.*

"But then why didn't she tell the police?" Perry asked. "Even with the earlier time of death window, if she'd met him straight after she'd left the tent, she wouldn't have had time to dispose of the chef's whites and the knife. He could have provided her with an alibi."

Bea's heart shrank. *He's right.* Why would Summer put herself through being questioned by the police as their chief suspect and then allow herself to be arrested if she had someone who could vouch for her?

"How much do you trust Isla's version of events?" Simon asked.

Bea looked at Rich. Did he have doubts about Isla too?

"I agree with Bea. I think she's hiding something, but I don't think she would've made up a story about seeing Summer with a man. After all, we know he was there as we have him on camera." He paused and glanced at his phone before continuing, "But we've hit a bit of a snag."

Have we? Bea leaned in.

"Spicer still hasn't been able to contact Isla. She's not answering her phone. When Spicer rang the hotel she's staying at, they said she hasn't been back since she left at lunchtime."

"Spooked, perhaps?" Perry suggested, swirling the wine in his glass, the ruby liquid catching the candlelight.

I hope not. Bea pictured Isla, alone and frightened—or worse, on the run. She felt strangely protective of the waif-like young woman. Had she and Rich scared her off?

"Let's hope not," Rich said, his tone carrying a shadow of concern. "We need her side of the story."

Simon glanced at his watch, then looked across at Perry. "Why don't we pop up to the pub when we're done here and see if she's there?" Perry raised an eyebrow. Then he smiled slowly and nodded.

Perry turned to Bea. "And what are you going to do about Summer and this man? Are you going to tell Fred?"

Tell Fred? Is he mad? She didn't want to be the one to

cause trouble between Fred and Summer. *Fred really likes her, maybe even loves—*

"Bea?" Perry's voice was insistent. "You *have* to tell him now that you know."

But I don't want to get involved. "Why? It's their business, isn't it?" *What if I tell him and he hates me forever?* Her mind retreated back fifteen years ago to when her husband James had been killed in a car accident along with Gill Sterling, the wife of Francis Court's estate manager. The speculation in the press about James and Gill's relationship and the not-so-subtle hints of a possible affair had shattered Bea's world. Despite the rumours, she had steadfastly believed in her husband's faithfulness. But when a letter had appeared some nine years later, seemingly from James, confessing that he was in love with Gill and they were running away together, the nightmare had become real. *Can I put Fred through that?*

"He's your brother, Bea. You'd want him to tell you if the shoe was on the other foot, wouldn't you?" Simon added on the pressure.

Would I? If someone had told her when James had died that he'd been having an affair, would that have been preferable to having believed for nine years that he loved her, only to find out she'd been living a lie? *I don't know…*

She looked over at Rich opposite her. *What do I do?* His brown eyes stared into hers. "Why don't you talk to Summer first? Maybe she could do with your help," he said evenly.

Gosh, he's good. I can do that! Then it hit her. How quickly she'd come to rely on his thoughtful advice and calm demeanour. His ability to see things from different perspectives, something that had caused conflict between them when their minds had still been prejudiced against each other after their uncomfortable start, was now something she valued.

Admired even. And as much as she'd had to dig deep to find it, underneath that sometimes brusk exterior was a man with a surprising amount of empathy, a strong sense of fair play, and a genuine desire to help others. As their eyes locked, she saw all that…and more. *He understands me…*

34

THE NEXT DAY, 10 AM, THURSDAY 22
APRIL

Bea dragged herself up the magnificent and imposing staircase that separated the second and third floors of Francis Court. Her boots thudded dully on the navy-blue carpet partly covering the stone stairs as she gripped the smooth brass handrail that rested on top of the ornately carved gold-painted balustrade. Her legs were heavy, as if they were made of lead, and a twitch behind her right eye suggested a headache was brewing. *This is what happens when you drink too much wine and don't get enough sleep,* she scolded herself. Although she was prepared to take full responsibility for the amount of wine she'd guzzled down last night, the lack of sleep wasn't altogether her fault. Something was bugging her. Something someone had said last night didn't quite add up, but she couldn't figure out what it was.

She gave a heavy sigh. And then there was the other problem keeping her mind from resting. *Rich!* As hard as she tried, she just couldn't get that man out of her head! And the fact he was being just so…well…adorable (that *was* the only word for it) at the moment wasn't helping. It had been so much easier when he'd been boorish and dismissive. Now he was attentive, charming, and really quite dreamy.

Oh goodness! This won't do…

She needed to focus on the investigation. Although it didn't feel like they were getting anywhere fast, they *were* finding out more about the day Vera had died. It would eventually all slot into place. She had to believe that.

At least they'd found Isla. Well, Perry and Simon had. Bea had been relieved to get a text from Simon not long after she'd got home last night telling her that Isla had been in the pub and had now spoken to Spicer to arrange an interview.

Arriving at the top of the stairs, Bea went through the wooden doorway below the gold-and-red painted arch and into a wood-panelled corridor. She glanced at her phone. Fred would be arriving at Rich's cottage now.

She'd seen him earlier from the window of her sitting room as he'd walked along the side of the Long Drive, so she'd known he'd been on his way before she'd left her rooms. It had been Rich's rather brilliant suggestion when they'd been in the car coming back from Perry and Simon's last night. In order to give her some time alone to talk to Summer, Rich would invite Fred over for a coffee this morning on the premise that he wanted to give him some feedback about the rehabilitation centre at Three Lakes after his visit there last week. *I hope Rich really* has *got something to say to Fred, or Fred will smell a rat.* She smiled to herself. Rich was resourceful; he would think of something.

Now it was her turn. She needed to get to the bottom of who Summer's mystery man was. She reached the large wooden door of Fred's apartment, pausing for a moment to collect her thoughts. *Maybe I should have brought Daisy, after all?* The little dog was a great ice-breaker. But then, she'd looked so sweet fast asleep and dreaming on Bea's bed, that she hadn't had the heart to disturb her. Bea took a deep breath and raised her hand. She knocked on the door, a rhythmic tap-tap that seemed to mirror her own thrumming pulse.

After a few seconds, the door swung open to reveal a slightly bemused looking Summer. "Beatrice? This is unexpected," she said, running a hand through her long dark hair.

"Hello. I thought I'd pop up and see how you're doing." Bea smiled as her eyes traced the lines of exhaustion etched around Summer's face, noting the pallid skin and the fragile set of her shoulders.

"I feel like a china cup sitting on the edge of a table and someone has just let in the bull," Summer quipped with a wry smile as she moved aside. "Come in."

Bea followed the slim woman through the hall and into the sitting room. The curtains were still closed, but patches of light were visible where the fabric didn't quite meet in the middle. Summer flopped down onto a blue-and-white striped three-seater sofa, and folded her legs beneath her as she plucked her mobile phone off the low coffee table in front of her and quickly glanced at it. "It's great to be out of that holding cell, but I'm just waiting for a call to say they want to see me again. Charlotte's number is practically burned into my phone screen," she said with a hollow laugh, tapping her mobile against her palm.

Bea bobbed her head in sympathy. "I can only imagine how horrid this must be for you."

Summer nodded slowly, then her eyes opened wide, alarm showing in her face, and she unfurled herself from the couch. "I'm so sorry, Beatrice. I'm a dreadful host. Would you like a coffee?" She gestured towards the coffeepot and mugs sitting on the sideboard along the wall.

I'd kill for one right now. "Only if you're having one."

"Er, yes. I think I will."

As Summer walked over to the coffee and poured two mugs of steaming black liquid, Bea debated if she should tell Summer the news about the more precise estimate of Vera's time of death. It wasn't really her place to share information the police had, but it was a great transition into discussing Summer's secret rendezvous.

"You take it black, don't you?" Summer called over.

"Yes, please."

Summer walked back, handed Bea one of the two mugs of coffee she was carrying, and returned to the large sofa.

"Thanks," Bea said, looking down at the white mug with 'Stolen from Gollingham Palace' in black lettering on the side. "Er, Summer," she said, taking the smaller sofa opposite her. "There's been an update on the investigation that I don't know if you're aware of. They've narrowed down the time of Vera's death to eleven o'clock, give or take five minutes."

Summer's eyes widened slightly. "Eleven?" she echoed, a tentative hope flickering in her eyes. "Well, that's...I wasn't in The Tent then."

"Well, that's good." Bea's gaze locked onto Summer's in a silent plea for the truth as she asked, "So where were you?"

The corners of Summer's mouth twitched downwards. "I've already told you. I was walking in the grounds."

"And are you sure you didn't see anyone while you were there?" Bea pressed, feeling the weight of the question like a stone in her stomach. *Come on, Summer. Just tell me the truth so I don't have to tell you I know.*

Summer shook her head, her long dark hair swaying with the motion. "Again. Not that I know of."

Bea stifled a groan. Fatigue was gnawing at her bones, but she pushed it aside. There was no choice now; she had to confront Summer with what she knew. "Summer. You were seen by someone."

Summer's grey-blue eyes widened in shock. "Who?" Her voice cracked, the word barely more than a whisper.

"A visitor recognised you. You were with a man."

The words hung in the room like a giant cobweb. The colour drained from Summer's cheeks, leaving her face ashen as she seemed to shrink in on herself. "It's not what you think, Beatrice," she stammered, her hands twisting together in her lap, her knuckles white with the strain.

"Then tell me what it is," Bea said gently.

Summer took a deep breath. "I was meeting Tom, my ex-boyfriend." She hesitated, her eyes pleading with Bea for understanding. "He wanted to see me before he left," she continued, her eyes downcast. "He's got a year's contract to work in the Galapagos Islands on a turtle conservation programme. He wanted me to go with him and give us another chance." Her voice broke, and she took a shaky breath before adding, "I told him no."

"Is that everything?" Bea asked quietly.

Summer nodded. "He was flying to Ecuador that evening," she said, almost to herself.

Ah…so that's why he hasn't come forward. He was half-way around the world and probably didn't even know Summer had been arrested.

"So why didn't you tell the police? He's your alibi."

"I hadn't told Fred. I was worried about what he would think of me for agreeing to meet Tom. I told him I'd been wandering around on my own to clear my head." Summer wrapped her arms around herself. "And I don't have any contact details of Tom's to give to the police, so he couldn't help anyway." Her eyes met Bea's as she bit her bottom lip. "Tom and I were supposed to get married; I still had feelings for him when we broke up…" She let out her breath with a *whoosh*. "And then, of course, when the police interviewed me, I had to stick to my story. Fred had organised a lawyer. He believed me. I couldn't face telling him I'd lied." She gave a little shrug. "I knew I hadn't killed Vera. I thought it would all just go away." Her face clouded over. "Oh, Beatrice, what am I going to do?"

Well, that depends on you… "Summer, how serious are things between you and Fred?"

Summer's eyes sprang open, then after a few seconds, they softened. "When Tom asked me to go away with him, it all became clear. I realised just how hard I've fallen for Fred. I've never met anyone quite like him. He's funny and thoughtful, and through all this madness, he's been there by my side. Reassuring me. Always in my corner." Her voice trembled. "And he never once believed that I could have harmed Vera." She looked down at her hands as she fidgeted with the hem of her sleeve—a quirky pattern of sunflowers and bees that was so distinctly Summer.

Bea suppressed a sigh. *Isn't that what we all want?* She absently brushed a strand of red hair away from her face. But Fred, like her, came with a unique set of challenges. "Are you ready for what comes next though?" she asked. Summer looked up. "The attention can be merciless, and they'll question if you're suitable for Fred. The press and the public will have an opinion on everything from how you style your hair to what clothes you wear. Believe me, it's brutal. Much worse than you can imagine."

"With Fred by my side, I think I can face anything." Summer sounded more confident now. She gave a dry laugh. "I've been grilled by the police and accused of murder. I think I can cope with what Karen from Surrey thinks of the colour of my lipstick."

Bea smiled, a warmth spreading through her chest. She admired Summer's spirit and her willingness to take on the world for love. "Then I think you'll make it work. Tell Fred about Tom. He'll be upset that you didn't confide in him right from the start, but I think ultimately he'll understand."

Summer's posture as she sat on the edge of the sofa betrayed her reticence.

"Look, Summer. I've known Fred for long enough to say he's never been quite so — well, besotted with anyone as he is with you."

Summer's grey-blue eyes searched Bea's face for certainty. "Really?" Her voice was barely above a whisper but laced with hope.

"Indeed." Bea smiled as Summer's face lit up. "But you must tell him everything. It's the only way forward."

"Okay, I will," she said, her face a picture of determination.

Bea stood. "After that, you must tell Charlotte. She'll give you advice on how to proceed. It's likely you'll need to give a statement to the police and provide them with Tom's full name and as many flight details as you know. If they know what plane he was on, perhaps they can work out how to reach him."

"Of course." Summer rose too. "Thank you," she said as she threw herself at Bea and wrapped her arms around her. "I'm so grateful you came up to see how I was. I feel so much better now."

Bea returned the hug, her heart swelling over knowing that she'd helped Summer. *After all, she might be my sister-in-law one day!*

Leaving Summer texting Fred to arrange to meet him, Bea descended the staircase from Fred's apartment. All her energy was now gone, and she was only a few centimetres away from draining her emergency reserve tank as well. She should feel lighter now that she'd spoken to Summer, but that persistent itch in the back of her mind about there being an inconsistency somewhere was still there; she just couldn't put her finger on what was weighing her down.

She paused mid-step, her boot hovering above the carpeted stair. It came to her in a flash, swift and unbidden. *Oh my goodness!* Could that be the key to unravelling who had killed Vera? *Stop, Bea! Don't get too carried away.* She needed to be sure. With a new sense of purpose, she grabbed the handrail and hurried down the stairs as if she was being chased by a hungry bear. There was no time to waste; she needed to speak with Cleo as soon as possible.

35

MEANWHILE, THURSDAY 22 APRIL

Rich stood by the window of Hope Cottage and watched Fred hurry towards the Long Drive that would lead him back to Francis Court. He turned away and sauntered over to the coffee table and picked up the two empty coffee mugs. If Bea had done her job, then the text Fred had just received had been from Summer wanting to see him. *I hope Bea has persuaded her to tell him the truth.*

He walked over to the kitchen sink and dropped the cups into it. He was sure Fred could take it. His earnest words from their earlier conversation echoed in Rich's memory. *"Summer's the one, Fitz. I'm in it for the long haul. I just hope she is too."*

Fred could have been summing up Rich's own feelings for Bea. Rich let out a slow sigh, his thoughts drifting to the woman who had unwittingly seized his heart. He returned to the sitting room, and moving past the coffee table and the two tartan-covered armchairs he and Fred had been using a short while ago, he plonked himself down on the overstuffed floral-patterned sofa by the fireplace. *What am I going to do?*

Fighting the pull towards her was like wrestling with his own shadow—impossible to get away from.

He closed his eyes. He could still feel the delicate weight of her hand as he'd helped her out of the car last night, their fingers entwining naturally as if they were two parts of the same puzzle longing to be whole. The thought sent a quiet thrill through him, though it was immediately tempered by the reality of their situation. Nothing could come of it while he still worked for PaIRS. It would be inappropriate, unprofessional, and career suicide for him. It would expose her to ridicule and judgement. *It can't happen.*

And anyway, did she even want it to happen? Looking at her face sometimes and the way her striking green eyes seemed to dance with the same hesitant hope, he was sure she felt it too. That pull. That connection. *But is it enough?* The possibility of threading their lives together was tantalising but fraught with the prickles of public scrutiny that she so hated.

He'd been surprised at how unbothered he was by the relentless flash of cameras and the hunger of the popular press wanting to get their story. His only concern had been on how it had made *her* feel. He opened his eyes and shifted his weight on the sofa. He knew his disregard for the press was a shield he could easily wield, but for Bea, it would be a tremendous challenge.

Can she brave the storm for a chance at what simmers unspoken between us?

His contemplation was fractured by the buzzing of his mobile phone over on the coffee table. He jumped up and tapped the screen.

Spicer: *I think Shelly's scared of Leah.*

· · ·

Leah? Rich's mind immediately diverted back to the case. Why would she be scared of her? Had Shelly witnessed something Leah had done? Had Leah been the one to set Summer up? But why? *Unless she's the murderer? But she has an alibi. Cleo heard the two of them talking...* Questions tumbled through his head like balls in a bingo machine.

Rich selected Spicer from his call list, and pressing the device to his ear, he listened to the ringing tone while his pulse quickened. Could this be the breakthrough they'd been waiting for?

The line clicked, and Spicer's voice came through, tinged with relief. "Fitz, thanks for calling."

"So where are we?"

"Something wasn't sitting right with me, so I've interviewed both Leah and Shelly at their hotel," she said, her words clipped and concise. "They're sticking to their story that they were together the whole time."

"Do you believe them?" Spicer had years of experience interviewing suspects. Rich trusted her instincts.

She sighed deeply. "Leah seemed quite calm but cagey. She said as little as possible. Shelly, on the other hand, was a bundle of nerves. She kept looking at the door as if expecting someone to run in at any moment and pounce on her. I'm worried she might be a little scared of Leah."

"And what does Saunders say?"

"He's not really interested. He's got his sights set on Harvey Jury even though we've found no stronger link between him and Vera than them both working on *Bake Off Wars*."

Saunders and his tunnel vision, Rich scoffed, picturing the DCI's bullish stance, his muscles straining beneath his shirt as he pointedly ignored alternative avenues.

"Why don't you keep pushing for him to take a second

look at Leah? In the meantime, I'll take a crack at the two women myself."

"That would be great, Fitz. They should still be at the hotel in Fawstead. I believed they're not expected on-site at the TV show until this afternoon."

"Okay, thanks, Tina. Let's keep in touch." He ended the call, sliding the phone into his pocket as he grabbed his car keys, and strode towards the door with a renewed enthusiasm to get to the bottom of the case, spurred on by Saunders' lack of vision and his own need to get to the solution before Bea put herself in harm's way. *Which she will undoubtedly do if I don't get there first…*

36

AT ABOUT THE SAME TIME,
THURSDAY 22 APRIL

Bea charged towards the garage complex on the Francis Court estate, hoping that Ward had already received her text message and would be waiting to drive her the short distance to Fawstead.

"Shelly and Leah won't be here until at least one." Cleo's words replayed in her mind. She glanced at her phone screen. It was only half-past eleven, leaving her ample time to intercept the women at their hotel.

Her boots clicked against the cobblestones as she turned onto the driveway leading from the garages. She smiled when she spied Ward cleaning one of the side mirrors of the Daimler with a rag. Hurrying towards him, she contemplated what she'd learned from Cleo.

Why did they lie?

Shelly and Leah had told Bea that the door had been closed while they'd been working in there. But when Cleo had gone past the practice kitchen for her second unsuccessful attempt to talk to her grandmother, she'd told Perry she'd seen the light on, heard a mixer and voices. Through a closed door? It turned out no. Cleo had been adamant just now that the door *had been* open.

What a silly, seemly unimportant thing to lie about…

And then there'd been the voices. On closer questioning, all Cleo could be sure of was that she'd heard people talking through the open door. What she couldn't be sure of was that those voices were definitely Shelly's and Leah's.

I have an idea about that…

As she reached the sleek black car parked on the fore-court, Ward opened the door to the rear of the car. "My lady," he said as he gave a quick nod of his capped head.

"The Fawstead Inn, please, Ward," she said, bending down to get in.

As she slid along the leather seats to the far side, her concerns about the barrage of press waiting to accost her as they left the estate took a back seat to her determination to find out the truth. *Time to get some answers…*

———

The shabbily grandiose lobby of The Fawstead Inn stretched before Bea as her gaze skimmed over the ornate cornices with peeling white paint and the weathered Victorian carpets. Her stomach clenched as she approached the reception desk. *I hope they're still here.*

The young man behind the wooden counter stared at her openmouthed. She stifled a smile. *It pays to be me sometimes*, she thought as he stammered out the room numbers for Shelly and Leah without even questioning why she needed to know them. *I'll just text Rich now and let him know—*

A familiar baritone made her start.

"Bea?"

She turned just as she heard a phone beep with a text. *Rich!* He closed the distance between them in five seconds.

"What brings you—"

"Why are you—"

They stood staring at each other.

"You go," she said, a smile playing on her lips.

"Spicer called," he said, his eyes dancing. "She's worried that Shelly is scared about something or someone. Saunders isn't interested so I said I'd check it out."

Her eyebrows arched. *Really?* Her pulse quickened. That supported her theory about Shelly and Leah being up to no good.

"You?"

"Shelly and Leah lied about the door to the practice kitchen being closed. It was open." She looked at him with triumph.

A frown creased his brow. "What?"

"Why did they tell a silly little lie like that?"

He shrugged.

"Exactly!" She looked at him with triumph.

He shook his head in confusion.

"And also Cleo heard voices, but she can't be sure it was actually *their* voices she heard."

Rich tilted his head to one side. "So there was someone else in there?" he asked tentatively.

"No. I think what Cleo heard was a podcast or something similar. Shelly and Leah were listening to one when I first met them in their practice kitchen."

Rich's eyes were now shining with excitement. "Could be. So what do you think happened?"

"Shelly told me the door was closed. I think it was, but then I think Leah went out and left it open. I don't think

Shelly realised. But Cleo went past after Summer had left, and it was open and—"

"You think Leah wasn't there because—"

"She'd left to kill Vera!"

They smiled at each other. Bea's chest felt light. *He gets me!*

Then his face clouded over. "And you were going to confront them by yourself, were you?" His brow furrowed, the protective edge to his tone not lost on her.

"I was about to text you to let you know. Honestly." She gave him a rather sheepish smile. "I just wanted to make sure they didn't leave before you got here." *Oh, but hold on…* "Wait. You didn't think to tell me about Spicer's call?"

"Er, I was about to…" He winked at her.

"Of course you were," she said, stifling a laugh. "Let's have a truce then, shall we? We'll agree that neither of us will act alone from now on. We tell each other everything. Okay?" she offered, extending a hand, which he shook firmly. A shiver went down her spine.

"Deal!" he said, his hand still lightly gripping hers.

She cleared her throat. "Shall we go then?" He nodded and dropped her hand. She wanted to offer it up to him again. *Bea!* She needed to concentrate on the *job* at hand. *Not his actual hand…*

Together, they made for the lift. Stepping into the mirrored enclosure, Bea caught a reflection of them standing side by side. She had to admit it. *We look good together…*

The lift dinged open on the third floor, and they were greeted by the unexpected sight of a door ajar down the corridor.

"Isn't that—" Rich began, but Bea was already moving in a hurry towards it.

"Shelly's room," she finished for him, reaching the door.

The scene inside struck her like a physical blow. Shelly Lovey sat slumped against the wall, her grey-blonde bob dishevelled around her round face. She was holding her right side with both hands, where a red stain was leaking through her fingers. Tears glistened in her blue eyes, her plump cheeks flushed with distress.

"Shelly!" Bea rushed to her side and knelt on the carpet carefully to avoid the knife lying on the floor by Shelly's side. "What happened?"

"Leah," Shelly gasped, her breath laboured. "She attacked me."

Just behind her, Rich barked into his phone, "Ambulance! Quick." He stepped away, speaking in hushed tones while scanning the room.

Bea looked around the room for something to stem the blood, which was now dripping through Shelly's fingers and onto the carpet underneath her. She jumped up when she saw the open bathroom door. *A towel!* She ran across the room and darted into the ensuite. She scanned the bathroom. It was empty apart from a bag on the floor. *Towels! Where are the towels?* She glanced down at the bath and saw two towels lying on the bottom. She grabbed the largest one. It was wet. *Rats!* She threw it back in and grabbed the smaller hand towel. It was only slightly damp. *Well, it will have to do!* She ran back into the room, balling the towel up as she went.

Dropping to the floor in front of a pale and slightly spaced-out looking Shelly, Bea gently prised the woman's hand away from the wound and pressed the makeshift plug to it. "Here, hold this," she said, guiding Shelly's shaking hand to the towel.

"Is Leah still here?" she asked gently.

Shelly slowly shook her head. "She ran off."

"And did Leah kill Vera?" Bea searched the woman's face for the truth.

"I don't know," Shelly whispered, her voice breaking. "I can't believe she would, but she wasn't with me. She asked me for an alibi... I've been so scared since I heard about the will…" Her voice trailed off, and her eyelids fluttered.

"Shelly!" Bea cried. "Stay with me, okay?"

Shelly's eyes opened fully as she stared at Bea, slowly nodding.

"Help is on the way," Rich said, crouching beside Bea and resting his lightly hand on her shoulder.

"Leah has fled," Bea told him.

He gave her a reassuring squeeze, then rose. "I'll let Spicer know."

"No need!" a familiar yet unwelcome voice barked from behind them. "She's here with me."

Saunders! Spicer must have persuaded him to reconsider Leah as a suspect.

"And what, may I ask, are the two of you doing here?" His distaste for the situation was clear in his voice.

Rats! How are we going to explain this away?

At that moment, the emergency responders arrived. *Saved by the bell!* As they piled into the room with shouts of, "Let us through, please!" and "Clear some space!" Bea quickly jumped up out of the way and allowed them to attend to Shelly as Spicer slipped out of the room.

Bea caught Rich's eye. *What do we do now?* He raised an eyebrow and subtly tilted his head towards the exit. They inched towards the door.

Saunders moved and planted himself squarely before Rich. "What are you doing here, Fitzwilliam?" His voice was sharp, accusatory. "You're supposed to be on sick leave."

Just say we were passing and found the door open.

Rich met Saunders' gaze and lifted his chin. "Well, I'm sorry, but I'm not one to sit idly by while someone gets away with murder."

Oh. I'm not sure that was a good idea…

"So you thought you'd do my job for me, did you?" Saunders scoffed, his thin lips curling into a sneer.

This is awkward.

"Well…someone…has…to!" Rich's jaw line was rigid as he enunciated each word slowly.

Saunders' small blue eyes squinted at Rich as a crimson tide seeped up his neck.

Gosh. That was brave!

"Sir," Spicer called out, her voice slicing through the strained atmosphere as she walked through the door. Her blonde hair bobbed with each assertive step she took until she was standing in front of Saunders. "No one in the lobby saw Leah leave."

Saunders stared at her for a second, then pinched his thin lips together, saying, "Well, organise a search then, sergeant."

"Yes, sir." Spicer gave Rich a look as she pulled out her mobile and walked over to the corner to make a call.

"Coming through!" A man and a woman, each in green overalls, rushed into the room. While one of the two men who had been attending Shelly walked over to Bea, Rich, and Saunders. "We've stopped the bleeding, and she's stable. We're taking her to the hospital now."

"Can I just have a quick word with her?" Saunders looked over at where the men were helping Shelly onto the ambulance trolley.

The man shook his head. "Sorry, mate. If you want to talk to her, you'll have to do it at the hospital." He turned without waiting for Saunders to reply and accompanied Shelly out of the room.

Saunders swore under his breath. He turned and shouted at Spicer, who was still on the phone. "Sergeant!" She paused talking and looked at him expectantly.

Bea caught Rich's eye. *Can we go now?* His eyes flickered to the door and back. He gave a brief nod. *Let's try again…*

"I'm going to the hospital." Saunders' voice boomed across the room.

Bea and Rich inched towards the door.

"You co-ordinate things here." Spicer gave Saunders a thumbs up and returned to her call.

"And you two," Saunders continued at full volume, turning back to Bea and Rich. "You will cease all involvement immediately. Or else…"

Rich stopped dead in his tracks. "Or else what?" he challenged.

A sinking feeling took root in Bea's chest. *This could get nasty…*

"Or else I'll have no choice but to report you to Blake." Saunders' stance was unyielding as he stared Rich down.

There was silence as the two men faced off.

The man's an idiot, Rich. Don't let him ruin your career, Bea pleaded with him in her head.

"Fine," Rich said through gritted teeth.

"Good," Saunders muttered as he stormed out of the door.

37

1:45 PM, THURSDAY 22 APRIL

The Breakfast Room at Francis Court had settled into a post-luncheon lull, its earlier bustle replaced by the occasional murmur from the few remaining patrons. The rays of the sun streamed through the tall windows, casting geometric patterns on the chequered floor and bathing the room in a warm amber hue.

"So Leah just stabbed Shelly, then ran off?" Perry asked Bea from across the table, slipping his last piece of chicken to Daisy, who sat next to him with her mouth open. "Do you think Leah tried to kill her, or was she trying to stop Shelly from following her?"

Good question. Bea looked to Rich, who was sitting next to her, absent-mindedly toying with the remains of his ham sandwich. His gaze remained fixated on the white tablecloth in front of him, but his fingers now stopped in their subconscious destruction of his lunch. *What's going on with him?*

He'd been quiet in the car on their way back from the hotel a short while ago. She'd thought that maybe Saunders' threat was bothering him, so she'd said, "Those threats from Saunders... They're just hot air, you know," but he'd kept his eyes on the road ahead and murmured, "Perhaps." He'd seemed to be in his own world, and somehow she didn't think it was the thought of Saunders whinging to his boss that was causing the unspoken turbulence beneath his calm exterior.

Picking up her coffee, she tilted her head to catch his eye, trying to read the thoughts hiding behind his rugged facade. She wondered if the shadows of the attack on him at Gollingham Palace still haunted him. He'd told her during one of their walks that when the gun had been pointed at him, he'd thought he was going to die. *Beneath his stoic mask, is he still battling that fear of being killed?* He'd been commendably strong when they'd found the injured Shelly, but was it possible that a latent trauma lay coiled within him, biding its time?

She cleared her throat. "Rich?" He turned his head, his eyes locking on hers. "Perry was just asking if we think Leah deliberately tried to kill Shelly or that poor Shelly just got in the way when Leah tried to run?"

The corners of Rich's mouth twitched in a semblance of a smile. Then he dropped her gaze and turned to Perry with a shrug. "It's hard to know until she's interviewed. Shelly said Leah attacked her, so it sounds like it may have been the former." He plucked a piece of ham from the remnants of his sandwich. As he bent down with the meat dangling between his fingers, Daisy wiggled through Perry's and Simon's legs to arrive by Rich's side just as his hand reached Daisy's head-height. She opened her mouth, and Rich dropped the morsel of food in. Bea sighed as Rich stroked the little dog's ears. *What's the point of me saying anything anymore?* Perry and Rich seemed determined to make Daisy a leftovers dustbin. *Well, they can have the pleasure of taking Daisy to the vets next time and be lectured about healthy diets for dogs!*

"Well, the good news is that Shelly's going to be alright,"

Simon said, shifting in his seat as he suddenly dipped under the table and gave Daisy a morsel of cheese. *Et tu, Brute?*

"The knife missed all her vital organs," he continued, ignoring the look Bea gave him. "They'll patch her up. She'll probably be released later today or tomorrow morning."

"Thank heavens for that," Perry said, relief audible in his tone as he leaned back in his chair.

"Indeed," Bea added. That should mean the police could interview Shelly soon. A tingle shot down Bea's spine. Would Shelly be able to fill in all the gaps for them about Vera's death? Bea had her own theory, of course, but it would be good to know if she was close. Also, something was still not sitting right for her, but whatever it was remained elusively hidden in the back of her mind. She took another sip of coffee. Hopefully, when they found Leah, she would realise the game was up and tell them exactly what had happened. *Does CID Steve know how the search for Leah is—* About to ask Simon that, she froze. She braved a quick side glance at Rich, but his mind was clearly elsewhere. He didn't appear like he was about to question Simon about where he'd got the information about Shelly from. *Phew!* They'd dodged that bullet again.

The sudden *beep beep* of text messages sliced through the air, startling them all. Rich and Simon reached into their pockets simultaneously. As they read their screens, Bea's heart quickened in anticipation of the impending news.

Simon's eyes met Bea's. A subtle tightening around his eyes betrayed concern. He said nothing aloud, a heavy breath escaping him instead.

"That's Spicer," Rich's voice cut through the silence, his jaw setting firm. "They've found Leah."

Great! At least now—

"She's dead," Rich continued, the words falling from his

lips like a stone into a still pond as he read aloud from the message. "She was at the bottom of the back stairs of the hotel. She had a bag." His brown eyes darkened. "It looks like she was fleeing and lost her footing."

"Oh my…" Perry exhaled, the words barely audible.

Dead? The finality of it reverberated in her chest. This wasn't how she'd expected it to end…

38

4:30 PM, THURSDAY 22 APRIL

Bea stood by the deep Belfast sink in the kitchen of The Dower House, her eyes roving over the sleek marble counter-tops and the chrome appliances that glinted like polished armour under the soft glimmer of pendant lights. Meanwhile, Daisy, her paws clicking against the porcelain tile floor, had her nose in and out of every nook and cranny she could find. The weekend move seemed tangible now, the anticipation curling gently in her stomach. *Our home…*

"And look at this, Sam." Simon's voice, rich and warm, carried through the space as he panned Bea's mobile phone around the room. "You'll be whipping up your favourite food in here in no time."

Through the phone's speaker, her son's youthful laughter filled the kitchen as Simon continued with the live video call. Bea's lips twitched into a smile at the thought of her son's homecoming next weekend, the image of them sitting at the new breakfast bar chatting or him cooking as she pottered about — a comforting domestic tableau.

"Ooh, look at the spice rack!" Sam exclaimed as Simon

zoomed in on the wooden fixture hanging elegantly on the wall, each jar inside it uniformly labelled. "I can't wait to use it."

As Simon moved to the other end of the room to show Sam the built-in chopping board, she ran her fingers along the cool stone countertop next to the sink, a thoughtful furrow knitting her brow.

"Bea?" Perry said, his voice gentle as he joined her. "You seem miles away. I thought you'd be doing cartwheels now the case is closed and this place is ready for you to live in. What's wrong? Don't you like it?" He leaned against the sleek new fridge, his arms crossed over his chest, a concerned look in his eyes.

She gave him a reassuring smile. "It's not that, Perry. I am thrilled with it, truly. But…" She exhaled. "It's just... Leah's death has left so many questions unanswered. It's like reaching the end a book and finding the last chapter has been ripped out."

Perry nodded slowly. "I know what you mean. It still feels unfinished, in a way."

"I can't wait, Simon. I'll start menu planning straight away…" Sam's voice was becoming more distinct as Simon walked over to join them. "…and I'll send you over my ideas tomorrow."

"Right, I'd better let you go, mucker," Simon said, bringing the phone back to his face. "We've got a bit more nosing around to do. You and your mum are going to love it here."

"Okay. I'll see you at the grand opening then!" Sam replied.

Bea looked at Perry and frowned. He shrugged. They both looked at Simon. He turned the screen around so Bea could see her son. "I'll tell you later," Simon mouthed from behind the phone.

"Bye, Perry! See you next weekend!" Perry waved. "Bye, Daisy!" Daisy barked, her sharp yap echoing off the walls as she jumped up to try to lick the phone screen. Sam laughed.

"Goodbye, darling," Bea said as she bent down slightly to wave. "Love you, Sam."

"Love you too, Mum." He waved, then the screen went blank. A hollow pit opened up in Bea's heart, as it did every time she had to say goodbye to her son.

"Grand opening?" Perry looked at Simon, an eyebrow raised.

"Ah, yes." Simon turned to Bea, a slightly apologetic tone in his voice. "Er, Sam wants to host a small party to celebrate you moving in to your first home together. A small do. Just us, Fred, Summer, your parents, Sarah, John, his cousins, Fitzwilliam, Ryan, oh, and Archie, if his parents allow him."

Bea stifled a groan. She would much rather have a low-key moving in, but Sam was much more like his father. James had loved to entertain. When they'd lived here together before he'd died, they'd often hosted drinks parties and lavish dinners for local friends and weekend guests.

"I told him that if you agreed," Simon continued, studying Bea's face for signs of her compliance as he handed her the mobile phone, "then Ryan and I will help with the food."

She smiled. Her heart swelling with a mix of pride and an odd sense of longing. James would be pleased to know their home would once again be filled with fun and laughter.

"Simon," Perry said, capturing his husband's attention. "Bea's feeling a little undone by all the loose ends around Vera's death. She's missing that definitive 'whodunnit' moment that we usually have when everything is revealed and we know all."

"Ah, the satisfaction of the puzzle solved." Simon scratched his beard thoughtfully. "Perhaps we should give Steve a ring? He might have more details by now to fill us in on."

Bea felt a twinge of guilt for sounding so dissatisfied when she had so much to be grateful for, but Simon's suggestion sparked a glimmer of hope. Previous cases they had been involved in had come to a satisfying conclusion. Every piece eventually had slotted into its rightful place, leaving little room for doubt or speculation. The ambiguity in this case was an itch she couldn't scratch, and it was driving her mad.

"Could we?" she asked Simon. "I hate to trouble him, but…"

"Say no more," Simon assured her as he moved to the breakfast bar and snapped up his phone. Bea and Perry moved to join him.

Simon dialled a number, then set it down on the counter. "Steve, mate, it's Simon," he announced into the phone. "I'm with Perry and Lady Beatrice. We were hoping you might have a moment to bring us up to date with the Vera Bolt murder case. Have CID interviewed Shelly Black yet?"

"Hey, mucker. Hi Perry, my lady," CID Steve said, his voice resonating from the phone's speaker. "Let me pull up my notes here... Ah, yeah. Mike interviewed Mrs Black in the hospital a short while ago. Right, so Shelly said that after she and Leah had had their meeting with Vera, Leah was visibly upset by some comments Vera had made. She said it got quite personal."

Bea leaned forward, her brow furrowed as she absorbed what he was saying. *Personal? Why was Vera being especially mean to Leah?*

"Oh yes. Here's something we didn't know. Apparently, Leah and Vera were more than just colleagues; they shared a home together. As a couple, you know. Except Shelly mentioned they'd had a major falling out before they came back to film this series, and Vera had ended the relationship. She'd told Leah to leave their house, so she was having to stay with her parents."

"Vera threw her out?" Perry quirked an eyebrow, exchanging a glance with Bea. *Well, that would give Leah a strong motive to want to harm her.*

"Yes, unceremoniously, I gather," Steve confirmed. "Leah wasn't coping very well with the rejection Shelly said. Okay, so here's her account of what happened that day. They were baking together—Shelly and Leah, that is—but at around five to eleven, Leah stepped out for some air and returned about ten minutes later."

"And how did she seem when she returned?" Simon asked, resting his elbows on the counter as he leaned over the phone.

"Shelly said Leah seemed composed and quite normal, but after, when they learnt about Vera's death, Leah became frantic, insisting that they vouch for each other, pointing out to Shelly that they would both be suspects if not."

"So they gave each other an alibi to evade suspicion," Bea said.

"Exactly," Steve agreed. "Although at the time, Shelly claims she believed Leah was innocent too, so they were just doing each other a favour to make life easier. Shelly said she thought at the time that Summer was guilty and that was that. But then after Summer was released, Shelly got cold feet and suggested to Leah that they come clean to the police about everything."

"So she still thought Leah was innocent at that stage?" Perry's voice held a note of scepticism, his blue eyes locked on the phone as if he could will more answers from it.

"So she claims. But Leah wouldn't hear of it. She was adamant they'd be fine if they just stuck to their story. Then this morning," Steve went on, "Shelly went to Leah's room and found her packing, ready to flee. She was upset and ran back to her own room. Leah followed her, and that's when she attacked Shelly."

Bea's stomach clenched. She could almost picture the scene: Shelly, mild-mannered and compliant, facing the betrayal of someone she trusted. Leah, cornered and desperate, trying to silence her.

Perry cleared his throat. "Will Shelly face charges as an accessory?"

"I think it's unlikely," Steve replied. "Given the circumstances, we're treating her as another of Leah's victims. She should be released from the hospital tomorrow."

"Thanks, mate. I'll speak to you later," Simon said as he disconnected the call. He looked up, meeting Bea's gaze with an unspoken question in his eyes.

She smiled. "Thank you, that helps."

Her phone buzzed against the fabric of her jeans. Rich's name flashed on the screen as she extracted it from her pocket.

Rich: *Spicer coming to Hope Cottage to say goodbye. Care to join us?*

"Seems I'm wanted elsewhere," she said as she typed a simple, *Yes*, in reply. "Perry, why don't you show Simon what we've done upstairs, and I'll see you both tomorrow? Just let Fraser know when you're done. He'll lock up."

The two men nodded as Bea called Daisy to her. The dog, sensing an outing, wagged her tail expectantly.

———

The brisk wind tousled Beatrice's auburn hair as she approached Hope Cottage, Daisy prancing excitedly at her side. The gravel crunched in front of her as a black BMW came around the corner and ground to a halt at the curb. Two figures emerged into the late afternoon light.

Daisy bounded towards them, her tail wagging as she veered around Saunders and ran straight to Spicer. Bea smiled to herself. Daisy was an excellent judge of character. As Rich appeared at the door, Daisy abandoned Spicer and went hurtling in through the open doorway as if it was her own home. *Daisy!*

Bea reached the top of the path at the same time as Saunders. "My lady," he said with the smug air of someone who'd just won a prize he didn't deserve. He held out his arm and let her go ahead.

"Bea," Rich greeted her with a nod, his brown eyes harbouring a softness that made her heart flutter.

"Rich," she said, feeling a little breathless as she stepped into the warm embrace of the cottage, the scent of fresh coffee wrapping around her like a familiar shawl.

"Drinks?" Rich offered as they followed him through the hall and into the sitting room.

"None for us, I'm afraid," Saunders said, his voice grating on Bea's nerves already. "We're on a tight schedule to get back to Surrey this evening—"

Good! She'd be happy to see the back of the bullish muscle-man who had turned out to be as useful as a chocolate teapot.

"—now that the case is closed," Saunders continued, puffing out his chest, smug satisfaction oozing from every pore.

Is he really that delusional? Doesn't he realise that without Spicer and Rich, he'd have never caught the right person?

She could no longer bear looking at his conceited round face with his silly pointy ears, so she shifted her gaze to Spicer. "So do you think Leah knew about the money?"

Spicer pressed her lips into a line. "It's hard to know for sure," she admitted. "I didn't find any evidence to suggest that she—"

"Of course she did!" Saunders barked. "Money—that was her motive!"

You would say that. It's the easy answer! But Bea wasn't so sure. "Or perhaps it was more personal," she suggested to Spicer, completely ignoring Saunders. "Maybe Leah grew tired of Vera's treatment of her but tried to make peace with her one last time. But when Vera dismissed her again, no doubt harshly, passion took over."

Saunders scoffed, shaking his head. "You've been reading too many detective novels, Lady Beatrice. Love doesn't get people killed, money does."

"Um." *I can't be bothered to argue with you.* She caught Rich's gaze. He winked at her. She stifled a smile.

"Well, goodbye then, Fitzwilliam. I'll no doubt see you when you're back at work," Saunders declared briskly, striding towards the door with a finality that Bea was grateful for.

"Thank you, both of you." Spicer's gratitude was genuine, her blue eyes meeting theirs in a silent acknowledgment of their shared journey. "We couldn't have done this without your help."

"Sergeant!" Saunders' impatient call echoed from outside.

Spicer rolled her eyes. "Take care," she said, her smile lingering before she turned to follow her boss.

"Are you going to stay for a coffee?" Rich asked, a smile tugging at the corners of his mouth as he glanced over at Daisy, who was curled up on the sofa, gently snoring.

"It would appear so," Bea said, following his gaze.

39

---

10 PM, THURSDAY 22 APRIL

The gentle lapping of water against the porcelain sides of the bathtub was the only sound in the softly lit bathroom. Bea lay submerged up to her neck, her hair piled high on the top of her head, a few red tendrils clinging to the dampened surface of her skin.

The heat enveloped her, seeping into every pore and untying the knots of tension that had gathered in her shoulders. Normally she wasn't a bath person; the efficiency of a shower appealed to her more. But occasionally, if she had a tricky problem to work through or her brain felt overcrowded, she found soaking in the hot water allowed her mind to open fully. Thoughts flowed through like a wave, allowing her to sift through them and let the unimportant ones go out the other side: *the empty knife block…the closed door…the open door…Rich's dazzling smile…*

Her heart fluttered, an inconvenient reminder of feelings she didn't have time to explore.

Concentrate, Bea.

She closed her eyes and trailed her fingers in the warm

water. *Isla…family…the open door…towels…the way Rich's brown eyes crinkled when he—*

Her eyes sprung open. *Come on, Bea. Focus!*

She sunk deeper until the water kissed her chin. She slowly closed her eyes again. *Shelly's bathroom…the closed door…white chef's jackets…gloves…toiletries…Rich's leather jacket hugging his well-built frame…*

She groaned, opening her eyes to the stark white ceiling. *Really?*

But the warmth of the bath had worked its magic, coaxing clarity from the chaos of clues. Something clicked in her mind, a gear snugly fitting into place. *The bathroom!* She couldn't quite seize the fully formed thought, which was as slippery as a bar of soap under water, but it was there, hiding within the shadows of her subconscious.

She needed to see Shelly again.

Her fingers, pruned from their watery deliberation, pressed against the edges of the tub as she hoisted herself out of the water.

"I need to tell Rich," she muttered, reaching for the fluffy towel on the rack.

Realisation hit her.

Towels in the bath!

She wrapped herself up and padded across the tiled floor. She went into her bedroom and grabbed her mobile phone from the bedside table. Daisy, lying diagonally across the bed, stirred, her legs extending out in a full stretch before she sighed and returned to the same position she'd been in before.

Bea's fingers tapped out a message on the screen.

Bea: *I need to talk to Shelly tomorrow morning. Can you come with me to the hotel?*

. . .

Her pulse quickened at the thought, a symphony of anxiety and anticipation playing in her chest. *What if I'm wrong?*

Her phone emitted a soft *ding.*

Rich: *Is this a woman's intuition thing?*

Bea laughed. He'd teased her so many times about her woman's intuition, but it seemed he was coming around to the idea of not immediately dismissing it. It had certainly helped them solve some of their previous cases.

Bea: *I guess so!*

Rich: *Then yes, I'll come with you.*

A smile teased the corners of her mouth. What had Summer said? *Always in my corner...*

40

THE NEXT DAY, 10 AM, FRIDAY 23 APRIL

Perry watched, a hint of irritation in his eyes as Peter Tappin bustled over to their table with the eagerness of a man who had spotted royalty.

The cafe owner's voice was a little too loud in the quiet morning buzz of Tappin's Tea Room. "I hope you enjoyed your breakfast this morning, Simon. The full English is always a solid decision, I must say," Peter proclaimed, whisking away Simon's empty plate.

"Thanks, Peter. It was spot on as usual," Simon replied with a gracious smile.

Perry traced the rim of his coffee cup —the ceramic cool against his manicured fingers— and allowed himself a silent chuckle. The irony wasn't lost on him; for all of his sharp suits and slick boots, it was Simon's rugged charm that commanded attention in this quaint establishment.

His gaze shifted back to Simon. He took in his husband's chunky frame and the way his well-trimmed beard moved when he spoke. There was a certain dishevelled grace about Simon that Perry found endlessly endearing. It was in moments like these, sitting across from each other in Simon's favourite corner of Tappin's Tea, that Perry felt a surge of pride. *I'm actually married to this man—this wonderfully genuine soul who can draw people in with a simple smile and a hearty laugh.*

"Can I get you anything else?" Peter asked, his tone suggesting he was ready to hop to the kitchen and back if Simon so much as required a grain of salt.

"We're good, thanks," Perry said before Simon could answer. But his words seemed to drift into the air, unacknowledged as Peter simply nodded towards Simon and turned on his heels.

"Did I accidentally put my invisibility cloak on again this morning?" Perry pouted.

Simon looked around the room. "Who said that?" he asked, his brown eyes twinkling.

The corners of Perry's mouth twitched upwards. He appreciated Simon's gentle ribbing; it was a sign of solidarity in the face of Peter's continued snubbing.

"It's because you blend in so well," Simon said, reaching across the table to give Perry's hand a quick squeeze as he looked up and down at his husband's roll neck blue cashmere jumper, his cream jeans, and his brown designer boots.

As they settled back into their seats grinning, Perry picked up his latte and let his eyes linger on the comings and goings outside the window of the cafe. His thoughts drifted to the case that had consumed their conversations of late. Despite CID Steve's briefing yesterday, Perry still didn't feel he knew enough about how or why Leah had really killed Vera to feel satisfied like he had after previous cases had closed.

"Roisin's just sent an update," Simon murmured, engrossed in his phone, his eyebrows knit in concentration as he read the text message from his best friend. The tenor of his voice dropped with concern. "It seems there's no trace of Shelly's blood on Leah, which is odd, considering—"

"Considering she attacked her," Perry finished for him.

Bea had said there had been a lot of blood when Shelly had been stabbed. Surely some of that would have transferred to her would-be killer?

"Exactly," Simon said, locking eyes with Perry before he looked back down at his screen again. "And there's more. Leah was covered in bruises from the fall, but, here's the kicker, they found no gloves on her. However, there wasn't a single print of hers on the knife used to attack Shelly. But Shelly's prints are all over it."

A shiver ran down Perry's spine, his mind whirring into action. He sipped his coffee, the warmth doing little to soothe the chill of doubt creeping up his core. "It doesn't add up, does it?" he said, a frown creasing his smooth forehead. "I get why Shelly's prints are on the knife; she must have pulled it out, but if Leah didn't wear gloves, why aren't her prints on it too?"

Mulling over this perplexing piece of the puzzle, Perry looked to the window, where his eyes caught a familiar figure sauntering past, her ginger hair unmistakable even from behind the glass. *Isla.*

"Simon, it's Isla." Perry's hand reached out and rapped on the pane. "Isla!" The young woman paused at the noise. "Come in!" he mouthed through the glass, gesturing emphatically.

A throat cleared loudly over by the counter, and Perry looked around to receive a disapproving glare from Peter Tappin. *Whatever!*

The bell above the door tinkled as Isla stepped into the tea shop and weaved her way through the hodgepodge of lace-covered tables to join them by the window.

"Hi," she said, her eyes darting around the room.

"Come and join us," Perry said cheerily, pulling out a chair for her at their table. "Would you like a coffee?"

"Er." She hesitated, looking down at Perry's half-drunk latte as she sat down.

"Or maybe a hot chocolate?" Simon suggested. "It has marshmallows, whipped cream, and a chocolate flake."

Oh my goodness, that sounds good. Perry licked his lips.

"Oh, yes, please!" Isla replied, her eyes lighting up.

Simon looked around and waved at Peter, who came scurrying over. "A hot chocolate with all the works, please." Then he caught Perry's eye. "Better make that two, please, Peter."

Perry beamed at him.

"So how did your chat with Spicer go yesterday morning?" Simon asked.

"Fine," Isla replied, a faint tremor in her voice. "You were right. She was very kind."

"And did you tell her everything?" Perry asked breezily.

"Er, yes. Why wouldn't I?"

Taken aback by her defensiveness, Perry looked at Simon. *What did I do?*

Simon stepped in. "I'm sure they were very grateful, Isla."

"Y-yes, I think so," Isla replied. "The sergeant asked me to stay in the area for a couple more days while they investigated the case, but then last night I got a message to say I could leave when I wanted to as the case was now closed."

"Yes. We were just talking about that," Simon said.

Perry leaned forward, his voice soft so as not to upset her again. "It was Leah Goldrich. She killed Vera Bolt and attacked her friend Shelly at their hotel yesterday. She—"

The colour drained from Isla's face. "At the Fenshire Inn? My hotel?" She gasped, her eyes wide with horror.

Perry frowned. He'd had no idea where Isla was staying. Simon nodded.

"Were they the ladies I saw...with their cases, leaving a room along my corridor yesterday morning?" Isla's voice quivered as she wrung her hands together.

"Just the one lady. Leah. She attacked Shelly, then fled with a case down the back stairs, but—"

"No," Isla corrected him with a sudden snap of confidence. "I actually saw two ladies, both with cases, heading towards the back stairs as I got out of the lift."

Perry exchanged a hurried glance with Simon.

"Can you describe them, please, Isla?"

Perry listened, his head to one side as Isla described Shelly and Leah to a tee.

The implications spun in his head like garden furniture caught in a tornado. *They were both fleeing? Shelly didn't tell the police that. Had Leah suddenly change her mind and attacked Shelly, or—*

"Bea and Fitzwilliam," Simon said sharply. "We need to tell them."

———

Rich shot a quick look over at Bea, who was sitting next to him on the back seat of the Daimler. With her legs crossed, she peered out of the window, looking poised and regal. *She's in a world of her own.*

This had been confirmed to him a short while ago when she'd barely flinched as they'd driven through the hordes of press surrounding the main gate at Francis Court, seemingly oblivious to the cacophony of flashlights and shouting.

When she'd picked him up from the cottage, she'd been vague about why she needed to see Shelly again, simply telling him she was still trying to figure something out. She'd said very little since. But knowing her as he did, he knew that whatever it was, she'd squashed her normal instinct to go running off on her own and tackle it. Instead she'd asked him to come with her. *This is progress,* he thought, shifting slightly to accommodate Daisy, who had moved to rest her head on Bea's lap.

Bea stroked the little dog's head gently.

I wish I was Daisy right now, he thought, not for the first time. To feel her soft hands as they tenderly ran through his hair, then— *Richard! Get a grip.*

As they approached the hotel in Fawstead, Bea turned away from the window and caught his eye. She smiled lazily at him. *Oh my goodness, that smile…*

She tapped the screen on her phone. "I'd better let Perry know where I am. I'm supposed to be meeting him at the house shortly so we can decide what needs moving from my apartment to The Dower House." She tapped out a quick message, then dropped the phone next to her on the seat. "Thanks for coming, Rich. I have some details in Shelly's story that I just want to clarify."

Her green eyes held his, a silent plea in them for him to just agree and not ask too many questions. As he lost himself in her gaze, he knew that right at this moment, he would do anything she asked of him.

A cough from the driver's seat broke their connection. Ward got out and opened the back door. Rich jumped out and pivoted around to offer Bea his hand. She took it with a smile, his hand enveloping hers. *I'll keep you safe, Bea. Whether or not you want me to!*

"Thank you, Ward. We won't be long, I don't think. Can you wait?"

"Of course, my lady."

She dropped Rich's hand. "Can I leave Daisy with you too? The hotel's not keen on dogs."

"Yes, Lady Rossex. I'll look after her."

Bea beamed at the older man, then looked at Rich. "Let's go, shall we?"

———

"Blast!" Perry said as he read Bea's text message. "She's at the hotel. She's gone to talk to Shelly."

"What?" Simon said, raking his hands through his short brown hair. "She's onto something."

Perry's heart jumped. "If Shelly—" He glanced at Isla, who had stopped mid-way through devouring her chocolate flake and was now staring at them both with a look of concern. "I mean, if what Roisin said about the fingerprints is true, then…you know, she shouldn't tackle Shelly on her own," he said, his wide eyes open as he tried to convey his concerns to his husband without alarming Isla.

"What's going on?" she said through a mouthful of chocolate.

What do I say? That my best friend is about to confront someone who may have been leading us all up the garden path, and I'm worried that someone will get hurt because they always do? And somewhere along the line, I will end up having to run. In these boots!! "Er, nothing for you to be concerned about," he said softly.

Simon, who he now noticed had his phone to his ear, shook his head. "I can't get hold of her. It's ringing out." He rose. "I'll run home and get the car while you settle the—"

"My car's just across the road if you want me to take you somewhere," Isla offered, downing the rest of her drink.

"I don't think—" Perry began.

"Great. That would save us a lot of time," Simon interrupted. He turned around and waved at Peter. "Can we have the bill, please, Peter?"

Perry studied Isla as she brushed cream off her chin with a paper napkin. He liked her. But he couldn't help feeling that she was orchestrating her involvement with them and this case somehow.

———

Rich switched his phone to silent as they stepped out of the lift and put it in the back pocket of his jeans. He didn't want a call to disturb them while they were talking to Shelly. When they reached the third floor, he allowed Bea to go ahead.

Does she have a plan? Or is this merely a fishing expedition?

He wished she would share what was going on with him.

"Bea," he said as they turned the corner and made their way along the corridor to Shelly's room. "What exactly are we doing here?"

She carried on walking until she reached Shelly's room. She stopped and turned to smile at him. "Sorry, Rich. Yes, I should probably tell you." She cleared her throat. "I think Shelly killed Vera and then pushed Leah down to stairs so that Leah would take the blame."

What the—

Bea reached out and knocked on the door.

41

A FEW SECONDS LATER, FRIDAY 23 APRIL

Bea's knuckles had barely grazed the wood when the hotel room door swung open abruptly, catching her slightly off guard. Shelly stood holding the door handle, shock etched on her face.

"Oh...Lady Beatrice. I wasn't expecting you—"

"We just have a few questions to ask you, please, if you don't mind." Bea took a step forward, forcing Shelly to retreat into the confines of her room.

"Bea!" Rich hissed by her side.

"Oh, and this is Detective Chief Inspector Fitzwilliam." She didn't dare look at Rich, knowing she had tricked him into this confrontation with Shelly, with only a few seconds of warning.

"Er, come in," Shelly stammered, a hand fluttering to her chest.

Scanning the room, Bea wasn't surprised to see a case situated prominently on the hotel bed, flanked by a smaller bag. It was that same bag, Bea noted with a tightening grip on her resolve, that she'd spotted in the bathroom just the day before. *I must be right.* "Oh, are you leaving, Shelly?" she asked, allowing the question to hang between them—an accusation veiled in a polite inquiry.

Rich had moved further into the room. He leaned against a chest of drawers and folded his arms across his chest. He looked intimidating. Bea swallowed, not sure if he was playing a role or just mad at her. His presence was nonetheless reassuring.

"The hospital suggested rest to ensure the wound heals properly. So I'll be off work for a few weeks, but I'll return to the show once I'm cleared by my doctor." There was a rehearsed tone to her assurance, like a line recalled from a well-worn script.

Bea's gaze dropped to Shelly's attire, the green tracksuit hanging loose on the woman's petite frame. It wasn't possible to see just how bad Shelly's wound was, but Bea suspected it was nowhere near as deep and as deadly as it had looked when she'd found her yesterday. Bea smiled to herself. She'd done a little research this morning over breakfast and had discovered that even superficial stab wounds could bleed profusely, but if properly and promptly treated, they weren't life threatening at all.

"Given Vera's royalties and the lump-sum inheritance you now have, work seems rather optional, doesn't it?" Bea watched Shelly closely, each word a gentle prod to see if she could break Shelly's fragile facade.

A flush crept up the woman's neck. "The will... Yes, the police mentioned it. It's a lot to take in. I keep forgetting." Her tone was light, but her eyes darted about, betraying her anxiety.

Bea's eyes narrowed slightly, her mind churning. Shelly's performance was compelling, almost enough to make her question her own deductions. *Almost.* The memory of the bathroom scene played across her mind's eye, an undeniable contradiction to Shelly's current portrayal of an exit due to hospital advice. *No.* Bea reassured herself. *I'm confident I'm right.*

"Why were your things packed yesterday, Shelly? When I fetched a towel from your bathroom, your bag was there, ready to go."

"I don't know what you mean." Shelly's response was swift, a little too swift.

"Your toiletries weren't out, and the towels were laid in the bath—typically how one leaves things when planning to check out."

For a moment, Shelly froze like a rabbit caught in the headlights. Her lips parted, but no sound emerged. Bea's heart thumped. *Have I pushed her far enough?* She held her breath.

Suddenly Rich stepped forward, his posture rigid. There was an air of authority around him that commanded attention. "Shelly." His voice was low and steady. "Did you kill Vera and Leah?"

The question, blunt in its directness, shattered any pretence of civility. Shelly's blue eyes darted towards her bag resting on the bed by her travel case. In a movement that betrayed a startling agility, she lunged for it, plunging her hand inside.

Bea's breath hitched in her chest, surprise rendering her momentarily still.

With a flourish that would have impressed a magician, Shelly withdrew a gleaming knife, its blade catching the sunlight streaming through the hotel window.

Bea felt her heart thud against her ribs. *Oh my goodness! Where on earth does she keep finding these knives?* Bea hadn't factored in that Shelly would have a deadly weapon on her. She'd reasoned that Shelly was a good four inches shorter than her and unlikely to have done the kidnap prevention training that Bea had done. Based on that, she'd been confident she could take Shelly if the woman had tried to run. And of course she had Rich too. *Now what are we going to do?* With Shelly, knife in hand, positioned with the door at her back, she and Rich were scuppered.

I need to keep her talking while I figure out what to do. "Did you do it for the money, Shelly?" Bea's voice was calm, belying the rapid drumbeat of her pulse.

Shelly's laugh, when it came, was a hollow sound. "Money," she scoffed, the word dripping with disdain. "Do you think this is all about the money?"

"Then what *is* it all about?"

"Money was never the end," Shelly insisted, her eyes glinting with a fervour that belied her usual mild demeanour. "It was about recognition from her for all the hard work I'd done. It was about taking back what was mine by right. After all these years of her scathing criticism, of all her promises, of her using me time and time again. I'd had enough of her and the way she treated me. And Leah. And everyone else. I mean, who did she think she was?" She took a deep breath, hardly able to keep a check on the torrent of pent-up emotions she had now released.

"I begged her to stop. Stop talking to Leah and me like that. Leah was so upset. Stop using me to make money." She paused. "We had an agreement, you know. She would front it all. The public loved her. Her name and face sell. I've never wanted to be in the spotlight. But she was supposed to share the profits with me. After all, I did all the work."

For a moment Bea's mind paused trying to look for a solution. *What's she talking about? All what work?*

"That hazelnut and chocolate sauce recipe was mine. It took me ages to refine. She didn't even know the secret ingredient! She was shocked when I wrote it down for the manu-facturer. 'Sherry?' she said, sticking her nose up. 'Why not brandy?' I told her I'd tried brandy, but it was too bitter. Sherry was sweeter. She'd tasted it hundreds of times and had never worked it out! That's when I knew something was wrong."

Bea frowned. Was that the sauce that had recently been sold for over three million? *Ah, does that explain the money Vera left Shelly in her will?*

"It's still incredible to think that she got away with it for so long," Shelly continued. "Seventeen years, in fact. That's why she needed me."

Bea shook her head. *What's she talking about now?* This stream of consciousness coming out of the baker was chaotic but at the same time compelling. Bea knew she should work out a way for them to escape. *But this is too good…*

"I was so excited when I saw the advert for a food researcher. Vera was charming at the interview, explaining that she'd been asked to write a cookbook to accompany her TV show *Vera Bolt Bakes*. It was a very popular show. She really was the Queen of Bakes back then. I was so flattered when she offered me the job. I was in my mid-forties, and my husband of twenty years had died six months before. He was a butcher."

Ah, her skill with knives.

"We had no children, but he never really wanted me to work. He was old-fashioned like that. I helped in the shop occasionally, but as far as he was concerned, a woman's place was in the home. So I cooked and baked. That was my life. WI. Church. Charity events. I baked for everything and anyone. When he died, I was left with the house and a small amount of savings, but no income. Cooking and baking were all I knew. I was so grateful to Vera for giving me a chance."

Her eyes glistened with unshed tears, then she sniffed, seemingly pulling herself out of her pity party. "All the way through that first book, I was pleased at how encouraging she was to me. She'd hand the spoon to me and ask my opinion. And when I gave it, she would nod and say, 'Good, you picked that up,' then she would make the adjustment. I was flattered that she valued my input so greatly. We were a team. I continued to help her work on new bakes for the TV show and was as thrilled as she was when the show got renewed for a second series."

Her face clouded over, the earlier tears replaced with a steely glare. "I was so stupid!" she spat out. "I was happy she cared enough to help me. Of course, I know now she didn't care at all. She was just using me." Her hand tightened on the knife.

Okay, I really need to focus on getting us out of here…

"A few months later was when I made the hazelnut and chocolate sauce for the first time. I was testing a new chocolate pudding recipe for a guest slot on *Sunday Roast* Vera had coming up. I thought I would offer her an alternative sauce to the toffee one she'd suggested. I tested and tested the sauce at home until I was happy, then I made it for her. She was a bit put out at first that I hadn't consulted her about an alternative sauce, but her agent, who was at the house that day, tried it and said it was amazing. Vera asked me to make some more so she could take it onto the show the next day. She was a guest chef. Ironically, Mark Jacobs was the host of *Sunday Roast* back then. She made the cake on the show, then brought out the sauce, which she said she'd made earlier. Mark loved it. The celebrity guest loved it so much, she told her she should bottle it and sell it. I was so proud."

She gave a satisfied smile, then continued, "A few weeks later, Vera and the show's producer told me they wanted to offer me the job of lead home economist on *Vera Bolt Bakes*. It was a good job. I would be employed by the production company; it came with sick pay and pension, things Vera said she couldn't afford to offer me. She stressed I would still work with her just like before. Again, I was so flattered to have been picked for the role."

She shrugged. "Vera took a break for a few months in between filming, but when she got back, she was different. She seemed to have lost some of her passion for baking. She was distant and more snappy than usual. We started on the new series, and more and more frequently, she asked me to 'suggest' recipes. Then she would use them, rarely making any changes. They asked her to do a second cookbook for the series. When I came to go through the proof, I remember thinking most of these recipes are mine. I mentioned it to her, jokingly saying that she should share the royalties with me."

Ah. So that explains the royalty payments. In death, Vera clearly wanted to make things right.

"Vera laughed too, then pointed out that without her name, no one would buy the book. And, of course, she was right. She arranged a salary increase for me though, so I didn't pursue it."

Shelly stopped and let out a deep breath. She shifted her weight slightly. "Just as filming for that third series was wrapping up, she asked me for the recipe for the hazelnut and chocolate sauce. She said she wanted to make it for a friend. I was cautious. Whenever she'd needed some before, she'd always asked me to make it for her. I said, half joking, 'Surely you can make it yourself by now; you've tasted it enough.' She got shirty with me. I was shocked. I was used to her sniping and grumbling, but that had always seemed harmless enough. In fact, she reminded me of my husband; he was like that too. I was used to it. But this was different. She was angry but seemed desperate at the same time. For the first time, I stood up to her. I said no. I said I was fed up with her using my sauce and passing it off as her own. And that's when she told me she'd arranged for a company to manufacture and bottle the sauce, and they needed the recipe.

"She'd spent the time she'd been off trying to recreate the sauce, but everyone she'd tested it on had said it wasn't the same. That's when she offered me a deal. If I gave her the recipe, she would fund all the processing, packing and marketing costs, then share the remaining profit with me. She said it had to be in her name as that's what would sell the product."

A smile flittered across her face. "It was exciting, you know. And I needed to do some work on the house. That would pay for it. I thought maybe I could even afford a new kitchen. So I agreed. I gave her the recipe. That's when she made the comment about using brandy. I challenged her immediately. 'How can you have spent so long trying to recreate this and not know there was no brandy in it?' I asked. She crossed her arms and refused to answer. I snatched back the recipe and told her the deal was off. And that's when she told me."

Told you what? Bea let out a slow breath. *This is better than a television soap opera.*

"She said that three years ago, she'd been in Brazil filming a segment for a TV show about South American desserts. When she returned, she was ill. She had a fever, and she lost her appetite. She wanted to sleep the whole time. It turned out, she'd picked up a virus over there. It took her three weeks to recover enough to eat again, but when she did, she couldn't taste anything. She was worried, but the doctors said it was most likely a temporary thing. So she waited. Then the BBC, who had been impressed when they'd seen a preview of her short film, offered her her own TV show. She was worried because of her inability to taste. so she started looking for a food researcher to help her. A second set of taste buds, if you like. And there I was."

She huffed. "Which was just as well as her ability to taste never came back. I felt sorry for her back then. She was so unlucky to lose something so vital to her career through no fault of her own. So I gave her back the recipe. She promised me we would make money. Every time I asked, she told me that sales hadn't paid back the costs yet. She said it might take years. So I waited."

42

MEANWHILE, FRIDAY 23 APRIL

"It's just ringing out too!" Simon leaned over from the front seat of Isla's car.

Perry's mouth went dry. Simon hadn't been able to get hold of Bea, and now he couldn't get Fitzwilliam on the phone either. *Is he with her, at least?*

Perry clutched at the neck of his sweater. *Are we nearly there yet?* A wave of nausea washed over him. Was it worry or the result of being a back-seat passenger?

To Perry's relief, Isla slowed down and pulled in behind a sleek black car. "That's Bea's Daimler!" Perry cried. He scrabbled with his seatbelt while Simon and Isla jumped out. Simon ran towards the car in front while Isla reached back and pulled her seat forward. Feeling like a contortionist, Perry unfurled himself and stepped outside with a sigh of relief. "Thanks, Isla," he said as he stretched his back.

Just ahead of them, he could see Simon leaning in, talking to someone in the driver's seat of the Daimler. *Ward!* Perry hurried towards them, Isla following behind.

Woof! Perry looked down and spotted Daisy on the back seat, now pawing at the side window to get his attention.

"Bea and Fitzwilliam have gone into the hotel to talk to Shelly," Simon told him. "Ward says they've been gone about twenty minutes."

Simon moved out of the way as the driver's door opened, and Ward got out. "Mr Juke. Hello, sir. I'm getting a little concerned as her ladyship said they wouldn't be long, and I can only park here for thirty minutes."

Perry suppressed a sigh. A potential parking fine was the last thing on *his* mind. "I think we'd best go up and see what's going on, don't you?"

Simon and Ward nodded. Perry raised an eyebrow. The older man lifted his chin. "If her ladyship is in trouble, then I'd like to help."

"What about Daisy?" Isla asked, her hand resting on the window as she stared into the back of the car where Daisy sat on the seat, her tail waving from side to side.

"We'll take her with us," Simon said.

Ward coughed. "I believe the hotel doesn't allow dogs, sir."

Well, you stay with her! Perry bit his tongue. "Er, well, if one of us carries her, I'm sure it will be alright."

"I will," Isla said excitedly.

"Great!" Perry yanked open the door and, grabbing Daisy, unceremoniously dumped her in Isla's arms. "Right, let's go."

They entered the lobby and hastily made their way to the lifts.

"Er, excuse me!" a young man cried out from the reception area. "I'm afraid you can't bring a dog in here."

Blast!

"This way!" Isla cried, and running past the lift, she pointed to a door. "The stairs. It's only three floors."

Perry halted. *Stairs? In these boots?*

"Excuse me!" The voice was now shouting.

Blast!

"Come on!" Simon cried as he pulled open the door and waited for them to go through. Isla was first, Daisy close to her chest, then Ward, who looked more spritely than Perry had given him credit for. Perry followed them both, his boots already pinching a tad by the time he reached the first half landing.

"Only five more to go!" Simon said as he overtook him.

Perry gritted his teeth. *Going upstairs is worse than running!*

43

MEANWHILE UPSTAIRS, FRIDAY 23
APRIL

Bea's mind raced. *Should we just rush her?* Shelly couldn't stab both her and Rich at the same time, could she? But Shelly knew her way around a knife—that controlled jab at Vera, then turning the blade on herself in calculated self-harm. She could badly hurt one of them. The risk was too great; she needed a better plan.

"Meanwhile, *Vera Bolt Bakes* was a firm favourite." Shelly was in her stride now, continuing to get her story off her chest. "What I couldn't figure out when I watched her was how she looked like she knew what things tasted like. Until I really studied it. I realised that she always waited for the other judge to start, then she would take what they had said and expand on it. She was so skilled at it, no one noticed."

Bea's eyes flickered to Rich, his frame rigid as if he was made of stone. He stared at Shelly as if his life depended on being able to see her at all times. *Well, I guess it does.* But was he totally engrossed in Shelly's story, or was it dredging up memories of his own recent brush with death, and he was paralysed with fear? *Can he respond in time if I make a move?*

Shelly took another deep breath and continued, "Then eight years ago, Vera was asked to judge a new show called *Bake Off Wars*. I was taken on as senior food researcher. That's when I met Leah. No one knew at that time if the format would work, but Leah's youth and enthusiasm was infectious and kept me going. Vera was worried too. *Vera Bolt Bakes* hadn't been recommissioned, so if *BOW* failed, then she would no longer have a regular place on TV."

She gave a dry laugh. "You know, at first Vera and Mark Jacobs worked well together. They had a different style, of course. He was younger, chattier, more encouraging to the contestants. She was the silent, judging presence who gave her verdict in solemn tones. The first season was a slow burner, but by the last episode, the ratings were good, and a second series was commissioned immediately. During that first break, after the series wrapped, was, according to Leah, when her and Vera got together. I never guessed. In fact, when we started filming the second series, Vera seemed to be rather harsh on Leah in my eyes, but when I mentioned it she told me it was just Vera's way of protecting her from any gossip. *BOW* really captured the public's attention during the second series, and by the end of it, everyone knew we had a hit on our hands."

While Shelly glanced down at the floor, a wry smile on her face, Bea edged subtly closer to Rich. Shelly looked up.

Bea froze. Her heart stopped. *Rats!*

Shelly stared at Bea for a moment, then opened her mouth. "Vera told me she'd been asked to do another cookbook and wanted my help. We were in between filming series five and six of *BOW*, and I was happy to take the extra money. Again, I seemed to do a lot of the heavy lifting, and by the time we got to the end of the recipe development stage, I was pretty fed up. We were working at Vera's newly acquired and remodelled country house in the Cotswolds. It has a state-of-the-art kitchen. I remember thinking that Vera must be being very well paid for *BOW*. I resented she was living this life of luxury while I could barely afford to go to the US to visit my sister every year."

She frowned. "I couldn't help but wonder why Leah wasn't the one helping Vera with the book. Then it occurred to me that maybe Leah didn't know about Vera's loss of taste. I subtly tried to find out in my chats with Leah, and eventually, when she told me she did all the cooking at home as Vera felt it was too much like a busman's holiday, I figured out I was right. I was shocked. They'd been together for almost six years. How could Vera have kept it quiet for so long?

It all came to a head one evening when Vera and I were going through the proof for the book. I was getting increasingly angry that eighty percent of the contribution was mine, and yet she would get all the rewards. I wasn't even mentioned by name in the acknowledgements. Leah was in the kitchen cooking when I asked Vera why she hadn't given me any recognition for my contribution. She said I was included in the thank you to her support team and pointed out that I had always said I didn't want fame and fortune. I told her I didn't, but a mention by name in the back of the book was hardly going to give me that. I then told her that as most of the recipes were developed by me, I should actually be credited as co-author and have a share of the royalties. She didn't like that. She shouted I was a nobody, and no one would buy the book if my name was on the front. Leah stepped in and calmed things down. She told Vera that she really should thank me by name for my help on the book. Vera stormed out. Later, I got a text from Leah to say Vera had calmed down and was sorry. She'd agreed to mention me in the acknowledgments. It felt like a victory even if it was only a minor one."

44

AT ABOUT THE SAME TIME, FRIDAY
23 APRIL

Perry's heart was beating out of his chest. *How much longer do these stairs go on for?* He looked up. Simon had disappeared, and Perry hadn't overtaken anyone. *I must be last!*

He winced. His big toes were being hammered against the inside of his super polished boots every time he put his feet down. *Oh, Bea! The things I put up with for you…*

At least the shouting from down below had stopped. The reception guy had obviously decided that it wasn't worth the effort to follow them up the stairs just for a dog. *Knowing my luck, I'll get to the top, and he'll be there with security, ready to throw us out.*

"Only a dozen more steps, Perry." Simon's voiced descended from above like a heavenly personal trainer. "You can do it."

Perry sucked in a deep breath. *Yes, I can!*

Perry burst through the door and hobbled towards the others who had congregated on the landing just outside. "That…

was…more…than…three…floors," he said, his breath ragged as he came to a stop beside them.

Simon reached over and patted him on the shoulder. "Well done!" *Why's he not out of breath?* "Isla says Shelly is in the room next to hers, so the plan is to go there and see if we can hear what's going on."

Perry, slightly bent over with his hand on his hip, nodded. "Okay," he panted. He looked up as Isla skipped ahead, Daisy still in her arms. *Well, what do you expect? She's young.* Following her, Ward, who Perry had worked out must be in his late fifties, if not older, was breathing normally as he walked just behind her. *Oh my goodness! I'm twenty years younger than him, and I can't breathe.*

"Simon," he gasped, stumbling over to his husband, who had hung behind to wait for him. "Next week…I'm going… to join that…fancy gym of yours."

"It's okay. Just take a deep breath and get some oxygen into your brain. The feeling will pass," Simon said, grinning.

With his husband helping, Perry made it to the open door of Isla's room. Limping in, he was surprised to see both Isla and Ward already with their ears to what looked like a connecting door.

He needed to sit down.

Joining Daisy on a small sofa at the end of the bed, Perry fell back onto the couch, the relief of not being on his feet almost making him cry. He tugged his boots off, his toes throbbing to their own beat. *Ahhhhh…..*

Simon had joined the other two now. "What's going on?" Perry whispered.

"I think someone's giving a monologue," Isla whispered back.

"It's Shelly," Simon added, his face pressed against the wood.

Perry rubbed his poor feet as his stomach churned. *Are Bea and Fitzwilliam in there with her?* He swallowed. *Are they in danger?* "Can you hear Bea or Fitzwilliam?" he hissed at Simon.

Simon shook his head.

It was no good. He couldn't just sit here while his friends were possibly in trouble. They needed to call the police, and they needed a plan. *And we need it now!*

45

MEANWHILE NEXT DOOR, FRIDAY 23 APRIL

Bea wanted Shelly to shut up now. What had been quite gripping fifteen minutes ago now seemed like the recounting of an epic saga. *But at least if she's talking, then she's not stabbing anyone.*

Her eyes met Rich's for a fraction of a second, a silent exchange amidst the chaotic retelling of Shelly's life story. His gaze, usually so sharp, now seemed clouded with hesitation. She needed to snap him out of it, to reignite the spark of action.

"It was at the wrap party for season seven that I found out Vera had been deceiving me," Shelly said.

Oh, okay. This might be interesting…

"Leah, without realising the implications, was telling me she and Vera were off travelling around Europe for six weeks, doing a sort of culinary tour. I said I wished I had the money to do something like that. She said it was all thanks to that hazelnut and chocolate sauce of Vera's. Vera had sold the entire operation to a well-known food company who had a deal to supply it to all the major supermarkets. 'She made a fortune,' was what Leah said. I was speechless. I tried to talk to Vera, but she left early, and the next day she ignored a text and a call from me. I sent her a strongly worded email telling her that as she'd sold the business, she could now pay me some money for my input. I said if she didn't, I would consider instructing a lawyer. She replied a week later to tell me we had no contract, so a lawyer wouldn't be interested."

Shelly paused and wiggled her wrist. The blade of the knife caught the light, reminding Bea that although listening to Shelly's story might be tedious, the alternative could be deadly. Shelly caught Bea's eye. Bea gave her a sympathetic nod.

Shelly carried on, "But I wasn't going to let it go, especially when I found out the deal was worth three-point-four million pounds. I wanted my share. The two weeks of rehearsals were so busy, it was impossible for me to talk to Vera privately. And Leah was no help. She and Vera had a falling out. It was something to do with Leah meeting up with an ex-girlfriend whose mother had just died. Vera accused her of cheating. Leah was devastated and was finding it hard to concentrate. I was angry on her behalf. Of course, she wouldn't cheat on Vera, although god knows what she sees… I mean, saw in her.

"Vera, meanwhile, was fairly poisonous towards me and Leah, one time telling us to 'pull our socks up' in front of everyone when we failed to make her recipe completed to her satisfaction in the time given, which was, by the way, at least fifteen minutes short of what it needed to be. Another time, she told everyone at an end-of-day wrap up that Leah and I were letting the show down. Leah took it much worse than I did. I felt bad for her."

Bea sensed a slight movement to her right. Rich had taken a half-step away from her but closer to Shelly's hand that was holding the knife. *Is he getting ready to disarm her?*

"It all came to a head on Monday morning. Vera told us during the production meeting to get our act together, and at our meeting with her in The Tent afterwards, she told us we were both useless and hanging on to our jobs by a thread. When we got back to our practice kitchen, Leah was in tears. She said Vera just wanted to show us she had the power to take our jobs away. I was worried it would be like this for the rest of the series, all the time wondering if I was going to be sacked at any minute. I couldn't live like that. Leah was still crying. She said after all the years she'd been there for Vera, now she was left with no money and no home. We were both so angry at her, we decided to confront her that very minute."

Bea's heart was racing. *Is Shelly about to reveal the moment she killed Vera?*

"We didn't even take time to take off our chef's outfits or remove our hygiene gloves. We stormed off to The Tent. I told Leah I would talk to Vera first, but asked her to wait outside and keep an eye out for anyone."

The person Cleo saw in the corridor was Leah?

"Vera was alone. I asked her how dare she play with my and Leah's lives like we didn't matter. I asked her what gave her the right to deny me my rightful money from the sale of the sauce. She said there were lots of expenses and costs, and therefore there was no profit. But I knew she was lying. No one pays three-point-four million pounds for something that isn't making a profit. I told her we would go to the papers. I would tell them about her taste issue and how she'd been deceiving everyone for all these years. Leah would tell them about their relationship and how Vera had kept it hidden. I told her she would be sorry for treating us like dirt. I turned and headed for the exit."

Shelly had sped up now, the words tumbling out of her mouth. "Vera grabbed me and spun me around. She told me no one would believe nobodies like us. She said she would get us both fired immediately." Shelly's eyes widened, her voice now deadly calm. "I was mad. So mad. I wanted to lash out. I looked around for something to hit her with. And that's when I saw the knife."

Shelly was shaking, her breath now slightly laboured.

Bea caught Rich's eye again. He nodded almost imperceptibly. Her pulse quickened. They understood each other without words; it was almost time.

Shelly shook her head slowly. "I don't really know what happened next. It was so quick. Like it was happening to someone else. I grabbed the kitchen knife with my free arm. I thrust it upwards. It was only when she let go, then moaned, that I realised I'd stabbed her with the knife. She fell to the floor. Blood was gushing over her hand as she clutched her middle. I looked down. The bloody knife was in my hand. I put it in my pocket, then ran."

Shelly's arms were now flailing at her sides, her eyes wild with excitement. "I grabbed Leah and dragged her back to the practice kitchen with me and slammed the door shut. There was blood on my overalls and the gloves. As I told her what had happened, I took the jacket off and put it in a plastic bag. I shoved it back deep in my holdall. Then I stripped off the gloves. I threw them in the sink. I washed my hands. Scrubbed them. Leah was in shock, but I told her to clean the sink. She did that while I went to the bathroom just off our room and was sick."

"Now!" Bea's shout came just as the door rattled with a sudden noise, swinging open with a momentum that seemed to carry the entire world with it. Shelly's face registered shock, her grip faltering for a precious heartbeat.

Adrenaline pulsed through Bea's veins as Simon, Perry, Ward, Isla, and Daisy burst into the room like a whirlwind.

"She's got a knife!" Bea yelled at them, seizing the moment of distraction.

As she launched herself at Shelly, Rich and Simon followed suit, their bodies moving in unspoken synchronisation.

Perry, a blur of motion, flung himself at Isla, pulling her out of harm's way by mere inches as Shelly and her three assailants tumbled to the floor.

The room became a picture of chaos, filled with barking, grunts, shouts, and the scuffle of shoes against carpet. Bea's heart thundered in her chest as she grappled with Shelly, her only thought to immobilise her before that gleaming blade found its mark.

46

TEN MINUTES LATER, FRIDAY 23 APRIL

Bea leaned against the wardrobe, Daisy in her arms, her eyes tracing over the floral wallpaper by the door of Shelly's hotel room, which was now scuffed by the commotion. Outside, the lingering echo of sirens confirmed Shelly's departure with the Fenshire Police. *This is madness,* Bea thought, her brain barely able to process what had happened in the last hour.

A hand on her shoulder made her jump. "Sorry." Rich's voice was full of concern. "I'm just checking you're alright."

She looked up at him and smiled. "I'm shellshocked still but no permanent damage done. You?"

He leaned over and stroked Daisy's head. "I've realised that next time you ask me to go somewhere with you, I need to insist you tell me what I'm letting myself in for before I say yes." He winked.

She grinned. "Sorry about that. I thought if I gave you too much warning, you'd try to change my mind, and I was so sure she was the killer. But I know how you like proof before—"

"You go barging in and accuse someone of murder?" he asked, still a tinge of amusement in his voice.

"Actually," she said, tilting her head to one side. "I believe it was *you* who did that."

He chuckled. "Okay, you've got me there. I rather let my impatience get the better of me."

His eyes held hers with an intensity that made her feel both seen and steadied.

"Seriously, you did well," he said. "Timing is everything, and you seized it perfectly."

"And thank you for letting me make the call," she replied, wrapped in the warmth of appreciation for his trust in her judgment.

A shared understanding seemed to pass between them. An exchange of trust given and earned.

The sound of someone clearing their throat jolted Bea back to the room. "Right, your ladyship. I'm off now." DI Ainsley gave her a reassuring smile. "We will need statements from you all at some stage, but it can wait until tomorrow. I'll send DS Hines over to Francis Court if that's okay with you?"

"Of course, Mike." Bea smiled at the inspector. "And thank you for responding so quickly."

"And thank you for apprehending the real killer." He looked at Rich. "I'm not sure how well DCI Saunders will take it. But I'll leave the pleasure of telling him to you, Fitzwilliam."

"Cheers!"

Daisy squirmed in Bea's arms. She gently set the little dog down on the floor. "You're not supposed to be here Daisy, so stay close, okay?"

Daisy trotted over to where Simon and Isla were sitting on the small sofa at the bottom of the bed.

"Are you sure you're alright, Isla?" Simon's voice was full of concern.

"It all happened so quickly," Isla said, her pale cheeks flushed from distress. Daisy nudged her nose into Isla's hand. She managed a shaky smile as she patted Daisy's head. "Thanks to Perry, I'm okay," she murmured, her gaze flitting towards the tall figure by the window.

Perry turned and smiled. His blond hair, usually so impeccably styled, bore the marks of the scuffle. He dipped his chin at Isla, a gesture both graceful and reassuring, as he shuffled over.

Bea and Rich moved to join them.

"Can you believe Ward?" Perry said. "Standing on Shelly's hand like that…"

Bea grinned over the image of the gentle giant, his face etched with determination as he'd pinned Shelly's wrist to the floor, immobilising her knife-wielding hand as the others had held her down. She shook her head; it was like a scene straight from a play where the understudy suddenly steals the show.

"He did ten years in the Army," Simon told them. Bea nodded. Perry raised an eyebrow. Simon shrugged with a grin. "It was a lot of stairs. We talked."

"Where is he now?" Isla asked, her voice more steady now.

Bea smiled. "He mumbled something about parking tickets and dashed out."

"Which reminds me," Simon said, glancing at his watch, his brow knitting slightly. "I'm due on the *BOW* set soon, so I'd better go." He rose.

"I can drive you if you want?" Isla said, standing up too, the colour having returned to her face.

"Thanks, Isla. That would be great," Simon replied, offering her a grateful smile.

"I need to get on too." Bea rubbed at the space between

her brows as she considered the looming task ahead. "I'm moving into The Dower House this weekend, and I'm woefully under-prepared."

"I promised I'd help you, and I will," Perry said. "But first, I need to retrieve my shoes from next door." He winced, glancing down at his socked feet. "Assuming I can get them on, that is."

"Right." Simon clapped his hands together. "I say we all deserve a good meal after today's drama. Dinner at ours tonight at seven?"

"That would be lovely. I'm not ready to face my brand new kitchen yet," Bea said.

"Yes, great. I'll be there," Rich added. "I'll need it after I've brought my boss up to date with what's happened today." His gaze lingered on Bea for a moment, then he smiled. "I'll give him the abridged version, of course."

"Isla?" Simon turned towards her. "Would you like to join us?"

Isla's cheeks tinged pink. With a gentle tug at the hem of her jumper, she looked at the floor, then back up to meet Simon's expectant gaze. "Er, thank you, but I—" She faltered. "I've got to head back to Scotland. There's a surprise party for my aunt on Sunday. I really should be there."

Bea could see the embarrassment fluttering in the young woman's eyes. There was still a small nagging doubt in her mind concerning Isla's intentions. She sighed. *It's probably nothing.* And anyway, she needed to concentrate on the mammoth task of getting The Dower House ready for her son's arrival next weekend and the grand opening party she'd been persuaded into having.

47

6:30 PM, FRIDAY 23 APRIL

"So what will happen now?" Fred asked Bea as he rested his arms on his knees on an edge of the blue sofa in her sitting room at Francis Court. Next to him Daisy dozed in a shaft of sunlight spilling in through the nearby floor-to-ceiling windows.

Bea, ensconced in her favourite armchair opposite them, shrugged. "I think there's a good chance she'll confess to both murders. She certainly didn't have any problem telling us all about why and how she killed Vera. If anything, she seemed to need to get it off her chest."

"Will she plead insanity, do you think?"

"Well, she seemed perfectly sane to me, but then her rambling account of her time with Vera spoke of someone with some deep issues. I would think a good lawyer could argue she'd faced years of abuse from Vera and thought she was defending herself."

Fred nodded slowly as he lounged back into the cushions and crossed his long legs. The waning sunlight highlighted the silver streaks just beginning to emerge in the dark tufts at his temples, lending him an air of distinction that suited his noble lineage.

Bea smiled. *It's the most relaxed I've seen him for days.*

Fred's hand slowly reached out and ruffled the wiry fur on the top of Daisy's head. She stirred, lifting her chin and opening one eye before she sighed and went back to sleep. Fred cleared his throat as his hands brushed some imaginary dust from the knees of his trousers. "I must thank you, Bea," he said, his voice thick with emotion. "Without your help in finding Vera's killer... Well, I just want you to know that Summer and I are extremely grateful." A pink tinge was appearing on his cheeks, and he glanced away from her gaze.

Bea suppressed a chuckle. The naughty little sister part of her wanted to prolong her elder brother's embarrassment. He was normally so composed. It seemed his relationship with Summer had brought out a softer side to her cool, calm, and collected sibling.

"It was nothing really. I'd have done the same for a friend." She grinned at him as their eyes met. He grinned back. "And anyway, it was very much a group effort."

"I've also spoken with Fitzwilliam and thanked him for his role in all this." He raised an eyebrow, his eyes still sparkling with good humour. "You two make a great team, you know."

I know! This case had shown very clearly that when they worked together, they were more than the sum of their individual parts.

The anticipation of seeing him later this evening stirred a flutter in her stomach; seeing him always had that effect these days, though she scarcely liked to admit it even to herself. With Rich's recovery nearly complete, and him returning to his role at PaIRS, there would be little room for...whatever was blossoming between them. His presence in Francis Court had become a comfortable constant, and the thought of its end filled her with an odd sense of loss she couldn't quite place.

"And there's something else—I owe you for advising Summer to come clean about meeting her ex. We had a heart-to-heart after that, and well, it feels like we're closer than ever." He paused and swallowed loudly. "I love her, Bea. After everything that's happened, that's the one thing I'm certain of. And now we can move forward. Together."

The conviction in his voice resonated in the quiet room, and Bea felt a warmth bloom in her chest. "I'm really happy for you, Fred. I like Summer a lot, and I think you've both got this."

"We have," Fred said as he rose. "Please also extend my gratitude to Perry and Simon when you see them later." He paused to peer out of the window. "We would have come to thank them in person, but with the press" —he gestured in the general direction of the main gates with a grimace— "out there, we thought it best to...you know, keep our heads down for the moment while we come up with a proper plan to go public with our relationship."

Bea stood. "Of course. They'll understand."

As she watched her brother leave, Bea couldn't help but consider her own life, and the solitary path she'd walked since becoming a widow and a single mother. Of course, she now had Perry and Simon, and they had brought so much warmth and love into her life, she couldn't imagine being without them. But what of romance?

Fred had found his 'one'. Someone to weather the storms of life with. But what did her future hold?

48

9 PM, FRIDAY 23 APRIL

Bea leaned back in her dining chair and languidly stretched her arms by her sides. Full of good food and a couple of glasses of wine, she was ready for bed. She raised her hand just in time to catch a yawn. After the day's drama, she knew she would sleep well tonight. Behind her, the gentle snoring coming from Daisy, who was curled up in her favourite chair by the French doors overlooking the now pitch-black garden at Rose Cottage, reminded her that she wasn't the only one who'd had an exciting day.

Her eye was caught by a glimpse of Simon through the partly opened door of the sitting room. In the far corner, he paced up and down with his phone to his ear. Hopefully, it was a further update about Shelly. When she'd arrived, Perry had taken her to one side and told her in a whisper that CID Steve had just texted Simon to tell them Shelly was *still* being interviewed. Bea hadn't been surprised. Shelly had clearly been bottling up a lot of hurt and feelings of being used for years. Now the floodgates had been opened, she had a lot to say.

Opposite her, Perry and Ryan were discussing *Bake Off*

Wars. Perry gestured at the last remnants of the chocolate ganache tart that clung to the edges of his plates. "Are leftovers from the set something we can expect a lot of over the next few weeks?"

Ryan smiled. "I doubt it. Normally the crew devour everything, but I think the shock of losing Leah and Shelly from the team in such dreadful circumstances means that some of them have lost their appetite for once. Ana baked that tart. I bet once the crew realises she's good, they will get their appetites back fairly quickly." Ryan had told them over dinner that Harvey and Ana had been temporarily reassigned to cover for Shelly and Leah until replacements could be found.

"Well, it was amazing," Rich, sitting next to Bea, said, dropping his fork on his plate and picking up a napkin. "I think Ana is wasted as a runner if she can cook like that." There were murmurs of agreement from around the table.

"Yes," Ryan agreed. "It's strange how well everyone is coping, considering we've lost Vera, Shelly, and Leah from the show in the last five days. You'd think that the total production would grind to a halt."

"Ah, but the show must go on. Isn't that what they say?" Rich said with a wry smile.

No one is indispensable. Bea had learned that when James had died so unexpectedly. As much as you expect life to stop, want it to even, it doesn't. It just goes on without the person you thought you couldn't live without. *It's a brutal lesson to learn.*

"Are you alright?" Rich whispered.

She turned to look at him. His brown eyes were full of concern for her. Her knees felt a little weak. *Maybe it hasn't been so bad that life's carried on...* She smiled at him. "Yes, I'm fine, thanks. Just tired."

"Well, it's not every day you jump a knife-wielding killer," he said. Then he paused dramatically, holding his hand to his chest in a gesture that Perry would be proud of. "Well, actually"—a huge grin spread over his face—"it's normally about what? Once a month?"

"Oh, ha, ha," she replied, trying to suppress the grin desperate to split her face. She tilted her head to one side. "And anyway, they don't always have a knife."

He threw his head back and laughed. Bea flushed. She loved to make him laugh. *Why is that?*

She grabbed her glass of wine and took a gulp. Over the other side of the table, Perry cleared his throat. She looked up at him. He winked. *Cheeky!*

"Er, so how's Simon getting on, Ryan?" she asked, giving Perry a look.

"He's really taken to the camera like a duck to water," the young chef said. "The only issue we have is that he's struggling to be the bad cop."

Bea frowned. *Why would Simon need to be bad?*

Perry laughed. "You're both too nice. But someone has got to reluctantly give that hard-earned praise, or else, what will motivate the contestants?"

Bea shook her head. *What's he talking about?*

"Oh, Bea!" Perry cried. "You really must watch the show, or I'm going to have to spend my life explaining everything about it to you." He gave an over-dramatic sigh. "One judge has to be the tough one who's hard to get a compliment out of. The bad cop, if you like. It's always been Vera."

"Well, I can't see Simon berating anyone over a soufflé," Bea said with a smile as she imagined her good-natured friend attempting to scold someone who had tried their best.

Ryan's laughter was deep and infectious. "Well, he'll have no choice. I've already sealed my fate as Mr Nice Guy on the show. I can't very well have a personality flip mid-series!"

"Hey, I can be the tough guy if I need to be," Simon chimed in, entering the room, his mobile phone in his hand.

"Love, you're more likely to patiently show them how to do it rather than tell them off for not doing it right!" Perry scoffed lightheartedly.

As the laughter died down, Bea glanced over at Simon, who had sat down next to Perry. *What did Steve have to say?* He caught her eye and tilted his head subtly towards Rich. A silent language passed between them, a shared understanding that as much as he wanted to say something, they couldn't have that conversation in front of Rich without compromising CID Steve's position.

"What did Steve have to say?" Perry asked brightly before taking a sip of his wine.

Perry!!

"Er, was that your friend Steve, Simon?" Bea said, her brain unable to catch up with her mouth. "The firefighter?" *What?*

"Er, yes. There's been a fire…" Simon was struggling.

"And there was me thinking you were on the phone to Steve from Fenshire CID," Rich said, chuckling.

He knows? She stared at him. *How?*

"Oh, come on. I am a detective. I've always known there must be someone keeping an ear to the ground at Fenshire CID for you. Although I didn't know their name until tonight." He looked across the table. "Perry, your whispering could use some finesse."

Bea's stomach went hard. *Will he say anything to anyone?* She turned to him and placed her hand on his arm. "We don't want Steve to get into trouble, Rich."

He covered her hand with his. "I know nothing, okay?"

Laughter bubbled up, genuine and unbidden as relief washed over her. *Thank goodness.*

Rich removed his hand and smiled at her. *Oh my goodness...this man!*

"So what did he have to say?" Perry asked, his eyes bright.

"Well, Shelly's finally finished giving her confession," Simon told them, reaching for his glass of wine. "Steve said she's not holding anything back. Even with her legal representative apparently sitting next to her with his head in his hands."

"Did she admit to killing Leah?" Bea asked.

Simon sighed heavily, his fingers tracing the grain of the oak table before he met Bea's gaze and nodded. "She pushed Leah down the stairs." His words hung heavy in the air.

Bea's heart clenched. *Poor Leah.* She could almost hear the thunderous echo of that fatal fall, could picture the horror in Leah's eyes as she realised Shelly had betrayed her.

"Shelly claims remorse," Simon continued, his voice strained. "Leah wanted them to come clean to the police. But Shelly... She pretended they'd escape together, only to—"

"Only to ensure that Leah took the secret to her grave," Bea finished for him, her full lips pressed into a thin line of disgust.

"Exactly." Simon dipped his chin slowly. "Shelly went back to her room after and stabbed herself to support her story that Leah was the killer after all."

"Wow. That takes some guts to do that to yourself," Ryan said, taking a drink of water.

Perry's eyes were wide. "Imagine sitting there and plunging a knife into your side like that." He gave an exaggerated shudder.

A silence descended on the room, punctuated only by the gentle snores coming from a dozing Daisy.

"Did she say what happened to the overalls?" Rich asked after a while.

Simon slowly scratched at his well-trimmed beard. "Only that Leah made the anonymous call and planted the overalls in Summer's car on Shelly's instructions. Shelly thought that as the police already thought Summer had done it, adding the overalls into the mix would close the case."

How callous. Shelly was more dangerous and calculating than she'd ever appeared to be. Even when she'd been rambling on to them about her mistreatment by Vera, Bea had been sure she was fundamentally harmless. How wrong she'd been. "And the knife?"

"Hidden by Shelly while she worked out a plan to get rid of it permanently."

"And what about Isla? Has she gone now?" Rich asked, breaking the momentary silence that had fallen.

Simon nodded. "She's been to give her statement about seeing Shelly and Leah with their cases at the top of the back stairs and she's been told she's free to go."

"She's a funny little thing," Perry said, a fond smile playing across his lips. "I'll kind of miss her around here."

"Ah, well," Ryan said abruptly, setting down his napkin with a flourish that seemed to shake off the sombre mood. "I've got to skedaddle. It's a big day tomorrow; filming's hard work, you know." His generous mouth stretched into his signature huge smile as he stood. "And Simon, mate." He clapped his hand on Simon's shoulder as he passed him. "Make sure you get some decent shut-eye tonight. You'll need it for your close-up."

Simon rose to see him out as Bea stood. "I should be off as well. Tomorrow's the big move to The Dower House, and I can't ignore any more how much there's still to be done." She sighed.

"I'll come and give you a hand tomorrow," Perry said, placing his wineglass down on the table and getting up.

Bea smiled at her best friend as she walked over and hugged him. "Big fat breakfast at eight to set you up for the day?"

He squeezed her tight. "You always know what to say to get me motivated," he said, grinning.

"Right!" Rich pushed himself up from the table. "Can I grab a lift with you back to Francis Court, Bea?"

"Indeed," she replied, a tingle running down her spine as she suppressed a smile.

49

FIFTEEN MINUTES LATER, FRIDAY 23 APRIL

Perry methodically stacked the last of the clean wineglasses on the polished mahogany shelf above the wine rack. He smiled to himself as his stomach gave a flutter. He'd seen how Fitzwilliam had been looking at Bea during the evening. Sneaky brief glances at her when he'd thought no one had been looking. But Perry had seen it.

And Bea is just as bad! Perry had watched her leaning towards Fitzwilliam as he'd spoken, her eyes fixed on his lips. *She so wants to kiss him…*

They really need to get a move on! Fitzwilliam would leave soon to go back to work. Perry bit his lip. *Could tonight be the night when they finally admit to each other how they feel?* Perry took a deep breath. *I really hope so…* "Love. If Bea and Fitzwilliam don't declare their undying love to each other tonight, then we need to—"

"Perry," Simon warned from over by the dishwasher. "You can't rush them. They'll come to the realisation of how they feel in their own good time."

"But he'll be going soon and then how—"

"They'll find a way." His husband's voice was kind but firm. He smiled. "Perry, I know how much you want this, but they have a lot of challenges to face if they want to be together, not least of all that he works for the organisation that's paid to keep her and her family safe."

Perry's stomach sank. "Don't you think they'll be able to make it work?"

Simon moved towards him and placed a reassuring hand on his shoulder. "If they want it bad enough, then I think they *will* overcome all the obstacles they'll have to face. They're both determined people. But it's not something they can rush into." He leaned in and kissed Perry's cheek. "Just give them time, love."

He suddenly clapped his hands, giving Perry a start. "In the meantime, tomorrow's going to be a circus, and I've got to learn to be stern and unimpressed."

The corners of Perry's mouth lifted in an affectionate smile as he gazed at his husband. "Just imagine you're trying to stop me from making an impulsive purchase that you know I'll regret. That should help."

The shrill ring of the doorbell cleaved through Simon's laughter as he said, "That will certainly do it!"

Perry's eyebrow shot up. *Who on earth is that at this time of night?*

Wiping his hands on a nearby tea towel, he moved to the door. "I'll get it," he called over his shoulder. His mind raced through a checklist of potential visitors, but he came up empty.

Unless Fitzwilliam has proposed to Bea, and they've come back to tell us and crack open some champagne? He hurried towards the door, a grin already spreading over his face.

The night air carried a chill that seemed to seep through the door as Perry threw it open wide. It wasn't Fitzwilliam and Bea.

It was Isla, swaying slightly on the doorstep, her mascara running in dark rivulets down her cheeks as if she'd been caught in a downpour. Perry looked up into the dark sky. It wasn't raining.

"I need to talk to Simon," she slurred, reaching out to steady herself on the door frame.

Perry quickly gave her the once over. Her usually tamed hair was a frizzy halo around her head, and her dress was crinkled as though she'd slept in it. But she wasn't bleeding. There were no bruises. She looked fully intact. "Isla, it's late, and Simon has an early start tomorrow. It's his first day filming *Bake Off Wars*," he reminded her gently, hoping his tone conveyed understanding rather than dismissal. "Can you come back another time? Maybe when you're...er... feeling a little better?"

The suggestion hung awkwardly in the air between them.

He watched her face crumple, the edges of her mouth quivering before pulling downwards into a frown. "No, it has to be now," she insisted with a hiccup, attempting to sidestep him.

Perry placed a firm hand on her shoulder, stopping her advance. "Isla, please. Let me get you a taxi back to the hotel."

She shook her head as tears began spilling over the top of her eyes.

No! Don't cry...

"I can't tomorrow," she sobbed, the words barely audible. "I won't have the courage to tell him."

"Tell him what?" Perry's voice was soft, almost a whisper, but it carried the weight of sudden concern. *Oh no, where is this going?*

Sniffling, she looked into his eyes, then her voice broke as she blurted out, "That he's my father!"

50

AT ABOUT THE SAME TIME, FRIDAY 23 APRIL

"So did you mean it earlier when you said this was the last time you'll get involved in a murder investigation?" Rich asked, a smile tugging at the corners of his mouth.

Bea nodded. "Honestly. A double murder? It's all just too much for me. So there will be no more, I promise." *But it will mean not working with Rich anymore.* Her heart skipped a beat. Was that really what she wanted? Was it too late to take her promise back?

"Good," Rich said, dragging his fingers through his short brown hair. "I don't think my blood pressure could cope with any more running around—"

Does my interfering really stress him out that much? She looked down at Daisy, who was curled up between them on the back seat of the Daimler, and gently stroked the top of her head. *Should I tell him I'm sorry for all the trouble I've caused him?*

"—trying to get to you before the killer does. Worried you're going to be injured or even dead. I'm too old for all that."

She looked across the car at him. *So he was worried*

about me rather than angry at me for getting involved? She studied his face. Still grinning at her, he looked more relaxed than she'd seen him in a while. "Don't play the too old card, Rich. You're not that much older than me. And in the past, you've easily outrun both Perry *and* Simon."

He shrugged. "Ah, but I hadn't been shot then. I think I'd be a tad slower now." Laughter lines creased the outside of his dazzling brown eyes, and his smile was infectious. She smiled back. Their eyes met. She felt lightheaded as his brown eyes gazed into hers. Everything in the car went slightly hazy. *What's wrong with me?* Was it the euphoria of having solved this latest case together? They'd not argued much at all recently, which was unusual for them. Her temperature was rising. *Oh my goodness.* Her heart rate increased. She wanted to lean forward and—

Click, click, click!

The light was blinding.

Click, click, click!

She jumped back in her seat, her heart racing as the Daimler slowed down for the police to let them through the trades entrance of Francis Court. Press swarmed around the gate like a pack of hungry wolves, their cameras flashing in a blinding cacophony of light. TV crews jostled for position, eager to catch a glimpse of who was in the car. *Do they think we're Fred and Summer?*

"Lady Beatrice! Can you confirm your brother is in a relationship with Summer York?" one reporter bellowed, thrusting a microphone towards the window.

"Is your family concerned about how this might affect the monarchy?" another voice shouted.

Bea hugged Daisy tightly, shielding her from the chaos outside. The little dog whined softly, burying her face in

Bea's shoulder as Ward expertly navigated the car past the gate, leaving the frenzy behind.

"Are you okay?" Rich asked, reaching out and touching her arm with an air of calm that contrasted starkly with the pandemonium they'd just encountered.

"Yes," she replied, letting out a shaky breath. "That was...unexpected. I thought they would all be at the main gates this time of night."

"I think they're everywhere at the moment," Rich said, dropping his hand. Bea shivered. Daisy squirmed in her arms, and she let the little dog go. The terrier let out a contented sigh as she settled into the gap between them.

The car glided quietly down the narrow road towards the mansion house. As darkness outside the Daimler enveloped them, Bea found herself acutely aware of the steady rhythm of Rich's breathing. *Oh my goodness!* Her gaze drifted towards him before flickering back to the window. Her heart rate quickened at the proximity of him, an involuntary reaction that she tried to suppress. *Get a grip, Bea!*

"Oh, I forgot to tell you." Rich broke the silence, his deep voice resonating within the car's interior. "I got a message from Tina Spicer while we were having dinner. She passed her inspector's exams. She found out today. She should be getting a promotion soon, then she'll be leading her own team."

"Really? That's wonderful news," Bea said, momentarily distracted from the maelstrom of emotions she'd been grappling with. "Please send her my congratulations."

"Of course," Rich agreed, his eyes meeting hers briefly before looking away again.

Bea attempted to focus on the lit up mansion ahead, but everything seemed to fade compared to the man beside her. The scent of his cologne filled her senses, stirring something within her. *Stop it!* She glanced over at him, struggling to read his thoughts as he gazed out of the car window. "So what happens now?" she asked tentatively. "Are you going back to Surrey?"

"Yes. I leave in the morning. I have my physio then an assessment at the end of this week. After that I can get back to work." His gaze caught hers, and she swallowed hard, unable to tear her eyes away from his face.

Don't go! Bea's heart ached with the realisation that their time together would end. *Please stay!* But she knew it was impossible. Images of Fred and Summer's ordeal flickered through her mind — the relentless media scrutiny, the invasion of privacy. It would be even worse if it was her and Rich, considering his role in protecting her family. She stifled a groan. *How can we ever be together without causing a scandal?* She dropped her gaze as her fingers absentmindedly stroked Daisy's soft fur. The little dog nuzzled up to her as if sensing her inner turmoil and offered a reassuring lick on her hand. *I'm being silly*. After all, she didn't even know how he felt about her.

Pulling up to the front of Francis Court, Ward got out and opened the rear door next to Bea. "Would you like me to drive you to your cottage, chief inspector?"

Bea held her breath, silently willing Rich to refuse. To her relief, he declined the offer. "No, thank you, Ward. I think I'll get out here and stretch my legs a bit." Rich glanced at her, his lips curving into a lopsided smile. Bea's stomach flip-flopped.

"Thanks, Ward," she replied as she stepped out of the car, Daisy hot on her heels. "Goodnight."

"My lady," Ward replied with a quick bow before closing the door and returning to the driver's seat. He slowly drove off, leaving Bea, Daisy, and Rich alone in front of Francis

Court. The night was warm and still, the air heavy with the scent of flowers. Rich looked over at her. "How about one last quick stroll around the gardens? They look great all lit up this time of night."

She swallowed. This would be the last time they would walk in the gardens together. She nodded, not trusting herself to speak. The soft radiance of the garden lights cast a warm otherworldly atmosphere as they strolled along the winding path, taking them away from the house, their footsteps echoing on the cobbles. Daisy snuffled along beside them, the gentle rustle of leaves in the still air the only other sound. Aware of the warmth of Rich's presence beside her, Bea sighed. *I should allow myself to simply enjoy this moment with him.*

"How are Fred and Summer coping with all this attention?" Rich asked, breaking the silence as they entered the formal gardens to the east of the main house.

"Surprisingly well," Bea said. "They're facing it together, and I have to say I'm impressed at how well Summer, in particular, is doing."

"I think she knows what she's getting into, and she's willing to accept it as part of being with Fred." Rich's voice was low and earnest.

That's all very well, Bea thought. But she knew from bitter experience that it was the relentlessness of it all that eventually got overwhelming. Could anyone really know what they were getting themselves into?

"If they want to be together, they have to navigate these challenges," Rich continued, his voice quieter now.

"Yes, but not everyone can handle that level of scrutiny, Rich. The press has been hounding Summer's family, digging up anything they can from her past to paint her as unsuitable for royalty. It's hard putting those you care about through that."

Rich tipped his chin solemnly. "I understand, but I'm confident they'll get through it. Sometimes, something special is worth fighting for, even when it seems impossible."

Bea frowned. *Are we still talking about Fred and Summer?*

A sudden irritation rushed over her, and she glanced away, biting her lip. Did he really think it was that straightforward? She stopped walking and turned to face him. "What if it was you, Rich? Could you handle the scrutiny? Would you be willing to put your sister, Elise, and her family through that? And what about your mum? How could you protect her from being harassed day and night by the paps?" She inhaled deeply. "What if the press declared you unsuitable, Rich? Not good enough to be part of our family? Could you cope? Or would you believe them? Would you give up and walk away?"

They stared at each other in silence for a moment. Looking deep into his brown eyes, she challenged him to be honest with her.

"It's not a straightforward question to answer," he admitted. Her heart fluttered. "But if I truly believed I had a future with someone, then I'd like to think we could face whatever challenges came our way."

Oh my goodness. Her heart stopped. In the soft glow of the garden lights, the atmosphere was charged with emotions long suppressed, and as they held each other's gaze, it seemed as though time stood still.

"Bea," Rich murmured, lifting his hand to her cheek. A shiver ran through her as his fingers touched her skin, but she didn't pull away. Instead, she leaned into his touch, her heart pounding in anticipation.

"Rich, I…" Her words trailed off, unable to articulate the whirlwind of emotions engulfing her. Before she could finish her thought, Rich closed the distance between them, his lips meeting hers in a tender kiss that left her breathless.

As the kiss deepened, Bea's mind went blissfully blank, every doubt and worry evaporating like morning mist under the sun's first rays.

Eventually, Rich pulled away. His eyes scanned her face. "I've wanted to do that for months," he admitted, his voice barely more than a whisper.

For months?

"But I wasn't sure if you would let me."

Bea grinned. *Months!* So she hadn't imagined it. He'd felt it too…

Suddenly, his eyes clouded with concern, pulling Bea back to reality. "But this is unprofessional of me," he said, his tone heavy with regret. "In my current role, I shouldn't be doing this. It's my job to protect you. To keep you safe. Not to take advantage of you."

Bea's heart clenched at his words, a surge of despair sweeping through her. She wanted to tell him she was happy to be taken advantage of. But he was telling her that when he went back to work, this would end. The thought of losing him just as she'd finally admitted her feelings for him was too much to bear. "Rich, please—" she protested, the urgency in her voice betraying her desperation.

He held up a hand to silence her, a mysterious smile playing at the corners of his mouth. "But, of course, it wouldn't be a problem if I had a different job…"

51

MEANWHILE, FRIDAY 23 APRIL

Perry's eyes flitted between Simon and Isla, taking in the tumult of emotions that filled the kitchen in Rose Cottage.

Isla was standing just in the entrance to the kitchen, her head down and her shoulders slumped as she stared at the floor. Simon had one hand resting on the work surface as if that was the only thing stopping him from falling over. His brown eyes were glazed over. Shock had settled into every crease of his face.

Hic! Perry looked back at Isla, who was now beginning to shake. *Oh my goodness, this won't do.* Hurrying over to a shelf by the fridge, he grabbed a tall glass, then thrust it under the cold water spout built into the fridge's door.

"Here, drink this," Perry said as he returned and handed the glass of water to Isla.

"Thanks," she mumbled in a low voice. Her shivering seemed to abate as she sipped the water, her eyes flickering up with gratitude towards Perry. He returned her look with a small, reassuring smile, though inside, his thoughts churned. Her nose was the same as Simon's. Why hadn't he noticed that before?

Perry turned back to his husband. Simon still hadn't moved. "Why don't we all sit down?" Perry suggested, holding his arm out towards the dining table in the far corner. He gave Isla a nod of encouragement, and she shuffled towards the large wooden table. Perry gently steered Simon after her.

Her hiccups having subsided, Isla placed her water on the table and pulled out a chair facing the kitchen. She slowly lowered herself onto it, then wrapped her arms around herself. Perry plonked Simon in a chair diagonally opposite her as he glanced at the drinks cabinet over by the wall. *Shock! What was good for shock?*

He skipped over and opened the glass door. *Gin? No, I don't think so. Brandy? Yes, that's it.* He scanned the bottles. *Rats!* He remembered now that it had all been used up in the Christmas cake and he'd not got around to replacing it yet. *Port? That will have to do.* He poured the liquid, rich and dark, into two glasses — one for him and one for Simon, then returned to the table.

As he sat down opposite Isla, he slid one of the glasses in front of Simon. "Here you go, love." Simon, still as a statue save for the occasional blink, seemed miles away, lost in a sea of bewilderment and silence.

Well, I guess it's up to me then. Perry took a sip of his port, then leaned forward, resting his elbows on the wooden surface. He steadied his gaze on Isla, the tremble in her lip mirrored by the slight quiver of her hands clasping the glass of water. "So, Isla. How much of what you've told us previously is true?"

The young girl's gaze drifted from Perry to Simon, then back again as if she was searching their faces for some sign of absolution or condemnation. Her breath hitched, and a single tear betrayed her attempts at composure, tracking down her cheek before she could catch it. "Almost everything I told you is true," she whispered, her voice cracking. "I *am* Isla Scott. I'm nineteen. My family do live on the east coast of Scotland, and I also have family in Spain, where I was raised. I am studying at the university in Barcelona, although I did make up the bit about doing a creative arts degree. I'm actually going to be studying international law."

She paused and took a sip of water. "I didn't want to lie to you. It's just that…" She swallowed hard and looked at Simon. "I made the course bit up so I had an excuse to interview you." When he didn't respond, she turned back to Perry. "I wanted to see what kind of person he was before I decided whether to tell him who I was or not." Her shoulders slumped as if they were weighed down by her deception.

Well, I get that. Perry could see how it would be sensible to vet the man who was your father beforehand. *After all…*

"And if he was a jerk?" Perry prodded gently.

A tear trickled down Isla's cheek. "Then I would have left." She looked up at Simon, a desperate plea for understanding in her reddened eyes.

Perry suppressed a smile. *She's smart, this one. Like her father…* "But you didn't leave…"

Her gaze met his. He glimpsed a moment of vulnerability in her face. "Because I like him," she said in a low voice. "The moment I met him, there was this…kindness. It wasn't just him either; it was all of you. You've been so welcoming." She drew in a breath. "I wanted to be part of that, to get to know you all better." Her voice cracked. She looked back at Simon. "I've wanted to tell you these last few days. I really have. But finding the right moment…and then all this murder stuff—"

A creak of wood signalled Simon shifting in his chair. His eyes locked onto Isla's face. "You're Bridget's daughter, aren't you?"

The question hung heavy between them, then the corners of Isla's mouth lifted into a hesitant smile. "Yes," she whispered.

Simon's gaze softened, the lines around his eyes deepening as he continued to stare at her. "You have her eyes," he murmured, almost to himself.

Perry took another sip of his drink. *Well, this is better. At least he's talking now. And he seems to know who her mother is…*

"I didn't know." Simon picked up his glass and took a gulp.

"I know." Isla nodded. "Mum said it was just a holiday fling, that you didn't even know her last name. She chose to keep me and raise me alone in Spain."

"And now? Is she still in Spain?" Simon asked.

Isla's delicate hands clasped together tightly, her knuckles blanching from the pressure. "Mum...she got sick last year — cancer." Her voice trembled. "When we knew there was nothing more they could do, she wanted to be in Scotland with her sister. So I put everything on hold and brought her over."

Perry swallowed. *Poor girl. She's so young to have had to go through all that on her own.* He fought the urge to jump up and hug her.

Next to him, Simon fell back into his chair. "I'm so sorry."

Perry watched his husband's face, compassion etched into every furrow of his brow. He reached out and squeezed his hand.

"Before...before she passed," Isla continued, her voice

hitching. "She told me about you. She wanted me to know my father."

A warmth spread through Perry. *Ah, Simon will be a great father.* Then, suddenly, the heat was replaced with a creeping chill of uncertainty. How would this revelation shape their life together? Simon would no doubt rise to the role of a father. *But what about me?* Nurturing wasn't his strong suit.

The thought sparked a flutter of panic in his chest. *Am I ready to share Simon?*

Stop it! Perry mentally chided himself. *This is Simon's moment, not a time for my insecurities.* What was important right now was to let the two of them talk. He rose. "Isla," he said gently, mustering a smile, "would you like a coffee?"

She sniffed and wiped a hand over her cheek. "Yes, please."

He headed over to the coffee machine and focused on the task in hand. The machine purred as the familiar scent of coffee beans washed over him. He leaned against the work surface, his posture relaxed but his mind far from it. A whirl of thoughts were colliding in his head with concern for Simon, curiosity about Isla, and the newly raised question of how he fitted into this new family dynamic. His heart ached. *We'll work it out. Won't we?*

The buzz of his phone cut through his worry-fog. He slid the device from his pocket. A text message lit up the screen.

Bea: *You'll never guess what's just happened!*

A smirk tugged at the corners of his mouth. With a swift movement, he typed his reply.

. . .

Perry: *Whatever it is, my dear, I can assure you I have news to top it!*

52

TWO WEEKS LATER

The Society Page online article:

<u>Killer of National Treasure Vera Bolt Pleads Guilty to Double Murder</u>

Shelly Black (61) today indicated in court a plea of guilty to the murder of national treasure and Bake Off Wars *judge Vera Bolt (66) and Lilian Goldrich (41), a home economist on the popular baking TV Show. Ms Black appeared at Fenshire Magistrates' Court yesterday morning in a brief session in King's Town. The District Judge immediately ordered the case to go to the Crown Court in Fenwich, where sentencing will be determined at a later date. Shelly Black was remanded in custody. She is likely to face a whole life sentence for the murder of the two women last month.*

Meanwhile Eat Cake Productions, who makes Bake Off Wars*, announced this morning that Mark Jacobs (49) will be returning as a permanent judge in series nine, alongside current judge Ryan Hawley (31). Jacobs, who left* Bake Off

Wars *at the end of series seven, will also be one of three guest judges who have been invited to join Ryan in the* Bake Off Wars *'tent' to judge the remaining episodes of series eight currently being filmed at Francis Court in Fenshire. Vera Bolt only recorded one episode of season eight before she died. Winner of* Celebrity EliteChef, *Simon Lattimore (40), stepped in as a temporary judge for three episodes, and the production company announced last week that Ryan's co-presenter of* Two Chefs in a Camper, *Finn Gilligan (33), will judge a further three after that. It is understood that Chef Mark will then judge the quarter-finals, semi-finals, and final.* Bake Off Wars *will be aired in August.*

In related news, Ryan Hawley and Simon Lattimore have confirmed they have closed on the sale of an empty beach-front restaurant at Windstanton in Fenshire. Announcing their joint venture, the duo told us they plan on opening a bistro-type eatery specialising in locally sourced ingredients with a seasonal menu. Simon's husband, Perry Juke (34), and his business partner, Lady Beatrice (36), the Countess of Rossex, will oversee the design and refurbishment of the restaurant, which is scheduled to open in July.

In royal news, rumours of a relationship between Lord Frederick Astley (39), heir to the Duke of Arnwall, and TV presenter Summer York (35) appeared to have been confirmed this weekend when Summer joined Lord Fred and the rest of the Astley family, including HRH Princess Helen, at the royal wedding of Lady Sophie Clifford (32) to actress and model Jessica Hines (30). The King's niece Lady Sophie is the youngest daughter of Prince David, the Duke of Kingswich. The wedding celebration was a private affair for 150 friends and family and took place at Francis Court in Fenshire.

In other royal-related news, Detective Chief Inspector Richard Fitzwilliam of the Protection and Investigations

(Royal) Services (PaIRS), who was injured in the line of duty earlier this year during the biggest international co-ordinated program of organised crime arrests ever seen, has been promoted to Superintendent in a move that will see him return to City Police to head up the Capital Security Liaison team there. Superintendent Nigel Blake paid tribute to Fitzwilliam, saying, "It is with a heavy heart that we in PaIRS say goodbye to an officer who is held in such high esteem as DCI Fitzwilliam. We know, however, that our loss is City's gain, and we wish him well in his new post."

———

I hope you enjoyed *Dying To Bake*. If you did then please consider writing a review on Amazon or Goodreads, or even both. It helps me a lot if you let people know that you recommend it.

Will the renovation for Simon and Ryan's new restaurant go without a hitch? What do you think! Find out in the next book in the *A Right Royal Cozy Investigation* series *A Death of Fresh Air*. Pre-order it on Amazon now.

Want to know how Perry and Simon solved their first crime together? Then join my readers' club and receive a FREE ebook short story Tick, Tock, Mystery Clock at https://www.subscribepage.com/helengoldenauthor_nls or buy it in the Amazon store.

For other books by me, take a look at the back pages.

. . .

If you want to find out more about what I'm up to you can find me on Facebook at *helengoldenauthor* or on Instagram at *helengolden_author*.

Be the first to know when my next book is available. Follow Helen Golden on Amazon, BookBub, and Goodreads to get alerts whenever I have a new release, preorder, or a discount on any of my books.

CHARACTERS IN ORDER OF APPEARANCE
DYING TO BAKE

Lady Beatrice — The Countess of Rossex. Seventeenth in line to the British throne. Daughter of Charles Astley, the Duke of Arnwall and Her Royal Highness Princess Helen. Niece of the current king.

Perry Juke — Lady Beatrice's business partner and BFF.

Daisy — Lady Beatrice's adorable West Highland Terrier.

Simon Lattimore — Perry Juke's partner. Bestselling crime writer. Ex-Fenshire CID. Winner of cooking competition *Celebrity Elitechef*

Ryan Hawley — Head Chef at Nonnina and TV chef

Sam Wiltshire — son of Lady Beatrice and the late James Wiltshire, the Earl of Rossex. Future Earl of Durrland.

Vera Bolt — famous pastry chef known as 'Queen of Bakes' and a national treasure. Judge on *Bake Off Wars*.

James Wiltshire — The Earl of Rossex. Lady Beatrice's late husband killed in a car accident fifteen years ago.

Lord Frederick (Fred) Astley — Earl of Tilling. Lady Beatrice's elder brother. Ex-Intelligence Army Officer. Future Duke of Arnwall. Special Observer (SO) for MI6.

Summer York — comedian and TV presenter. One of presenting duo on *Bake Off Wars*.

Charles Astley — Duke of Arnwall. Lady Beatrice's father.

HRH Princess Helen — Duchess of Arnwall. Mother of Lady Beatrice. Sister of the current king.

Queen Mary The Queen Mother — wife of the late King, mother of HRH Princess Helen and grandmother of Lady Beatrice.

Lady Sarah Rosdale — Lady Beatrice's elder sister. Twin of Lord Fred. Manages events at Francis Court.

Richard Fitzwilliam — Detective Chief Inspector at PaIRS (Protection and Investigation (Royal) Service) an organisation that provides protection and security to the royal family and who investigate any threats against them. PaIRS is a division of City Police, a police organisation based in the capital, London.

Ana Halsall — runner on *Bake Off Wars*.

Adrian Breen — head of security at Francis Court.

Hamilton Moore — One of presenting duo on *Bake Off Wars*.

Characters In Order Of Appearance

Mark Jacobs — renowned TV chef and ex-judge on *Bake Off Wars.*

Nicky — server in the Breakfast Room restaurant at Francis Court.

Archie Tellis — Sam's best friend from school.

Claire Beck — Francis Court's human resources manager.

Ellie Gunn — Francis Court's catering manager.

Emma McKerr-Adler — Detective Chief Inspector, investigations team PaIRS. Friend of Fitzwilliam's.

Izzy McKerr-Adler — Emma's wife and ceramics expert.

Elise Boyce — Richard Fitzwilliam's sister.

Rhys Boyce — Elise's husband. Richard Fitzwilliam's brother-in-law.

Dylan Milton — landlord of the pub *The Ship and Seal* in Francis-next-the-Sea.

Isla Scott — student visiting the area.

Austin Matthews — director of *Bake Off Wars.* Suggested by reader Laura Morga.

Harvey Jury — food producer on *Bake Off Wars.*

Lilian 'Leah' Goldrich — lead home economist on *Bake Off Wars.* Suggested by reader Heather Sharp.

Shelly Black — food researcher on *Bake Off Wars.*

Cleo Barrington — runner on *Bake Off Wars.*

Ward — the Astley family driver and overseer of maintenance at Francis Court.

Alex Sterling — the late Francis Court's estate manager.

Mike Ainsley — Detective Inspector at Fenshire CID.

Eamon Hines— Detective Sergeant at Fenshire CID.

Nigel Blake — Superintendent at *PaIRS.* Fitzwilliam's boss.

Charles - local building contractor

Tina Spicer — Detective Sergeant at *PaIRS*

Hayden Saunders — Detective Chief Inspector, investigations team PaIRS.

Steve Cox (CID Steve) — ex-colleague of Simon Lattimore at Fenshire CID.

Roisin — Simon Lattimore's best friend who works in Forensics at Fenshire Police.

Peter Tappin — Owner and manager of Tappin's Teas, a teashop in Francis-next-the-Sea.

Charlotte Mansell — Summer York's lawyer as arranged by Lord Fred.

Tom — Summer York's ex-boyfriend.

Finn Gilligan — TV chef and co-presenter of *Two Chefs in a Camper* along with Ryan Hawley.

A BIG THANK YOU TO...

…my friends and family who continue to offer encouragement and support. I couldn't do it with you.

To my editor Marina Grout. Your counsel is invaluable to me.

To Ann, Ray, and my lovely friend Carolyn for being my additional set of eyes before I publish.

To my ARC Team. For the reviews. For the great feedback. For spotting mistakes. For being part of my support team. I appreciate everything you do for me.

To you, my readers. Your emails, social media comments, and reviews encourage me to keep writing. I appreciate your support more than you can imagine. I must mention two readers in particular, Heather Sharp and Laura Morga, who won a competition to name a character each in this book. Thank you for taking part, and I hope you enjoy seeing your name in print.

As always, I may have taken a little dramatic license when it comes to police procedures, so any mistakes or misinterpretations, unintentional or otherwise, are my own.

ALSO BY HELEN GOLDEN

A short prequel in the series A Right Royal Cozy Investigation. Can Perry Juke and Simon Lattimore work together to solve the mystery of the missing clock before the thief disappears? FREE novelette when you sign up to my readers' club. See end of final chapter for details. Ebook only.

First book in the A Right Royal Cozy Investigation series. Amateur sleuth, Lady Beatrice, must pit her wits against Detective Chief Inspector Richard Fitzwilliam to prove her sister innocent of murder. With the help of her clever dog, her flamboyant co-interior designer and his ex-police partner, can she find the killer before him, or will she make a fool of herself?

Second book in the A Right Royal Cozy Investigation series. Amateur sleuth, Lady Beatrice, must once again go up against DCI Fitzwilliam to find a killer. With the help of Daisy, her clever companion, and her two best friends, Perry and Simon, can she catch the culprit before her childhood friend's wedding is ruined?

The third book in the A Right Royal Cozy Investigation series. When DCI Richard Fitzwilliam gets it into his head that Lady Beatrice's new beau Seb is guilty of murder, can the amateur sleuth, along with the help of Daisy, her clever westie, and her best friends Perry and Simon, find the real killer before Fitzwilliam goes ahead and arrests Seb?

A Prequel in the A Right Royal Cozy Investigation series. When Lady Beatrice's husband James Wiltshire dies in a car crash along with the wife of a member of staff, there are questions to be answered. Why haven't the occupants of two cars seen in the accident area come forward? And what is the secret James had been keeping from her?

When the dead body of the event's planner is found at the staff ball that Lady Beatrice is hosting at Francis Court, the amateur sleuth, with help from her clever dog Daisy and best friend Perry, must catch the killer before the partygoers find out and New Year's Eve is ruined.

ALSO BY HELEN GOLDEN

Snow descends on Drew Castle in Scotland cutting the castle off and forcing Lady Beatrice along with Daisy her clever dog, and her best friends Perry and Simon to cooperate with boorish DCI Fitzwilliam to catch a killer before they strike again.

A murder at Gollingham Palace sparks a hunt to find the killer. For once, Lady Beatrice is happy to let DCI Richard Fitzwilliam get on with it. But when information comes to light that indicates it could be linked to her husband's car accident fifteen years ago, she is compelled to get involved. Will she finally find out the truth behind James's tragic death?

An unforgettable bachelor weekend for Perry filled with luxury, laughter, and an unexpected death.
Can Bea, Perry, and his hen's catch the killer before the weekend is over?

Even in a charming seaside town, secrets don't stay buried for long as Bea and Perry discover when they uncover the remains of a chef who disappeared 10 years ago. As they unravel a web of professional rivalries and buried grudges, they must race against time to solve the murder before the grand opening of Simon's new restaurant.

ALL EBOOKS AVAILABLE IN THE AMAZON STORE.

PAPERBACKS AVAILABLE FROM WHEREVER YOU BUY YOUR BOOKS.

Printed in Great Britain
by Amazon

49307625R00189